I recognized Carioca Jones

although she had been absent from the
3-V alcoves for several years; there was no
mistaking that long hair, falling by her
downturned face in a jet cataract. She
seemed to be wearing a tight black sheath
dress, thigh length.

A land shark lay at her feet.

I saw all this briefly, very briefly, because nobody looks away from Carioca
Jones for long. The star had shifted her
position as her boat drifted nearer. As she
straightened up from her scrutiny of the
wreckage, we saw, startling and dark-
tipped, her bare pale breasts. On a late
September afternoon . . . I think every
man on my boat drew a sharp breath as
desire punched him in the stomach.

She sensed us. That sort of woman always does . . . She sensed us and looked
up as a female animal hears a mating call,
and her eyes met mine.

She was old, horribly old, and her black
eyes knew me for a necrophile.

A land shark lay at her feet.

THE JAWS THAT BITE, THE CLAWS THAT CATCH

Michael G. Coney

DAW BOOKS, INC.
DONALD A. WOLLHEIM, PUBLISHER

1301 Avenue of the Americas
New York, N. Y.   10019

FIRST PRINTING, MARCH 1975

1 2 3 4 5 6 7 8 9

PRINTED IN U.S.A.

1

We picked the pieces of Harry Alberni out of the cold green waters of the Strait early one September evening, laid him on the deck and gathered around to hear his last words, if he were capable of uttering them.

"Make for port, Sagar!" somebody said to me, his voice canine with urgency. "Give the man a chance. What the hell are you thinking about?"

The water was dribbling away from Alberni's clothes into the scuppers as his broken body rolled with the motion of the boat. I knelt beside him. The others, freemen and state prisoners alike, were silent, watching, listening. Nobody had ever listened to Alberni before. Why should his words have this new special value, merely because he was dying?

Alberni spoke, the words little whispers, puffs of evanescent steam in the September air. "It hurts like hell, Sagar," he said.

We all knew that. We could see it in the lines of his face, in the grotesque attitude of his body. The steel spinal support which sling-gliders wear to guard against such an accident as Alberni's was twisted, projecting from under his body like a compound fracture.

"We have no dope, Harry. I'm sorry. I just brought a few people out for the afternoon to watch the gliding. I didn't expect—"

There were tears in his eyes. "Oh, God, I didn't think it would be so *bad*. Why the hell should it hurt so much?"

There was a rescue boat in sight now, skipping over the waves. I looked at the eight men standing above me. Their faces showed concern of one sort or another; Tranter, the man who had wanted me to head for port, was still fidgeting, face twitching as his eyes flickered from Alberni to the approaching launch. I didn't know the other men, but I could place them. There were two worried freemen whose afternoon's pleasure had been spoiled—or fulfilled—by the tragedy. And there were five prisoners from the state penitentiary. Two of these were immediately identifiable by their dark green coveralls marked *S. P.* in large white letters front and rear. The other three—

Like their uniformed comrades, they were smiling.

That's how I knew they were prisoners, despite their plain clothes. They were bonded men under the care of the three freemen, so uniforms were not necessary. But they were smiling as a freeman died—and that was identification enough. The Penal Reform Act had divided mankind into two classes.

I could hear the rescue boat now—that bouncing, thumping whine of fiberplast and turbines hopping waves. I turned back to Alberni and for a moment I thought he heard it too, because his eyes had widened and he was regarding the sky intently. But there was no change in focus as my head cut off his view.

I stood up as the rescue launch cut engines and fell to the water, slowing abruptly and wallowing toward us in a wide turn. Fenders bumped lightly and two men leaped to my deck.

"Alberni, is it? How is he?" The mediman had set down his bag and was already selecting a hypojet. The other man was a state prisoner and he was staring down at the body with an intensity which told me he was Alberni's personal bonded man.

Two men, bonded together in unequal partnership until death intervened—or the senior partner canceled the contract.

"You're too late," I told the mediman.

He shrugged and turned away but the S. P man remained, gazing at the body, his expression changing to one of incredulous, transcendental joy.

"You bastards!" he shouted, a high cracked yell of ultimate delight. "I've beaten you all, you bastards!"

He climbed back aboard the rescue launch. His contract was over. He was a freeman. I heard him laughing as the stretcher-bearers arrived and scooped up Alberni.

By now the curious had gathered; a half dozen boats bobbed around us as the occupants strove to get a glimpse of death. Off the port bow the bright remains of the glider drifted away like a dead macaw.

I heard someone whisper, "Carioca Jones."

The 3-V star's hydrofoil was there, idling beside the splintered alloy and torn fabric of Alberni's glider. Her boat was about forty feet long, sleek and black; across the stern the name *Flamboyant* was painted in luminous white letters a foot high. Two women leaned against the stainless-steel after-rail, gazing at the wreckage. I recognized Miss Jones although she had been absent from the 3-V alcoves for several years; there was no mistaking that long hair sprayed midnight with Ultrasorb, falling by her downturned face in a jet cataract. She seemed to be wearing a tight black sheath dress, thigh length. A land shark lay at her feet.

The girl 'by her side was in contrast fair, and her hair short. She looked across at us and smiled slightly, ruefully, as though to say: This is what you get for indulging in dangerous sports. Her eyes were blue and she had a snub nose and, I'll swear, freckles. Her youthful appearance was belied by full breasts beneath the blue pullover.

I saw all this briefly, very briefly, because nobody looks away from Carioca Jones for long. The star had shifted her position as her boat drifted nearer; the wind threw a curtain of hair across her face and she shook her head. As she straightened up from her scrutiny of the wreckage we saw, startling and dark-tipped, her bare pale breasts. On a late September afternoon . . . I think every man on my boat drew a sharp breath as desire punched him in the stomach.

She sensed us. That sort of woman always does—it's basic. She sensed us and looked up as a female animal hears a mating call; and her eyes met mine.

She was old, horribly old, and her black eyes knew me for a necrophile.

That was the end of the summer when everybody on the Peninsula tried sling-gliding, and some fared better than others. I had tried it myself, from the training catapult, borrowing the gear from Doug Marshall and being lucky, because gear must be individually tailored and an incorrectly balanced glider can mean death. After that one flight I kept my feet on the deck and spent the weekends cruising spectators among the offshore islands in my ancient double-ender, while the tiny bright gliders fled silently across the sky like swift paper darts.

Pausing for an instant to gather the appreciation to which she was accustomed, Carioca Jones turned away from the rail and sat down beside the other girl in the cockpit. I heard the faint silver tones of an orchestrella. A weatherbeaten Adonis in S. P. coveralls handed them drinks, then took the wheel and gunned the motor. The craft leaped away, climbing its hydrofoils like stilts.

"Lucky guy," said a voice. It was one of the freemen; the state prisoners had not ventured any comment. "What a way to serve your sentence." He chuckled. "Almost makes it worthwhile, eh, Tranter?"

Tranter, the officious type who had tried to take command when we picked Alberni up, grunted. "Not like you think, I reckon. They say she's gay. Shops around, too. That blonde's the latest. . . . Nice-looking kid. Pity."

Somewhere, somehow, there is always someone who will claim personal knowledge of the homosexuality of a public figure. Tranter was talking garbage, a proclivity of his type. There had been nothing queer about the way in which Carioca Jones's eyes had met mine; I still felt faintly nauseated.

By Monday I had forgotten about Alberni, Tranter, Miss Jones, and the rest of them, and was back in the weekly routine. I was standing at the window looking at the frosty morning when I caught sight of a movement among the bushes on the opposite side of the tiny bay. Then there was stillness again and a noise from the sea and after a while Doug Marshall's boat came past, towing some fool on water skis with a glider attached to his back.

I finished my coffee and went out into the keen air. Silkie trotted to greet me, pink with happiness and uttering that high-pitched whine which is the slithe's way of exhibiting delight. I picked him up, stroking his incredibly soft skin while his reptilian eyes regarded me with cold joy. I carried him to the workshop door where Dave Froehlich was waiting.

I said, "I saw Carioca Jones yesterday."

"She's moved in, over Deep Cove way." Dave knows everything that happens on the Peninsula. "I was meaning to tell you. You ought to cultivate her."

"Have you seen her? Close up, I mean?" I uttered a short laugh.

He regarded me steadily. "She could be a customer, Mr. Sagar," he said.

The small factory was emerging from the mist, a gaunt timber structure at the waterside, its cedar shingles silver and black with age. Through the windows I could see the uniformed S. P. girls working. Behind the building, merging into the bushes, were the slithe pens where the little reptiles scuttled.

"Look here, Dave," I said suddenly. "I saw a slithe in those bushes over there earlier, from my window. They're escaping again. How the hell do they do it? That's what I'd like to know."

"I'm sorry, Mr. Sagar. I'll inspect the pens again." His face was wooden.

"Forget it, for God's sake." A phrase came into my mind, a phrase from decades, centuries ago when Man found that he was surrounded by equals, and so invented Class Distinction. The phrase: He Knows His Place.

Dave Froehlich Knew His Place and, by God, he was never going to let me forget it.

He is my personal bonded state prisoner for a period of three years—the standard sentence for embezzlement of a sum of not more than two thousand dollars, which was Dave's crime. I think I am a reasonable master. I provide him with accommodation and pay him a small amount for pocket money, which is more than many bonded S. P. men get. In return he must make himself useful to me in so many ways that one wonders at the possibilities for abuse of the Penal Code. But at least the moral is clear. Stay honest.

The other prisoners, those uniformed girls in my small factory, are not so lucky. I hire them from the state pen at an hourly rate. They receive no pay themselves and they live in the deplorable prison accommodations. A state prisoner's only hope of escape from this existence is to elect for bondage—which carries an automatic one-third reduction of sentence and the right to live in accommodations provided by his principal. But principals are not always easy to find, since many freemen do not like the idea of having a crook around the house.

"Maybe you ought to realize just how goddamned lucky you are," I once said to Dave.

"Maybe," he grunted, helping a slithe to shed its skin.

"I suppose you'd rather go back to the old system," I said with some heat; it was one of my bad days. "You'd like to sit around on your ass doing nothing all day, kept by society.

Is that what you're saying? You're saying that because you stole somebody's cash you have a right to a three-year vacation?"

He flushed, and for once I had him going. "I made one mistake, Mr. Sagar, just one. OK, so I've got to pay for it. But the way things are now, you *own* me. You can do what you like with me. It's degrading."

The slithe skin was hanging from his fingers; he released the reptile, dropping it over the wire into one of the pens. I glanced at the fine, almost transparent membrane which the slithe sheds every six months or so. It possessed that grayish, curiously inert look which is characteristic of the shed skin; a sort of waiting look, waiting for a host, waiting for an emotion to latch on to.

And where Dave's fingers touched, the skin glowed bright blue.

Just a small area, the size of a fingerprint—but it told me what Dave was thinking, what his emotions were concerning me, concerning everything. It showed, just for a moment, that Dave hated—and there was no way he could fool that membrane.

Yet he had *elected* for bondage. I'll never figure that.

It took us an hour or more to examine all the netting, repair the holes and retrieve a couple of escaped slithes, and by that time I hoped Dave's mood had improved because nobody can go on hating forever; and he is a damned good foreman. He has the interests of the farm at heart, and I'm sure he will be glad when his time is up and he can stop hating, and take up that partnership I've half-promised him. We walked slowly toward the factory.

"Hi, there! Have I come to the right place?"

I swung around and saw her standing at the gate. Maybe leaning against it would be a more accurate description, leaning in such a way that the top bar pushed into her breast and made me think of her as a woman. And from the direct stare I received from those aged and ageless eyes, I knew she knew she had come to the right place.

Beside me Dave drew a sharp breath and I tried not to look at the skin he was holding.

Instead I looked at Carioca Jones, and I said, "I hope so. I'm Sagar and this is my slithe farm. Can I help you?"

I moved to open the gate but she was already through,

twisting to shut it behind her, then smiling directly at me like a death's head. "What Sagar?"

"Joe."

"I'm Carioca Jones. Didn't I see you . . . ?"

"Out in the Strait yesterday. I'd just pulled the body of Harry Alberni out of the water," I said brutally.

"God, did he *die?*" She was an actress; her expression of horror at the death of a perfect stranger was well done.

"It was an accident, one of those things. The mediman didn't get there in time. Nobody could be blamed."

The flymart landed in the yard, rattling off a list of the day's bargain offers almost before the rotors had stilled. The hatch slid open, displaying shelves of groceries. I handed my list to Dave and moved away from the din, drawing Miss Jones with me. Today she was wearing a sober brown, neck to knee.

"So these are the slithes. I've heard *so* much about them. Where do they come from?"

"They're imported."

"Slithes . . . what a curious name."

"Lewis Carroll. From slithy, meaning lithe and slimy. I think it's quite apt—but it tends to distract from the fact that they're friendly and pleasant little things. And unusually intelligent, for reptiles. Silkie, now—" I picked up my pet, still pink, and held him out to her. She reached out a tentative finger and prodded him behind the ear in that slightly embarrassed manner of the non-animal-lover.

"Oh, look at that. He's changed color!"

"They do. That's their attraction."

"Yes, I suppose so. It's funny"—she laughed girlishly—"I'd never thought of the *animals* changing color. I mean, I knew the *skins* changed color, that's what they're, uh, *for.* But the animals themselves . . . I'd never really thought about *animals,* you know."

She thought the skins grew on trees, was what she meant—if she'd ever thought of trees, that is. But she looked more like a customer every minute. I continued the spiel which had been interrupted by Silkie's involuntary display of distaste. "The chameleon effect fulfills a number of purposes for a slithe on its home planet. It's a mating display, for one thing. When the animal turns red it lets the love-object know of the attraction. Then, as a defense mechanism, when the slithe feels itself threatened it will turn a livid purple in an attempt to frighten its enemy."

"How positively *fascinating*, Joe."

"The skin holds the secret. It's triggered by changes in the body, by heat, sweat, adrenaline, or whatever. But the most remarkable thing is, it lives even after it's been shed. Put it against human flesh and it's sensitive to human emotions."

And, I refrained from saying, slithe skin has learned some new colors, that way.

We entered the small showroom and she admired the displays; fingering the bandannas, kerchiefs, muffs, pendants, wristlets, all those things women wear when they hope to display an affection they are too shy to put into words. Or, as frequently happens, when they are so completely the exhibitionist that they want to parade their emotions—any emotions—in front of the world.

Carioca Jones stood too close to me and handled all these things, and turned them deep pink.

"I want a dress!" she cried suddenly. "I want a whole dress made out of your skins, and I want it to fit *close*. What do you think of *that*, Joe?"

"We don't really do that sort of thing," I mumbled as she arched her back over the display counter and looked up at me, her throat wrinkled like a condor's. "There's a lot of work in joining skins so the seam doesn't show. And it's difficult to match the tones. The cost is out of all proportion. We restrict ourselves to things which can be made out of one skin."

Her eyes had narrowed slightly. "And why do you think the cost should worry me?"

"Well, I . . . I like people to know what they're letting themselves in for."

"Listen to me, Joe Sagar. I never go into anything with my eyes closed, not anything, I want you to remember *that*." Then suddenly she was smiling again, toying with a slithe-skin bandanna which had undergone as rapid a color transformation as I had ever seen—pink, blue, pink almost as quickly as you can say it. "Make me a nice dress, Joe. I can afford it."

"I'll let you have the estimate tomorrow, Miss Jones."

She turned away and I accompanied her across the yard to the gate; Silkie trotted at my heels. Her car was parked under the trees; there was a faint sound of music. I opened the door for her.

The blonde snub-nosed girl was sitting in the passenger seat, an orchestrella on her bare knees. She wore a light gray sweater and a no-skirt skirt. She looked up and smiled, but her smile was for Carioca Jones. The music changed tone, became gay as her long fingers shifted and worked inside the egg-shaped instrument.

Somehow I managed to bid Carioca Jones a polite good-bye, then the car rose from the ground in a swirl of damp autumn leaves and glided away, taking the girl and the music with it, leaving me with the aftersight of beauty.

2

─────◆◆────◆◆◆◆────◆◆─────

Of course I had to find an excuse to call on Miss Jones—
and the blonde girl—as soon as possible. When the estimate
for her dress was worked out I persuaded Doug Marshall to
take me gliding, and contrived to make a clumsy landing
near the beach which backs onto the Jones residence. I
fought my way clear of the harness and waded through the
shallow water to the shore, dragging the tiny glider after me.
Then I climbed the steps above the high-water mark and hurried through the trees in the direction of the house.

I heard the music while I was still among the trees, that
melodic yet unearthly tone which characterizes the orchestrella. For a second I paused, trying to establish from which
direction the sounds came, then I walked on again, turning
left through a pergola which gave onto a tiny sunken lawn.

The girl was sitting on a rustic seat, the instrument in her
lap. She was totally oblivious of my presence as I stood behind her waiting for a break in the flow of the music, reluctant to interrupt. It was like a setting from an ancient oil
painting: the lawn, the shrubs with their late September
flowers, the girl dressed all in white—as though I had stepped
into a dreamlike past. So I waited for just a little while, and
the music flowed on from her sensitive fingers.

At last I recalled myself to the present. I coughed, thinking
what an ugly masculine noise it was in the midst of this
beauty. The music stopped. The girl swung around, eyes
widening in surprise.

"I'm sorry to interrupt," I said. "I've brought the estimate
for Miss Jones."

"You startled me. How did you get here? I didn't hear a
car."

She had spoken without any particular warmth; indeed, I
don't think she recognized me. I introduced myself.

14

She told me her name was Joanne Shaw and for a while I thought things were going well—then I told her about the glider on the beach.

If I'd hoped to impress her with my daring, I failed. Her manner became stiff and she made a few pointed remarks about playboys with bonded men at their beck and call. I tried to explain that I normally worked on Thursdays but lacked the nerve to tell her I'd come in the hope of meeting her.

"What's going on here? Oh, it's you, Joe. I heard voices."

Carioca Jones stepped down to the lawn.

"I was just telling Joanne. My glider came down off your beach."

"Oh, do you *glide?* How *thrilling!*"

We made our way down to the beach and I showed her the glider, then Marshall and his man Charles swept around the Deep Cove headland in the hydrofoil. I removed my wet suit while they loaded the glider on board. Marshall glanced at me inquiringly.

"Why don't you come up to the house and have a drink, Joe?" Carioca Jones said. "You don't have to go, not yet. I can run you home. Then we can talk about the dress in comfort. Joanne, you bring him up in a minute or two."

She departed without waiting for a reply—after all, who could refuse an invitation from Carioca Jones?—leaving Joanne and me standing on the beach and Marshall grinning at us from the stern of the launch as he headed out to sea.

In fact we were not quite alone yet. An obscene shape flopped past, undulating like a sea lion, and a cold eye dwelt on me in passing. I shuddered, feeling a sudden chill.

"I suppose she keeps that brute around so that she can look beautiful by comparison," I observed as the land shark disappeared among the bushes.

Joanne walked away from me without speaking and sat down on a tree stump, placing the orchestrella on her lap. I heard a few sad chords.

"Is it any use telling you Carioca is a very fine person?" she asked quietly. "A lot of people don't understand her, you know."

"Why did she go off like that?"

She smiled faintly. "She doesn't want our company right now. I rather think she's going to . . . change into something more suitable to entertain a male visitor."

"She's wasting her time. I didn't even notice what she's wearing now."

"Didn't you?" Joanne murmured wonderingly, and began to play again. I saw her slim fingers shifting as they caressed the interior of the instrument and the melody flowed all around, bathing us like the warm sea of a tropic summer as we sat on that chill September beach.

She played for a long time although it seemed just a moment; I knew this because suddenly when she finished it was dark and I remembered we were supposed to be up at the house. Joanne remembered at the same time; she jumped to her feet with a gasp of alarm and I climbed stiffly from my heap of driftwood. We hurried up the path, the wet misty webs of night spiders drawing cold lines on our faces.

The house was ablaze with light. I hesitated as one does before entering a large and ominously noisy party.

"I could do with a drink," I muttered from force of habit.

Joanne laughed. "You'll get one, don't worry." She hesitated. "In fact I'll get you one myself. I think Carioca still isn't ready."

A hint of stiffness, of embarrassment, in the way she said this caused me to look at her, then follow her glance to an upper window. Miss Jones moved past, whitely naked in the brightness. We went into the house and Joanne made me sit on a low couch. "Because I rather think Carioca will want to sit next to you," she said with a real, genuine grin. She brought me a scotch and ginger ale.

It was a large, comfortable room; in common with many Peninsula residences the motif was based on the historic Western Seaboard Slide. I suspected the featured spiral staircase came from the beached liner *Princess Louise,* and the floor was original sediment. Polished and glazed, the rich brown ooze showed a multitude of species of marine life which had been stranded decades ago when the tidal waves swept over the low peninsula.

"Look. Uh, Joanne, what exactly is your function here?" I asked bluntly.

"Carioca would call me her companion," she replied, unoffended. "I suppose I'm a sort of agent, secretary, bodyguard . . . I just keep her organized, I guess."

"Does she . . . work much now?"

"Oh, now and then when she feels like it; not a lot. Hardly at all, I suppose. Oh, hell. If you really must know, she doesn't work. She's not . . . in fashion now, if you know what I mean. It hurts her. That's why she sometimes seems a little abrupt, you know. She's a wonderful person, really. She's been great to me, like a . . . like a sister," she said defiantly, daring me to interrupt with a less tactful simile.

"I'm glad you're happy," I said helplessly; there was something disarming about this girl which voided the mind of smart answers.

"Carioca likes to be the center of attention—hadn't you noticed? She always has been, and now she's having trouble realizing things just aren't like that anymore. I rather suspect," she said sadly, "that her ordering a slithe-skin dress is just another bit of compensation. After all, you can't get more flamboyant than that."

"You don't approve of the dress," I surmised.

"Not for her. I think it's a shame she has to call attention to herself that way. But there it is. She's used to being the center of attraction."

And when Carioca Jones made her grand entrance a few moments later, I could see what Joanne meant.

For a start, an open spiral staircase is a revealing item of furniture for a woman in a short dress to descend. The impression of stark cold metal against warm soft flesh heightens the effect. But, as Joanne had said, it was a shame. It was a shame that I was thinking, as she moved down the stairs so slowly, that maybe she was getting on in years and didn't want to fall. I wasn't intended to think that at all. So by the time she reached the bottom and began to make her swaying way across the petrified sediment, I was feeling quite sorry for her. And, to be honest, her figure was good—obscenely good, like one's mother; and just about as interesting. I averted my eyes from the exposed flesh.

She held her face up to be kissed, at least giving me the choice of splashdown area. Then she proceeded to chatter away as though I'd only just arrived, and led me to the couch.

"Joanne darling," she cooed, "play for us while we talk, there's a dear. Something nice and slow and smoochy."

I'd only met her once before today, and that had been a business meeting. I wondered how she would behave if I were a close friend—and then I wondered how many close friends she had, and I felt sorry for her again.

Joanne had moved over to a piece of furniture which, at

first glance, I'd taken for a 3-V alcove. It was a sort of half-dome which somehow suggested excellent acoustics, or the womb, according to how introverted you felt at the time. Like a quarter of an egg. She moved inside and, I think, sat down; it was difficult to tell, as the interior was coated with the new Ultrasorb compound which absorbs all light. Then her hands appeared, slipping into the orchestrella which sat on a low stand. The effect was most spectacular—hands appearing from the blackness, holding the instrument.

I excused myself from Carioca and walked over, standing directly in front of the alcove. Still I couldn't see Joanne. Just her hands were there, right in front of me, caressing the orchestrella. It was uncanny. Then she began to play, disembodied hands moving, astral music filling the room, and I returned to Carioca with some reluctance.

"*Well,*" she said, smiling. "Now here we are. Isn't this *delightful?*"

"Interesting piece of furniture you have over there."

"*Quite,* but we don't want to talk about boring old furniture, do we? Tell me about yourself, Joe. Why does a man like you hide himself away among those funny little animals?"

"It's a living." The music, which Carioca had intended to remain in the background, had impressed itself on me by its sheer power and beauty. I couldn't help but listen to it. "Has Joanne ever thought of taking that up professionally?" I asked.

"My dear, why should she need to, when she has *me?*" There was more than a hint of acid in her voice.

"She's very good."

"Oh, let's forget Joanne, for heaven's sake, Joe. I didn't invite you here to talk about *her.*"

The trapped feeling flustered me and I said something foolish. "Why did you invite me here?"

"Well now, aren't you the forceful one?" She edged closer, all thighs and shoulders. "I asked you here because I like you, Joe. And because you're making a nice dress for me." Her voice hardened again here and I took the point. The dress was far and away the most profitable order we were likely to get this year, and it looked like being a long, hard winter.

"I'm very flattered, Miss Jones."

"Carioca."

"Can I get you a drink?"

"Oh, not *now*. Not when you're just going to tell me all about yourself."

So I sighed inwardly and began to tell her my life story, making it as interesting as possible in the hope that she would concentrate on the abstract past instead of the physical present, while all the time those dark eyes were fixed on mine like mating slugs. After a while she changed the subject.

"But how can you make the dress if you don't know my *measurements*?"

She jumped up and made for the stairs, presumably in search of a tape measure. I heard a chuckle clearly amid the music and looked quickly toward the semidome. "For God's sake come and help me out, Joanne."

In answer the music swelled to a derisive crescendo with undertones of the "Wedding March" as Carioca began her descent of the staircase. "Here!" she cried. "I've found a tape measure. Now we can get it over with. Come on!"

She took my hand and pulled me to my feet—or more correctly I got up, otherwise she would have landed in my lap. She led me to the darkest corner of the room, out of sight of Joanne. "This will be fine here," she said. "I'd ask you to come up to my room, but it wouldn't be quite *right*, would it?"

And suddenly I wasn't worried anymore. She had no thought of getting me into bed, whatever impression she might give. She was Carioca Jones, playing her part. She was a born exhibitionist and it had been quite a while since she'd displayed herself. Now she was virtually alone with a captive audience and she was going to make the most of it. Was I feeling sorry for her again? Maybe, but I was annoyed too. She was using me, taking me for a ride.

The music changed.

"After all, the dress is worn next to the *skin*, isn't it? So the *measurements* must be taken next to the skin."

A most repulsive creature was humping its way across the vitrified past in our direction.

Joanne was playing Duncan's *Allegro in E*.

"I've always thought that's one of the most uplifting pieces ever composed, haven't you, Miss Jones? And doesn't Joanne play it well? So lively, my God, it makes you want to do calisthenics."

She wriggled back into her shoulder straps instantly, coloring. She strode across the floor toward the semidome while I hurried after her, fearing mayhem. The land shark snapped at my heels, dislodging a shoe.

She took the orchestrella from Joanne's hands and held it before me. Her voice had become quiet, very quiet. "It's quite easy to play, Joe, and very interesting. I used to be able to play it myself one time, but you need young hands for that. Soft, like dear Joanne's. You see"—she plunged her fingers into the holes in the egg-shaped instrument—"the depth of the fingers—how far you push them in—controls the pitch. The position of the fingers—which sides of the holes you press—controls both tone and volume. Each finger can produce a sound like a violin, a piano, a guitar, a drum, even. Ten fingers—a ten-piece orchestra, in the hands of an expert."

Her hands were hooked into the instrument like talons.

"I'm afraid my hands aren't what they were. The sensitivity has left them, you see."

Joanne's face appeared from the blackness of the semidome, stricken.

"No, nowadays I'm just a little bit ham-fisted."

The orchestrella screamed in discord as she squeezed and kneaded; then it was silent.

I treated that team of slithes like children. Immediately after Carioca Jones placed her order I had chosen ten prize animals and Dave had built a separate pen for them, with heating in the hutch and a temperature-controlled pool in the small yard. It's odd, the way we tend to regard the animals from a human standpoint. In point of fact, it didn't matter a damn whether the slithes were happy; the important thing was that they all felt the same. If one of them had a bad day, then it was better that they all had a bad day in order to remain empathetic.

Very soon I found that my slithe team needed to be strengthened—something I should have known from the start. It takes more than ten slithes to make a ten-slithe-skin dress. The first disaster occurred two days after my fraught evening with Carioca Jones.

The morning mist was cold and hung in beads from the chicken wire of the pens; I don't know what prompted me to look out of the window at six A.M.—or even to get out of

bed. Anyway, as I gazed on the peaceful scene I saw a movement among the hutches. Something was amiss.

Soon I stood dressed and with shotgun in hand, in the yard.
I looked around, hefting the gun. They can say what they like
about the advantages of the fanbeam laser rifle—it has none
of the excitement of the good old-fashioned twelvebore with
its thunderous discharge and wicked recoil. At this hour of
the morning I was itching to kill, and to have killed quietly
and efficiently would have been no sop to my temper whatever. There was something prowling around my pens, and I
wanted to blast it all to hell.

In point of fact it was a moray eel. He came around the
corner of the prize hutch in a twisting slither, and in his jaws
was struggling a member of my hand-picked team, vivid yellow with fear.

The eel saw me and stopped, watching me with cold
knowing eyes. He was a stray. An oxygenator pulsed near his
gills and I wondered how long he had to live, in his de-
pendency on a human machine. I couldn't shoot him, not
while he had the slithe. I watched him and he watched me,
and at the same time I tried to see where he'd got through
the chicken wire. Then I saw a small gap where the mesh met
the damp soil. I reached it before he did; he dropped the
slithe in order to bare sharp teeth in a soundless gape, and
came on. He must have been seven feet long and he looked
savage and relentless, and I backed off nervously. I'd always
understood morays were idle creatures, spending their time
sitting in rock caves waiting for food to come their way. This
one was acting out of character and it threw me. I had forgotten the shotgun. It was man-to-man stuff now.

Uttering a vicious hissing noise, he came under the wire,
threw me an icy look as he passed, slid across the yard, and
disappeared among the driftwood on the shore. I called it an
honorable draw, because I had the slithe.

I entered the pen and picked the reptile up. He was trembling violently, his skin still yellow; it looked as though it
had been permanently dyed that way.

This strange region of Earth, half land, half ocean, which
we call the Peninsula, abounds in characters equally as
strange. They come here to escape, to retire, to write, to
paint, to live, to die—but mainly to play. A few come here
with the genuine and honest intention of making a profit;

in fact the city of Louise is just like any other North American city on the surface, with stores and lawyers and used hovercar dealers and all the trappings of civilization. Yet there is no escaping the underlying strangeness which dates, I suppose, from the Western Seaboard Slide so many years ago. It is as though the ocean is reluctant to surrender the low-lying land which it briefly occupied during that disaster. Marine images are everywhere; from the barren landscape which the tsunami swept clean of land-born life, depositing its legacy of shells and fossils and the corpses of great fish and even greater ships, to the images of the mind; the compulsions which force the inhabitants to surround themselves with reminders of their prehistoric surroundings.

Naturally enough, the craze for terrestrial fish began on the Peninsula, and although it has since spread nationwide, the person chiefly responsible for the distasteful fad is still with us.

The afternoon following the incident with the moray eel I called at the premises of Pacific Kennels, to lodge a complaint.

The Kennels are situated some three miles from my farm, and consist in the main of a rectangular arena bordered by cages; the entire affair measures some forty yards by twenty. Nearby stands a mock-Tudor house, a tombstone to good taste. A kennel maid greeted me and, after passing on my message, led me into the presence of Miranda Marjoribanks, the proprietor of Pacific Kennels.

She stood statuesque in the center of her large living room, wearing something flowing. "Good afternoon, Mr. uh, Sagar," she said with faint distaste. She has pretensions toward the cultural image whereas I am only a rough farmer. An emotion mobile flickered and murmured in the corner of the room; I knew without looking at the signature that it would be an original Hector Bartholomew.

"Good afternoon, Miss Marjoribanks," I replied, pronouncing her name as it is spelled, which always annoys her.

"Please be seated."

"I'd rather stand, thanks." There was a big horse mackerel on the nearest chair, breathing hard and shedding scales. "I'm afraid I have a complaint. Your fish have been frightening my slithes again. I must ask you to keep them under closer control." I spoke stiffly. I knew that, whatever I said and however I said it, the matter would shortly become unpleasant.

"Oh? And how can you say they are *my* fish, may I ask?"

"A moray took one of my animals this morning. Nobody around here owns a moray. And it can't have come far, otherwise the oxygenator would need replacing."

"I'll have you know the latest oxygenators are *most* efficient, Mr. uh. A fish can live for months, years, without recharging. I don't think I am boasting when I say that my fish are now as well-adapted to land as the domestic cat—and they make just as good a pet. If not better. And they would most *certainly* not attack other animals. Most certainly not."

"How do you know? They have to eat, don't they?" I was thinking of Carioca Jones's objectionable land shark. "My God, if enough of them get loose they'll be roaming the countryside in packs!"

She stared at me furiously. "That, Mr. Sagar, is just the sort of ill-informed comment which can stir up prejudices against the most good-natured and lovable of animals. They said the same thing about the paracat, years ago. Come with me." She swept from the house and I had no option but to follow.

We crossed the open area of rough scrub and stopped at the chain-link fence of the fish enclosure. All manner of brutes lay comatose in the September sun: sharks, rays, barracudas, octopuses, tunas. Among them, unconcerned, moved the kennel maid, feeding a tidbit to a sailfish, rubbing moisturizer into the rough hide of a hammerhead. "Rosalie!" called Miss Marjoribanks.

The girl approached, stepping carefully among the dozing forms. She smiled at me; she was quite pretty.

"Mr. Sagar seems to think our fish are savage beasts, Rosalie," said Miss Marjoribanks. "I'd like you to demonstrate just how wrong he is."

The girl smiled again, glancing around the enclosure. She spotted a barracuda nearby; a six-foot bastard at least one-third of which was head and jaws. She sat down beside it; the fish watched her with one eye, oxygenator throbbing lazily beneath the silver scales. She reached out a finger and tickled the fish. The jaws gaped, the sharp teeth were exposed.

Then Rosalie lay back on the grass and the barracuda's eye followed her as she approached nearer, nearer until her face was within the angle of those terrible jaws and the fish had only to snap them shut in order to disfigure that pretty face for life.

"You see, Mr. Sagar?" Miss Marjoribanks cried triumphantly. "The barracuda is just one of those creatures which Man has granted an undeserved reputation. Newspocket has reported attacks on skin divers. Now, I took the trouble to do a little research. You know what I found? There were two types of incident involving barracudas and skin divers. Firstly, when the diver had speared a fish, the barracuda scented the blood, moved in, and took the fish from the end of the spear.

"And secondly, when the skin diver was stupid enough to shoot the barracuda himself. Then the fish would dart away but would be brought up short by the spear in its side, attached to the line from the gun, and it would be forced to turn. It would tend to swim in a circle, faster than the diver could turn around, gradually wrapping the diver in the line, shortening the distance between them until fish and man were tied together. Then, crazed with fear and pain, the fish would naturally snap at the nearest object."

She went on for some time in this vein while Rosalie moved among the fish, feeding them. I was unconvinced, but she is not the type of woman on whom it is wise to use logic. It was apparent to me that the fish were harmless because they were not hungry, because they were constantly fed. It seemed to me that the average fish-owner might not be so careful. Carioca Jones, for instance. I would hate to be around her land shark if it had missed a meal.

But the most significant point involved Rosalie herself. In the course of the lecture it emerged that the girl was a state prisoner, bonded to Miss Marjoribanks.

I felt that here was a case where the penal laws were being abused, but there was nothing I could do.

3

———— ►◄ ◄■► ►◄ ————

I had replaced the frightened slithe with the others and given him a couple of days to recover, but it was no use. The terror had had a traumatic effect on him and his presence made the others uneasy. He could not lose the yellowish tint which the rest of the team were taking as a warning signal, causing their own skins to fluctuate in unhappy sympathy. In the end I removed him and placed him in isolation.

As a result of this event I doubled the size of the team. I could now afford ten individual disasters without threat to the dress project; and a large, communal disaster did not matter unduly, provided all the animals suffered alike.

Carioca Jones came to see me the day after the moray incident and my visit to Pacific Kennels. By the time I was told she was around, she had already pumped Dave and was leaning over the prize pen in a proprietorial manner.

"Hi, Joe *darling.* Your man tells me these are my *creatures.*"

"That's right."

"But aren't they a bit *variegated,* Joe darling?" Her sharp black eyes scrutinized the tiny herd as the animals scuttled about. "It wouldn't do for Carioca Jones to go dressed in *motley,* would it?"

"I told you about that. They have to get used to each other."

"Oh, dear, they're not like us, are they? I mean, we sort of hit it off immediately, didn't we? I think you felt that too, didn't you, Joe?"

"Of course. Look . . . Carioca. Unfortunately I have a hell of a lot to do."

"But I understand! I've only dropped by for a minute, Joe. I thought we might get the fitting done." She opened up a minuscule purse and dangled a tape measure which I re-

25

garded as one regards a krait. She smiled knowingly. That goddamned measure was becoming almost symbolic.

So I took her into the house and, unchaperoned, got it over with—the measurements, I mean. I don't think she really expected anything else. She just had that knack of making anything appear sexual, which was why her career had been so successful and why it was over, now the bloom had gone. Sad? It was almost pathetic; I kissed her briefly as a compulsory compliment and got her out of the house.

"Well now, that wasn't so bad, was it, Joe?"

"Uh."

"I'll get out of your way now. I have to go into town and do some shopping. I wonder. How would you like to come along? It would do you good to get away from this smelly old farm for a while. Eh, Joe? Maybe we could have a drink somewhere?"

She had dropped the overemphasized manner of speech, she had dropped the coquettishness, she was suddenly, genuinely trying to get through to me. She was lonely and she wanted company for the rest of the afternoon. I wondered what had got into her—then I remembered the episode of the orchestrella.

"Where's Joanne?" I asked.

Her gaze shifted; she looked away. "Back at home."

So there had been a split-up; it was not surprising. I wondered if Joanne was packing her bags and leaving—and I think I felt lonely too, then.

"I'm sorry, Carioca," I said. "I'd like to come. But I've got a hell of a lot to do here, like I said. Maybe some other time."

She smiled. "You really mean that, don't you, Joe? How nice. We must make a date sometime."

"Great."

I walked with her to the car and held the door open. She couldn't resist vouchsafing the usual thigh display as she got in; then she looked at me and said in completely flat, neutral tones: "I must hurry. I have to buy an orchestrella before the stores close."

I've often wondered about the way she said that. That not-quite-casual remark of hers became almost an obsession with me when months later I lay on the warm sands of Halmas and tried to remember and to forget—and even now there is nothing I can pin down, nothing which might have given me a clue as to what her intentions were, that September afternoon. Nothing to tell me whether I was terribly to blame for what happened subsequently.

Was she saying she was sorry? At the time I thought so; but then, she is an actress.

The car rose and whined off, and she was gone. I was left thinking about Joanne again, as I did so often. And as I thought about Joanne and the wrecked instrument, which it seemed Carioca had achieved the decency to replace, I suddenly thought I would make some recompense also. After all, I was partly to blame.

I went into the workshop and gave Dave careful instructions. I wanted to give Joanne a present; not something ridiculously expensive like Carioca's goddamned dress—just something small and appropriate.

But as I went outside again, feeling Dave's amused gaze on my back, I wondered if maybe I just wanted to be around when Joanne wore slithe skin for the first time.

I was so engrossed in this speculation that I jerked in dangerous proximity to heart failure when her voice spoke right next to me.

"Good afternoon, Mr. Sagar."

"Uh, God. I . . . I didn't see you arrive, Joanne. Call me Joe. What . . . how did you get here?"

"Oh, I borrowed a car. Look, Joe. Have you seen Carioca?"

"You've just missed her."

"Did she say where she was going?"

"Louise. She was—" I stopped in time. Maybe the orchestrella was supposed to be a surprise. "Is it anything urgent?"

"I . . . I don't know." She hesitated. "We haven't spoken very much, you know, since— Then she went off this afternoon without saying a thing, not a thing."

"Don't worry. She was perfectly normal when I saw her."

"Oh, thank goodness." She looked around, at a loss. "Well, I must get going. I'll see if I can find her in town. When we . . . when we go to Louise together, we usually split up for shopping and meet at the *Princess Louise* bar, at six. That's where I'll find her, I'm sure. She'll be there."

"Joanne, I tell you she's OK." She was fidgeting around and twisting the strap of her bag between her fingers and it was driving me mad. I mean, here she was on my home ground, and all we could talk about was an aging 3-V star who was more than capable of looking after herself. "Come in and have a drink, why don't you?"

"Oh, I couldn't. Really, not now. I must go."

"I'll come with you," I said. "We can all have a drink."

But with luck, I thought, we won't be able to find Miss Carioca Jones.

Time has been kind to the *Princess Louise.* The records of its arrival are sketchy as the ship's log was destroyed—along with the entire crew, so it is said—at the time of the Slide. Soon afterward it was discovered by the few survivors of the tidal waves which had cleaned any other form of shelter off the surface of the Peninsula. These frightened wrecks huddled together for months, maybe years, until they gradually drifted back into communication with the rest of the world.

Their first contact doubtless came by means of the roving bands of Indians who had hunted the more northerly regions since time immemorial. By then, it is supposed that the *Princess Louise* had become a village in its own right. Then suddenly the world returned and a city grew around the beached liner. And with the arrival of people, history began to move forward again on the Peninsula.

"Look. I'm sorry if there was some sort of trouble," I said as we sipped our drinks in the busy bar. "I feel partly to blame, you know."

"I . . . I don't see why."

"Well, you know . . . I was maybe a bit tactless praising your playing, knowing Carioca can get jealous. I just didn't think."

"I haven't noticed she's particularly jealous," she said. "She likes to be the center of things, yes. But jealous?" At last she grinned, a good straightforward grin. "I think she was annoyed because she wasn't getting what she wanted, so she took it out on me—or rather my orchestrella." She hesitated oddly then, and the grin faded.

"I'm not sure she, uh, wanted anything. She just wanted me to think she did. It was an act." And it could be a dangerous act; this was when I experienced my first real twinge of uneasiness about Joanne's position. "Can't you see what she's really like, Joanne?"

I had lost her again. "I know what she's like, and she's always been very good to me."

She was loyal to Carioca Jones and she was damned if she was going to denigrate her in front of a comparatively casual acquaintance like me. Apologetically I reached across the table and put my hand over hers.

That was the moment Carioca Jones chose to arrive. As I tried to collect my thoughts I remembered I had told her previously I was too busy to come out.

I often saw Carioca Jones during the next few weeks. When we met, her manner was not unfriendly, and she never referred to the meeting with Joanne and me—or the public scene that had ensued. She dropped by every few days to check on the progress of her dress and chatted pleasantly about the promising appearance of the slithes. By now the little reptiles were identical in their reactions; it was a pleasure to see them all change color, simultaneously, from dull brown to warm pink when I approached with food. I calculated they would all be due to shed in a couple of weeks' time, and within two or three days of one another.

Just once she made an oblique reference to Joanne. She let drop the news that she was practicing the orchestrella again; I presumed Joanne was giving her lessons. She held her knotted fingers before her as she said this, flexing them as though playing an imaginary instrument. It put me in mind of an eagle swooping on a lamb.

I found an excuse to call on the house, once. I got Doug Marshall to take me for a run in his hydrofoil and persuaded him to anchor off Carioca's beach. He, myself, and Charles Wentworth sat in the cockpit drinking while I kept my eyes on the shore. Marshall was talking about his new glider which he expected to be delivered later in the week, and Charles and I listened, although from time to time I caught Charles glancing at me with a faint grin, as though he knew what I was looking for.

"I think I'll just slip ashore for a minute," I said suddenly.

They looked knowing. "Not longer than an hour, right, Joe?" said Marshall. "I want to get some practice in later, before the new glider arrives."

It seemed a long time before I was hurrying through the trees but it was probably only a few minutes, such is the time-scale of love. The carport was empty, so I could safely

assume Carioca was out, and that it was Joanne I had caught
a glimpse of from the boat. Then I heard the sweet sounds
of an orchestrella being played as only Joanne knew how. I
slipped through the open French windows and crossed the
floor quietly. The interior of the semidome was the antithe-
sis of light but I could see her hands stroking a new and
ornate orchestrella. I watched and listened for a while,
then I spoke. Time was short and Carioca might return at any
moment.

"Joanne."

She stepped from the blackness and smiled at me. "Hello,
Joe. I didn't hear you come in. I'm afraid Carioca's gone out
for a while, but she'll be back in about half an hour, I expect."

"I came to see you, Joanne."

I had been too direct. A flicker of alarm crossed her face.
"Whatever for?"

"I see Carioca's bought you a new orchestrella."

"It's not mine. It's Carioca's. She's playing again. The one
she smashed was hers too; I'd like you to understand that."
She looked around the expensive room. "Everything's Carioca's. Everything."

"Don't be so goddamned humble, Joanne. She's not a god-
dess. It's not a privilege for you to work for her. She's just
an ex-star, a has-been. You're worth a dozen of her. You're
young and you're very pretty. You could be a star yourself,
if you had half the luck she had."

"Look, Mr. Sagar. There's nothing wrong in Carioca's
having been successful. I don't like to hear people running
her down because she isn't maybe . . . working so much these
days. Look at it this way. She could have been just another
married woman, an average housewife. Would you say a married woman was finished—a has-been—just because she's decided not to have any more children? The only person who
knows if Carioca is finished is herself; and judging from the
way she is I'd say she's OK, she's fine. She used to be a 3-V
star but now she's changed her angle. She's moved to the
Peninsula with plenty of money; she doesn't need to work,
and now she's well on her way to becoming a pillar of local
society, a person who people want to know because she's
famous and interesting. How many people seek *you* out, Mr.
Sagar? How many people make an effort to get to know
you?"

I wondered why she was talking like this. I'd seen no evidence of Carioca's sudden popularity. It seemed that everything had gone wrong. I shouldn't have come. "That's not fair, Joanne. Maybe I don't want people to seek me out."

"Hey, but you wouldn't mind, would you, Joe? You wouldn't mind people pointing you out to each other and saying, 'There goes Joe Sagar, the world-famous slithe-farmer.'" Suddenly she was laughing. "Oh, Joe, why the hell didn't you choose a more impressive name, and job?" She looked at me, face flushed, and she was incredibly beautiful, infinitely desirable.

I put my hands on her shoulders. "I'm happy the way I am. I don't think Carioca is. I'm on an even keel but she's on the way down. But I'd rather not talk about her."

I drew her gently toward me. She disengaged herself and walked back to the semidome.

"I'll play for you, not with you, Joe," she said.

When Carioca arrived she found us just like that. I was standing, listening to the music and watching Joanne's hands, because that was all I could see of her.

Two weeks later the slithes shed their skins, and a week after that Carioca Jones's dress was finished. I had a female state prisoner in the factory at the time who was about Carioca's size, so we gave her the dress to try on. When she reappeared she was smiling and radiant, and the dress was a warm, uniform pink. The seams were invisible and the fit perfect; the dress seemed almost to blend with the girl's own skin. She looked a hell of a lot better in it than Carioca would—and she knew it.

"Betty, you look fantastic," breathed Dave, popeyed with admiration.

Eventually we had to get the girl and the dress separated. I supervised the packing; I didn't want anything to go wrong at this stage. I had previously packed my personal gift to Joanne and I sat looking for some time at the small box, wondering what the hell to write on the card.

I hadn't seen either Carioca or Joanne for over two weeks and had, in fact, been getting nervous over the order for the dress. There had been no answer to my calls and on the one occasion I summoned up the nerve to visit the house, it was all locked up. I couldn't understand why Carioca hadn't told me she was going away.

Then, a few days before the dress was complete, her face had appeared on the visiphone screen.

"Terribly sorry, Joe darling, but I had to go away for a couple of weeks. Rather nasty, actually. Everything's all right now, though." In the background I caught sight of Joanne moving about, and felt a huge relief.

"What do you mean? What happened?"

"Oh, such a *silly* thing. I was feeding Wilberforce and he bit me, and I had to have shots and surgical treatment and all sorts of stupid things."

"Wilberforce?"

"You know him, my land shark. He's such a pet really, and *so* good-tempered."

"You ought to have the bastard put down."

"Oh, I *couldn't*. Anyway, I thought I'd better call and tell you everything's all right here. And my dress. Is it finished?"

"Almost. Just two or three days."

It was, in fact, four days later when I called and told her it was ready. She went into hysterical transports of delight and insisted that I bring it over right away for a ceremonial trying-on. By then it was four o'clock in the afternoon, so I washed and changed and left Dave instructions to close up. As I drove over to Carioca's place there was a tingling knot of nervous anticipation centered around my solar plexus. I hadn't seen Joanne for three weeks. I wondered if she'd thought of me during that time. I wondered if she would like her present. Then I managed to think business again to the extent of hoping Carioca liked the dress.

The lights were on in the house when I arrived and I could hear the soft sound of the orchestrella. Twilight was all around me as I hurried across the wet grass, then up the crunching gravel path to the front door, clutching the boxes. The air was chill and damp and I started at a rustling in the bushes; it was probably the carnivorous Wilberforce on a foraging expedition. The front door was ajar; I stepped inside.

"It's me!" I called.

There was no reply so I entered just the same, sure of my welcome now the dress was finished. The vast living room echoed to the glorious tones of the orchestrella and a drink stood on the table near the semidome. This was something of a royal welcome; obviously Carioca meant me to make myself at home while she slipped into something easy to slip off again. I took the glass and strolled over to the semidome, watching Joanne's pale, beautiful fingers working gently as she changed subtly from the buoyant tones of the welcoming music into the melody of a tender love song.

For a while I just stood and listened, trying not to think about Carioca and the fact that she had told Joanne what to play; instead I said to myself—this is for me. Joanne has chosen this song herself, for me, because she loves me.

And the way she was playing it, so softly, so expressively, I could almost believe she did. It was not a matter of technical perfection; in fact, I'd heard her play more correctly. It was an emotional thing; the occasional uncertainty, hesitancy, only serving to heighten the spell—the endearing tremulousness of a young girl in love. She played it how it is.

At last the slender fingers were still and she was finished. She was waiting for me to say something but I didn't know what to say.

"Hello," I murmured at last. "That was beautiful."

A pale shadow appeared within the light-absorbing semidome as she stood. She stepped forward and the room lighting fell upon her black hair, accentuating harshly the wrinkles about the eyes, the hard lines of the mouth.

"Hello, Joe darling," said Carioca Jones. "You never believed me when I said I could play."

Just for an instant the room seemed to shake itself about me and my stomach gave one single, great throb of horror and disgust. I turned away so that she couldn't see the shock in my eyes, and clutched at the boxes on the table. Dumbly I handed the larger one to her.

She took it in her young, soft hands and began to undo the wrappings with little squeals of delight, while I watched in fear, seeing the thin scars around her wrists.

Dimly I heard Joanne's voice behind me and dragged my gaze away.

"Joe! How nice to see you again. Carioca tells me you've had a present made for me. You shouldn't have, you know."

Joanne was walking across the room, smiling at me; then she turned and watched affectionately as Carioca went into paroxysms of delight over the dress. She looked at me again.

"Well, aren't you going to give it to me?"

Of course, I should have guessed. I should have known that Carioca would have a bonded S. P. girl, and I should have guessed that neither the friendless ex-star nor the female state prisoner would advertise the fact.

I was still clutching the small box. I suppose I must have blinked and half pulled myself together, tried to smile, and offered it to her.

Joanne reached to take it.

With glittering, steel prosthetic hands.

4

Winter came to the Peninsula and the sling-gliders were dismantled and stowed away in the clubhouse, and the racy hydrofoils were winched up onto the slipways to stand poised on their stilt legs like greyhounds in the traps, waiting for the start of the first race of the season. The chill rain drove across the flatlands and low scrub, and the November gales pounded the shore. It became uncomfortable to drive the hovercars in the sweeping crosswinds and most people stayed at home, relying on the flymart for supplies, wishing they had gone south before all this happened. There were News-pocket reports of starving fish prowling the bush.

I missed most of this, because old Doc Lang recommended me to take a long vacation. "You need a change, Joe," he said, after I described symptoms which ranged from headaches and indigestion to bouts of screaming in the night. I can laugh about it now, almost, but at the time I reckon I must have been pretty sick. The very fact that I can remember so little of those months must prove something.

"I can't leave the farm," I think I said.

"If you don't want to end up in the funny house you'll have to leave the farm," he replied, drinking my scotch.

Later I approached Dave Froehlich. Despite the cold, the animals were all fit and well in their heated quarters, and the factory had orders for several weeks ahead. Everything was running smoothly; the question was, would it all fall apart as soon as my back was turned?

"Dave, I'm taking off for a spell. I don't know how long. Will you be able to cope?"

"Yes," he said shortly, evincing no surprise.

"You won't forget about the new consignment of breeding stock? They arrive at Sentry Down on the fourteenth.

And Mrs. Lambert's stole; I promised delivery in two weeks. Those animals in pen E are for—"

"Just get the hell out of here, will you, Mr. Sagar? I've been running this business almost as long as you and I reckon I ought to know how to handle things by now."

It would be nice to record that this was said with manly gruffness which failed to conceal a deep concern—but this was not so. It was my bonded man Dave Froehlich speaking, and he spoke with cold dislike. I looked in on the S. P. girls in the factory, was about to say good-bye to them all, then thought better of it. Soon enough, they would notice that I was not around.

Doc Lang had been eager to suggest a place for me to hole up in; it seemed he knew a small hotel down south where, I suspect, they understood people who suddenly and inexplicably began to cry into their soup, or stand on high ledges. It was called Dingle Dell, which in itself gave me cause for suspicion, with its undertones of coziness, of sympathy. "I'm sure they can fit you in," he said.

So I loaded the hovercar and caught the early ferry to the mainland. It was a rough crossing with high seas and a stiff breeze, but the huge old hovercraft rode the steep waves well. I sat in the restaurant during most of the voyage, watching the weather outside, and all the time the thought of my hovercar down in the car deck was nagging at me. The thing was a responsibility, and I didn't want responsibilities. I would have to collect it, and drive it off, and find parking spaces, and observe speed limits.

The waiter brought me another coffee and by the time I had finished it the matter of the hovercar had become an obsession. I took out my Newspocket portovee and tried to concentrate on the news items but there were road warnings here and accidents there, and it seemed that anyone who drove a car at this time of year was even more insane than I. There was snow in the mountains and floods in the valleys. I began to wish I was back at home on the farm.

By the time the ferry docked I had made up my mind. I contacted a porter, gave him instructions to have the car taken back to Roberts Bay at my expense, and caught the bus south. I left all my possessions in the car, apart from my wallet and the clothes I wore, and as the bus nosed through the traffic I began to feel better.

I stayed for a few days in several towns, but something always happened to make me move on again. Either the weather was foul, or the hotels full, or I would see a paraplegic being wheeled down the street. On one occasion I found myself in the midst of a Foes of Bondage convention. I met a few of these people in the bar of the hotel; they seemed to be mostly women with burning eyes and incessant cigarettes and a rabid hatred of the Penal Reform Act and all it stood for.

It was a pity. Although I was in sympathy with much of what they stood for, I couldn't stand the individuals themselves. They seemed to be suffering from a bad case of oversell; if I'd admitted to them that I had a bonded man who was running my farm right now, I think they would have strung me up on the spot.

But the weather improved as I traveled south by hoverbus and monorail and hoverbus again, until eventually I wound up at Halmas. It was literally the end of the road, a small hot ancient village on a rocky promontory with a sandy beach, and there was no place else to go; there didn't need to be. I climbed down from the bus to the dusty street and I didn't see a land fish anywhere; in fact the only living creature in sight was an old man sitting in the dirt outside what looked very much like a bar.

Several beers later I knew I had found what I was looking for. I checked in at the little town's only hotel and spent the next few days lying on the beach in the sun; and gradually I began to feel better. I didn't forget the events of the past months on the Peninsula because, strangely, I hadn't properly been able to remember them for some time. I merely found that my amnesia didn't worry me so much.

The hotel was simple and comfortable, and the owners pleasant. I think they were excited at having a foreigner in the place and they spoke English for me and would have cooked northern food for me, but I insisted that I would rather eat the local dishes. Their names were Aldo and Jinny Carassa and they had a son named Jon, a swarthy Latin-looking lad of twenty who looked as though he knew how to use a knife. They also had a daughter whose name, oddly enough, was Marigold.

The scene was therefore ripe for the development of the type of situation common in many of the early Carioca Jones movies. During the fall season the local 3-V station had

rerun several of these classics and I had been amused by the
style of melodrama, and interested by the dark beauty of the
young Carioca who appeared to spend her time being rav-
ished by a succession of strangers in town. The ravisher was
in due course dispatched by a thrust from the knife of
Carioca's brother of the time. The brother was then executed
by members of the Nordic subrace. The father took to drink.
The mother committed suicide. Meanwhile Carioca became
pregnant and a nun, in that order.

It was all terribly sad and I didn't want it to happen to
these good folk, so for a time I kept my hands off Marigold.
This was not always easy, since it was her habit in the evenings to walk abut the hotel in scanty night attire, invari-
ably meeting me in some narrow, twisting corridor.

Added to which she would frequently wake me as I lay
dozing on the beach, and I would find her kneeling over me,
falling out of her bikini. "Wake up, Joe, and speak to me more
about the Peninsula," she said one day in her strong accent.

"Marigold, would you mind sitting back a bit? Your brother's over there."

"You don't like my—" She looked down at herself. "How
do you say it?"

"I don't say it." I couldn't decide whether she was totally innocent or totally carnal, and I didn't intend to find
out. "What do you want to know about the Peninsula?"

I had already told her everything I knew, described every
square mile, told her about Louise and the beached liner, the
state pen, the Peninsula Sling-gliding Club, Pacific Kennels—
and she was still hungry for more. It was sad that she should
regard the phony sophistication of the Peninsula as some sort
of romantic heaven—to the detriment of the beautiful, real
simplicity of Halmas.

I once told her, joking, that when she came to visit me
there would be no need to meet her at the ferry terminal.
She would be able to find her way to my house blindfold.

She stretched out her leg and examined it, stroking the
brown flesh. She had a small star-shaped scar on the big toe
of her right foot; the result of an accident with a spear-gun,
she told me. "Tell me all about the sling-gliders."

"I've already told you all about them."

"You tell me what they do, but you don't tell me what they
are. It seems they risk their lives for fun, is that not so?"

"Well, yes, but they don't think of it like that. I mean, you don't keep thinking a shark will get you, when you're out spear-fishing, do you?"

"I fish for food, not fun. It is not the same thing. These pilots, do they not fear being broken up?"

"That's half the fun, Marigold. And if they do get hurt—" I hesitated; suddenly the Peninsula seemed a long way removed from this warm beach. "If they do get hurt they might have a bonded man. If not, we have a thing called the Ambulatory Organ Pool, where they can get replacement parts for themselves." Images began to flicker through my mind.

"Please tell me what is the matter, Joe."

"It's nothing to do with you, Marigold. Can I tell you something? I love you." I laughed so that she wouldn't take me seriously, because I didn't love her for herself. I loved her for the life she stood for.

I had remembered my own life. It still hurt, but I could face it now, here on this beach.

I remembered leaving Carioca's house and, after a short interval, getting into my hovercar. I remembered the way the light from the front door slanted across the grass which was already sparkling with dew, while the two women watched me from the doorway, black silhouettes and long black shadows which I tried not to see, in case I saw details I wanted to forget.

I remember being able to think again, to think slowly and begin perhaps to understand. I was somewhere in a suburb of Louise, although I forget how I got there. I saw pale houses and dark shadows, and here and there the lissom shape of a guard shark. I drove out of Louise then, and along the Marine Drive.

I remember stopping somewhere, lighting a cigarette and looking out at the blackness of the night sea. I took a flask of scotch from the glove compartment and drank, and I remember being scared that there wasn't enough in the bottle. Something caught my eye on the seat beside me; it was the small box containing Joanne's present. I tried not to blame her for what had happened; she was a bonded S. P. girl and she had no rights in the matter; such is the law.

I remember watching some fool night-gliding, slipping quietly across the sky like a pale, swift bat. Somewhere a state prisoner might be watching that tiny shape, too. He might be wishing the pilot dead, but he would never wish him injured. I remember wondering just how badly Carioca's hand had been bitten.

There is a derogatory nickname for state prisoners based on the initial letters; it is seldom heard, but it came into my mind that evening.

At least I'd had the wit to bring Joanne's present away with me.

What good was a pair of slithe-skin gloves to my used Spare Parts girl?

"I know you don't mean that, Joe. You don't mean that, do you, Joe?"

I looked into her face. I've often wondered why Marigold was so fair, while her parents and brother were such typically dark Latin people. She had pretty blonde hair and a golden tan which made the darker girls on the beach look merely dirty. "Not in the way I wish I meant it," I replied.

"It is good; you feel better now. I think a ghost was walking on your grave."

"You're right. But it's gone now." It would be back, of course, but at least I felt I could look it in the face. "Come on," I said, standing and pulling her to her feet too. "Let's go for a walk. I want to go where your brother can't find us."

"I think I know the place," said sweet Marigold.

We climbed the hot rocks at the northern end of the beach and walked along a brown rutted path beside a banana plantation; the tall plants were beginning to bloom and the tops had bent over with the weight of the heavy, suggestively shaped red flower. Marigold walked ahead of me, and I watched her provocative bottom moving under the thin cloth of the bright bikini. She led me between the rows of plants; I glanced back once but brother Jon seemed to have lost us. The leaves were dense and I turned back to follow Marigold, satisfied that we were safe from pursuit.

She stopped and turned to face me, a faint smile on her lips. The sun dappled her body as she reached up and took hold of one of the firm, heavy banana flowers, weighing it in her hand. I could see the undercurve of her breast as I stood beside her, and moving my viewpoint slightly, I caught sight of a pink nipple.

"You didn't look at me like that before," she said softly, still feeling the red flower, pulling it down toward her, laying it against her cheek as she watched me. Her bare feet shifted in the coarse grass, her left arm cradled under her breasts, lifting them from the scanty cloth, bringing hard little pink tips into plain view. "Why don't you, if you like to?"

"Your brother . . . was always around." I was having difficulty in speaking; my hand reached out of its own volition while a huge pulse hammered in my chest. My fingers were stroking the erect nipples; I found my breath was coming faster. I wondered briefly how this foreign girl whom I didn't love could affect me like this; then my mind seemed to stop thinking and I think I groaned as I pulled her toward me, and she let go of the red flower which sprang up and away, and she took hold of me instead.

We must have stayed in that plantation for three hours or more and yet, as I watched her lead the way back toward the sea, I was still overcome with desire at the sight of her and had to seize her from behind while she struggled and giggled and at last gave in with a groan of delight. Afterward we slipped down to the beach and quickly into the sea, before Jon, who sat on a nearby rock in saturnine frustration, could see us. The cool water brought us to our senses, and by the time we emerged, I think we were quite lucid. Anyway, after a brief glance of suspicion Jon appeared satisfied, and made no move toward his knife.

That afternoon of pure, unthinking lust was the catharsis I needed, and the following day I decided I could face the return to the Peninsula. When they saw me off on the bus Marigold kissed me in brief sisterly fashion, while Jon scowled and shook my hand. I invited them all to come and stay with me at the farm, and they accepted. As the bus moved off I was hoping they would come, although I knew they wouldn't. They were poor, the fares high. I tried, later, to work up a guilt feeling over Marigold, but I couldn't achieve anything worth condemning myself for. I took the slow route back, and a few days later arrived home.

Dave Froehlich greeted me with a question about the new breeding stock; he spoke as though I'd never been away. There was a different bunch of S. P. girls working in the factory; it later emerged that we had suffered a strike over working conditions while I'd been gone. Dave admitted this grudgingly and it gave me no small satisfaction. Although the method of solving a dispute with the S. P. girls is simple—we merely hire a different crew—the fact that any problem should have reached strike proportions bore testimony to Dave's lack of tact. Maybe it was not just me he hated. Maybe he hated everybody.

That evening as I sat in my living room, back to the realistic view of the stormy winter Strait with the euphoria of the south just a memory, I wondered how to face the Peninsula again. I called the state penitentiary for a start, and soon the face of Heathcote Lambert appeared on the screen.

"Joanne Shaw?" he repeated. "Yes, I recall her. She was bonded to Carioca Jones."

"Was? You mean she's been released now? She's a freewoman?"

"Oh, no. She's back in the pen. Wait a moment." He disappeared from view and I found I'd finished my scotch without remembering the first gulp. "Here we are," he said after a while, holding a card. "Yes. She drew a stiff sentence in the first place—I can't tell you why, of course, Joe. Then she had a one-third remission for contracting into bondage, plus a further one-third for— I see she made a donation."

"That's right," I managed to say.

"Then Miss Jones released her from bondage with a good reference and she came back here to serve out her term. She's due for release in September. The sixth, it says here."

September the sixth . . . it was about eight months away. "Why did Miss Jones release her from bondage?" I asked.

"I've no idea. Provided the references are good she still gets her remission, and that's all that concerns us. Although—" He hesitated. "I hear Miss Jones has been speaking out against the Penal Reform Act recently."

"Christ, that's a switch. Are you saying she doesn't believe in bondage anymore?"

"I'm just throwing out a suggestion, Joe. You can make what you like of it. But there was a lot of trouble while you were away and it transpired that Miss Jones had made herself unpopular over the, uh, circumstances of Miss Shaw's donation. A whole lot of people reckoned the donation was unnecessary and Carioca Jones found herself socially ostracized."

"Oh, now isn't that just too bad."

"Seriously, Joe, it means a lot to a woman like Carioca Jones. My betting is that she's trying to make amends, and the first step was to release Miss Shaw. Then she made a big thing out of sending her damned shark to the Kennels for psychiatric therapy. I see her name around a lot; she seems to be trying to get involved with the Fine Arts Club, and the Louise Amateur Dramatics, and the Victims of Tycho Fund, and all that crap."

I thanked him, told him I'd see him at the club on the weekend, and hung up. I poured myself another scotch and watched the lights of an antigrav shuttle glide across the black sky. Joanne was due for release on September sixth. I wished I'd asked Lambert about visiting days. The scotch, plus the undeniable pleasure of being back in familiar surroundings, induced a sensation of optimism. Cautiously I thought again of Marigold and found only pleasure in the recollection, allied to a considerable amount of honest lust.

It occurred to me only briefly that I would have been better advised to love Marigold, rather than the enigmatic and disabled girl in the state penitentiary.

5

On the following morning I awoke refreshed and alert, a sign of having consumed exactly the right quantity of alcohol the previous night. My bedroom was bright with watery sunlight and the ceiling reflected moving ripples from the murmuring ocean outside; there was almost a touch of spring in the air. It occurred to me that I might go along to the club later in the day; it was time to start making arrangements for the start of the new sling-gliding season. I dressed, watched Newspocket while I drank my coffee, then went out to the yard.

Dave Froehlich was squatting beside one of the pens, repairing the netting. He looked up as I approached.

"We lost two animals last night," he said shortly.

"Sharks?"

"I don't think so. Look. The netting has been pulled away from the post. No shark could do that."

In one corner of the pen the remainder of the slithes huddled uneasily, their skins still bearing traces of the yellow tinge of fear. They regarded me with sad, reptilian eyes and even the sight of Silkie at my feet could not persuade them to approach.

"So what do you think it is?"

He rose to his feet, dusted his hands off, and accompanied me toward the workshop. "I don't have any idea," he said. "There's been a lot of talk recently about people abandoning their pets, turning them loose." He opened the factory door and we entered. The S. P. girls were working quietly and, so far as I could tell, efficiently. "Some of these people think it's cute to have a tuna as a pet—then after a few days they find tunas need constant moisturizer and food. And they're boring; all they do is lie around gasping and stinking. So they have the choice of turning them loose, having them

put down, or eating them. It's easiest just to turn them loose
and forget about them. I hate to think what might be out
there, in the bush. Somebody ought to do something about
it. We need an active organization, like the Foes of Bondage. They'd close down that Marjoribanks woman quick
enough."

"From what I've seen of the Foes of Bondage I'd call
them a bunch of nuts," I said incautiously.

There was a twitter of indignation from the S. P. girls and
I found myself the center of instant hostility. One rat-faced
woman had sprung to her feet.

"The Foes are the only thing that keeps bastards like you
under control!" she shrilled. "The Foes are a fine body of
women and I won't have any goddamned freeman saying
otherwise. You're just an idle slave-owner, going off on vacation and leaving poor Dave here to run your goddamned
farm for you!"

It was too early in the morning for this kind of thing. "Take
her name and send her back to the pen, Dave," I
snapped. "How the hell did you get to pick a weirdo like
her?"

"Don't let him tell you what to do, Dave!"

The women were all on their feet now, crowding around
me, and I wondered who was going to throw the first punch
or whatever it is that enraged women do. I had a hunch that
someone would hit me from behind first—and only then
would the rest of them summon up courage to attack me
from the front. So I backed quickly against a bench and
bunched my fists. In such a situation I have no scruples whatever; it was, quite simply, them or me. I still found time to
be surprised at how quickly the storm had blown up.

Apparently there was still some talking to do before the
action began, however. "Look at the coward, frightened of
us women," someone shouted uncertainly.

I felt a rising tide of temper at the unfairness of this confrontation. "Dave," I snarled, "I want you to tell these fools
the score. As a freeman there are three ways I can make
things hot for you people. Firstly, I can misuse you as a
bonded man. Have I ever done that? Secondly, I can ill-
treat these S. P. girls. Have I ever done that? Thirdly, I can
apply to the Ambulatory Organ Pool for a graft or a transplant. Have I ever done that? Tell them, you bum. Tell them

that you elected for bondage of your own free will, because you wanted the remission. Tell them that!"

He swallowed as they all turned on him. "Yes, but you go sling-gliding. How do I know you won't get yourself smashed up? Because you have a bonded man they won't let you use the Pool. I'm the one who'll have to donate."

"Then why the hell did you apply for bondage?"

"I . . . I guess I wanted the remission."

"Look, Dave. I keep you here because you're a good worker, and I've told you I'll see you right when your sentence is up. Isn't that worth waiting for?" I stared at him; his eyes dropped. "I just can't understand your problem."

The rat-faced woman reentered the fray, sensing that the battle was degenerating into a logical discussion. "You've created a race of second-class citizens!"

This was a new one to me; it sounded like a slogan of the Foes of Bondage, but I hadn't heard the group down south use it. "Have I?" I asked, puzzled.

An unexpected male voice spoke. "Of course you haven't, Joe. That's Evadne Prendergast's latest catch-phrase, designed to make you feel guilty." Doug Marshall stood in the doorway, large and comforting. With him was his man Charles, equally stalwart. "It conveniently ignores the fact that the reason state prisoners are second-class citizens is because of the crimes they committed—not because of anything honest men did."

"You!" squealed the rat-faced woman. "You there, Charles Wentworth. You're a bonded man. Are you going to stand there and take all this horseshit? What sort of a man are you?"

Charles was leaning against the door, grinning lazily. "Too much of a man for you, lady. I got five years for rape." He scrutinized her scrawny frame with pretended interest, then shook his head. "Although I think I'd draw the line at you."

The scream of temper was drowned by the general outburst of mirth from the other girls and the bad moment was passing. Charles followed up his thrust with a short pep talk on the advantages of playing ball with one's employer, and the whole affair fizzled out.

As we left the factory I asked Doug Marshall, "Who the hell is Evadne Prendergast?"

"President of the local chapter of the Foes of Bondage—although not for long, if Miss Carioca Jones has anything to do with it. I think our movie star has her eyes on the title."

I stared at him. "Are you seriously trying to tell me Carioca Jones has joined the Foes of Bondage?"

"Casting aside all worldly possessions, including Joanne Shaw," he affirmed. "There's nothing strange about it. Politicians change viewpoints all the time, so why not aging 3-V stars? I tell you, your friend Carioca is really going places."

"I just don't get it," I muttered. "I can't even understand why they should admit her to membership."

"A convert is the best advert," he said. "Particularly a notable like Miss Jones. Her presence will have more impact than a dozen ordinary honest women. I only hope they don't take it into their heads to foul up the opening day of the gliding season with some goddamned demonstration. The Foes have been making their presence felt around here, recently. By the way, we have a Club Committee meeting later this afternoon. Are you coming?"

"Sure." It would be good to talk gliding again. We discussed the President's Trophy—which is awarded to the winner of the first race of the season—then we caught sight of a hovercar moving through the scrub.

"I'm getting out of here," said Doug abruptly, hurrying toward his car. "That looks like Carioca Jones." Charles followed, the doors slammed, the car rose and fled down the track in a scattering of dead leaves.

I leaned against the gate, waiting for Carioca Jones and wondering how the hell to handle her.

Her car sank to the ground and there was a pause while she collected her things from the seat beside her; I could see her tucking gloves and keys into her purse and making a show of peering under the dash for her shoes—but I knew that she was playing for time; that, like me, she was uneasy about the confrontation.

She walked toward me, dressed soberly in black. "Hello, Joe," she said quietly.

"Let's go into the house," I said.

She sat by the window in the living room and I handed her a drink, taking a large one myself. My hands were shaking and I didn't know whether I hated her or pitied her. I didn't know why she was here; I could see no reason why we should ever have needed to meet again—except that we both knew Joanne.

She watched me with her hard black eyes but the usual calculation was not there; rather, she looked uncertain. Not surprisingly.

"Joe, I don't know what to say," she said at last. "I want you to believe me when I say I'm truly sorry for what happened. I was a stupid and jealous woman and I should have been imprisoned for what I did, but the law doesn't work that way."

"No, it doesn't."

"How . . . are you? I mean, how are you feeling, Joe? I heard you were . . . sick, before you went away."

"I needed a change, that's all."

Her drink was finished, as was her first cigarette. I re- filled her glass and she fumbled another cigarette from the packet and held it to her lips with trembling fingers, with young fingers, looking to me for a light. I saw a bright tear starting around her lower eyelid; they teach actresses to do that. She looked beaten, like an old prostitute.

"You loved her very much, did you, Joe?"

"I guess I did . . . I mean I do."

I was staring at those shaking fingers and I was thinking to myself: Those are Joanne's fingers. How can the law allow a thing like this to happen? How can humanity? I could see the pale graft scars at her wrists.

"Joe—" She hesitated. "You know we were . . . sort of rivals for her love, you and I? You understand that, don't you? But she liked you very much, Joe."

"Why the hell do you keep talking as though she's dead?"

"She cried a lot when I sent her back to the . . . back to— She was unhappy; she wanted to stay with me, but I couldn't have her there, not when I knew what I'd done. That wasn't very brave of me, was it, Joe?"

"You could hardly keep her around, if you wanted to join the Foes of Bondage now, could you?" I said bitterly. What- ever she said now, whatever she had done these last few weeks, I was going to make damned sure she understood she was wrong. Carioca Jones could do no right. I stared at her; she was weeping softly but in an hour's time she would be laughing. She was evil, and no amount of clever stageplay could disguise that.

Later we were able to talk more normally; I think the scotch loosened us up. It was early in the day to start drink- ing, but we both needed it. In time the mask of remorse began to slip—or maybe nobody can keep apologizing, keep abasing themselves all day. She said in businesslike tones that she wanted to order a slithe-skin wrap. She peered into her mirror as she said this, making the final reparations to her face, then closed her purse with a snap. The apology was over. Life goes on. She was buying my forgiveness with a large and expensive order.

And what the hell was I supposed to do? Refuse to take her money?

I took her to the factory and Dave sketched out what she needed—he's clever at designing. I noticed the S. P. girls treated her with respect, which bore out Doug's theories. Her crimes against morality were forgotten. She was Carioca Jones, member of the Foes of Bondage, valiant fighter for the rights of the underprivileged. It was the here and now that mattered.

"And now you can take me to Pacific Kennels, Joe *darling*," she said with a complete reversion to normal. "I have to pick up dear Wilberforce who has been having treatment for his little tantrums, and I need a man in the car to handle him, as he can get *fractious* when traveling."

We experienced a certain amount of unpleasantness at Pacific Kennels, which I think was partly responsible for the unfortunate accident which marred the later stages of our visit. Carioca started off by needling the stately Miss Marjoribanks about her bonded girl, Rosalie.

"The first objective of the Foes is to ban the use of bonded state prisoners for dangerous work," she stated.

"Are you suggesting that my fish are dangerous, Carioca?" asked Miss Marjoribanks distantly, her gaze playing over the peaceful scene in the enclosure.

"You never can tell with fish. Why, even my Wilberforce is unpredictable, as you very well know, Miranda. Otherwise I wouldn't have brought him for treatment, would I?"

"The only trouble with Wilberforce is that you overfed him, and it is a well-known fact that the fat fish is the bad-tempered fish."

"*Nonsense*, Miranda. It's the hungry fish that snaps."

Miranda Marjoribanks actually tossed her head, an unusual gesture which I did not at first recognize for what it was. "Really, Carioca, it's quite obvious that you know nothing about fish. I'm sure I don't have time to argue such a ridiculous issue. Rosalie! Get Wilberforce, will you?"

"Be careful how you handle him, you *poor* dear."

"Carioca, I assure you that Wilberforce is perfectly tractable now that I've slimmed him down. A child could handle him, he's so docile. Oh, and just in case you should have any trouble"—she handed Carioca an ornate little box—"there's a denticure set for him. It's specially made for fish such as Wilberforce."

Carioca opened the box suspiciously. Inside was a little file with an inlaid jade handle, for filing down the brute's teeth, and a crystal pillbox containing dope to facilitate this dangerous procedure. There was also a small pack of hypodarts. Carioca sniffed and shut the box without comment.

In due course the kennel maid reappeared pushing a two-wheeled cart, in which lay the menacing form of the land shark.

"What's the matter?" asked Carioca sharply. "Can't he move himself?" She bent over the fish and tickled him anxiously around the oxygenator. "What's she done to you, my pet? What's the trouble, old boy?"

"Well, really . . . I took the trouble to sedate him for the journey and this is the thanks I get. Please take him away, Carioca. I'm just too upset to want to see him around anymore."

Carioca Jones seized the cart handles, pushing aside Rosalie. "I'll *not* have him wheeled out of here like a *cripple*," she stormed. "He'll go under his own steam or you'll keep him here until he's well. You know what I think? I think he's too weak to move. I'll swear I can see his *ribs,* poor dear."

So saying she lifted the cart handles violently and Wilberforce slid to the grass, instantly galvanized into snapping fury. We backed off quickly, but Miranda Marjoribanks caught her foot in a tussock and went down with a squeal of alarm.

Wilberforce moved in purposefully.

It was good to be back in the clubhouse of the Peninsula Sling-gliding Club. I sat with the other members of the Committee at the long table, drinking scotch while the sky darkened outside the big windows. I had been relating the incident at the Kennels, the main business of the afternoon having been disposed of.

"So we called the ambulopter and they took her away," I concluded. "Her foot was badly mauled, I'm afraid."

"Pity it wasn't Carioca Jones," somebody said.

"Can't you do something about that woman, Sagar?" boomed Ramsbottom, the noisy building contractor. "You seem to have some influence there. Get her to call off this goddamned demonstration, otherwise she'll ruin the President's Trophy."

I shrugged helplessly. "So far as I'm concerned she's a business acquaintance. You know she's not the sort of woman to listen to reason anyway, Walter. I can't do a thing."

"I wish we knew what form the demonstration is to take," muttered Bryce Alcester worriedly. "I heard someone talking about picketing. What do you suppose that means? To me it sounds actively hostile. It could frighten a lot of the visitors away."

Doug Marshall laughed. "They'll just stand at the marina entrance and shout a few epithets as we go through, like they always do. It's harmless enough. Hey, Joe, have you seen the catapult since we've had it all fixed up?"

Drinks in hand, we walked out onto the concrete jetty at the seaward side of the club where the catapult equipment stood. The rest of the Committee stayed behind, for which I was grateful. I didn't want to discuss Carioca Jones. There was a faint hissing from the catapult; a thin wisp of steam arose on the cool air. It was a fine evening; the sky was clear and a single star glittered near the horizon. I found myself thinking that a good exhilarating glide was what I needed. I examined the catapult; it looked in good shape.

"We were using it this afternoon," Doug said.

The catapult is used mainly for training purposes, but it is also useful if the equipment or crew for sling-gliding proper are temporarily unavailable, since it will provide a reasonable launch and an enjoyable flight—although without the total thrill involved in the more skilled sport of sling-gliding. The catapult is what its name implies, a simple device for throwing a man and his glider into the air.

It comprises a gas-fired stationary boiler which powers the piston. Rails point seaward; on these sits a trolley, and on the trolley the horse to which the pilot attaches himself, glider strapped to his back. On depressing a lever, the piston accelerates the trolley and its passenger to a speed of around one hundred and sixty miles per hour. After the fifty-

yard run the glider, pilot, and horse rise into the air, the pilot
releases the horse which falls back into the water, attached
to a cable by which it is retrieved. He then streaks off across
the Strait, makes a wide turn among the offshore islands, and
returns to stall and drops neatly into the sea beside the clubhouse—into which he then goes to get out of his wet suit
and calm his nerves with a drink.

"Care to give it a try, huh?" asked Doug coaxingly.
"There's a good head of pressure in the boiler, still."

"I'm a little out of practice, Doug."

"Listen. I want you to be my observer in the President's
Trophy and I'd feel much happier if you'd had recent experience. You know how an observer can panic and call for
an abort. You did that on me once last year."

"Doug, I wasn't happy with your flying attitude."

"I probably have one of the best takeoffs in the club, second to Presdee, of course. The truth of the matter was, you
hadn't flown yourself for a few weeks and you began to
imagine things. The less you fly, the more dangerous it looks.
Go on, your wet suit's in the locker room."

A few minutes later I was buckling a training glider, dart-
shaped and about twelve feet long, onto my back. I harnessed myself to the horse, shut my eyes, kicked the lever,
and tried not to black out as the acceleration hit me. The
trolley roared down the track, the horse wobbled, and I was
airborne. I pulled the release pin and the horse dropped away.

Lying facedown in the slender fuselage, I flew across the
Strait.

It is difficult to describe adequately the thrill that is gliding.
The tiny craft are little more than aluminum tubes with
sharply swept-back wings of wood or aluminum framing covered with tough plastic. There is no tailplane; the control
surfaces are on the trailing edge of the delta wing. The tube
of the fuselage is open at the underside; the pilot lifts himself into this slot and grasps the simple controls within the
transparent Plexiglas nosecone. Since the entire glider is little
bigger than the pilot himself the sensation is the nearest
thing to true flying yet devised—with the additional spice of
danger. The gliders are built for speed and are innocent of
safety devices. Once a man is in the air, the rest is up to him.

I headed across the Strait in a shallow climb, rising above
the blackness of the first offshore island until the horizon
paled and the rim of the sun reappeared to gild the wing-

tips and haze my visibility through the Plexiglas with a crimson glow. I banked and dived, leaving the sun behind, the scattering of islands floating below me as I headed northward with the dark tongue of the Peninsula to my left. I passed over the gaunt concrete boxes of the state penitentiary at the edge of Black Bay.

I wondered about Joanne briefly, but a man in a glider has no time for sentiment. I was losing speed and the tip of the Peninsula was a dark hump beneath me; farther ahead I saw the late hoverferry plowing its silvery furrow toward the mainland. The wind whined over the wings as I dived still lower, picked up speed in a wide turn, and skimmed low over the rippling sea. I swept past a lonely yacht with pale sails and a bright masthead light, and Black Point, the promontory which guards Black Bay, loomed before me. I held my course; my speed was falling and I wanted to be sure of setting down as near to land as possible, if I found that I couldn't reach the clubhouse in Roberts Bay.

Now I could see the lights of the state pen to my right and I turned toward them slightly. A freakish wind was rocking the glider and I dived lower, as low as I dared with the dark waves flashing by, beneath my nose. I swept past the broken water and jagged projection of Wolf Rock.

The accident happened so quickly that I can't recall the exact sequence of events to this day. My speed by this time was comparatively low, probably sixty miles per hour, and this was what saved me.

There was a sudden scream from the structure of the glider; it was instantaneous and deafening and at the time it seemed to come from everywhere; only later did I discover that the left wing had been sheared completely away. The glider slammed left so abruptly that I think my head must have smashed into the Plexiglas; then it went into a crazy spin. I fought the controls for an instant, numb with shock; then immediately I was in the water. The glider was sinking around me as I clawed my way clear; the buoyancy chambers had ruptured and the black cold water bubbled around me as the little craft disappeared.

I coughed up stinging water and looked around as my head cleared. There was a huge black wall moving beside me; it was an old displacement coaster. Lights showed at the portholes and on the decks. Distances can be deceptive in the dark, and I realized too late that I had mistaken these lights for those of the state pen, a mile away.

I shouted but my voice was drowned by the rumble of ancient diesels and swept away by the wind. I looked up and saw the upperworks silhouetted against the sky; several heads were outlined there. Men were looking down at me. A searchlight sprang into brilliance and I found myself blinking and isolated in a pool of brightness—then just as suddenly the light went out.

But the ship slid on and soon there was a terrifying threshing and the water roiled about me as the huge propellers churned past. I saw pale letters against the black of the stern, *Ancia Telji,* as the old ship forged on.

I yelled obscenities at the *Ancia Telji* as she merged with the dark coastline.

6

Perhaps there are few situations so lonely as being adrift at sea, at night. The shore may be seen, certainly, and the lights of houses and towns where sensible lucky people are talking and drinking and copulating—but those lights serve merely to enhance the sensation of being totally alone; they are as inaccessible as the farthest star. My morale had dropped sharply as the ship drew away from me, and now I found myself thinking of the depth of water beneath, and the alien things which wriggled down there, and the cold which was steadily penetrating through the insulation of my wet suit. I shouted a couple of times but soon gave up; the sound of my voice yelling into emptiness was unnerving.

The lights of the state penitentiary went out, all at the same time, leaving a few glowing at isolated windows where the night staff worked and wished they were at home in bed. The moon hung low on the horizon, casting sinister shadows among the waves and soon I was seeing the tall triangular fins of killer whales in every ripple. These creatures are common visitors around the Peninsula coast and are said to be harmless—but their large mouths are endowed with a plentiful supply of teeth. I would imagine that only their great size deterred Carioca Jones from keeping one as a pet.

Time went by and I tried to figure out which way I was drifting, but I had nothing to reckon by. I would swim toward the shore for a while and then rest, floating on my back while, I imagine, the current stole the few yards I had gained. My face and hands were numb with cold and I was becoming drowsy. Several times I found I had slipped below the surface; immediately I struggled up again, panicky and coughing, feet thrashing as fear restored me to total alertness. Then I would swim on again, slowly with token movements of arms and legs while some small devil was whispering slyly in my mind, advising me to give up.

A narrow shape fled overhead.

I yelled, treading water and waving at the disappearing glider which banked suddenly against the dark sky and came in for another low pass. I heard it, the roaring hiss of wind on fabric, then a voice.

"Hold on there! We're bringing a boat!" The last words I guessed rather than heard as the black dart slid behind the promontory in the direction of Roberts Bay. Slowly the water around me was changing color, brightening with an eerie blue fluorescence as the marker dye dropped by the glider spread over the ruffled surface.

A long while later I heard the boat, but by that time I was semiconscious and staying afloat by will alone. I remember coughing violently as the wake rippled about me and filled my mouth and lungs with water, then the hands were around me, lifting; and the wet suit was being peeled from my body. I was rubbed vigorously with a towel which was then left wrapped around me while focus returned to my eyes and I found that I was in a boat cabin, lying on one of the berths. I lay still, waiting for someone to force brandy between my teeth.

After a while I became tired of waiting and sat up. "I could do with a drink," I mumbled petulantly.

Doug Marshall was already busy at the tiny bar in the corner of the cabin. Charles and Tranter and Rennie were there too; they all had drinks. "What the hell happened, Joe?" asked Charles. "Where's the glider?" The boat was drumming comfortably to the impact of waves at speed.

Marshall handed me a scotch and ginger and I drank gratefully, while they waited for me to explain. It struck me that they were irritated at being called out; they probably thought the mishap was my own fault—and certainly they would be annoyed at my writing off a glider.

"There was a ship," I said. "I think I ran into one of the mast stays. It was a coaster, an old vessel. I couldn't see the outline against the shore. They turned the searchlight on me, but they kept going."

"They what?" exclaimed Charles, while they all regarded me incredulously. "Are you saying they left you to drown?"

"That's what I'm saying."

"Do you think you could identify the ship again, Joe?" This came from Warren Rennie, our local police chief.

"I'm goddamned sure I could. I saw the name. It was the *Ancia Telji.*"

They looked blankly at one another. "What sort of name is that?" asked Tranter skeptically. I'm sure he thought I'd made the whole thing up, as an excuse for losing the glider.

"How the hell should I know what sort of name it is!" I snapped. "It's just some sort of goddamned foreign name." Tranter always annoyed me with his supercilious manner; even his name was irritating, sounding like the gait of a hurried pig.

"It's just that none of us have heard of it, that's all," said Tranter. "After all, we know most of the ships which call around these parts, particularly the old ones—there aren't so many left now."

"I'm going to make sure I catch up with those murdering bastards," I said with heat; the drink was turning fatigue to bravado.

The engines died and the boat slowed as we came alongside the wharf at Skipper's Marina. Back at the clubhouse, I dressed and we all had a final drink. Before long we were outside again, the clubhouse locked up and the hovercars hissing away homeward. I hardly remember getting back to the farm; I must have passed out cold once I reached my bed.

The next morning I called on Heathcote Lambert, the Governor of the Northwest Regional State Penitentiary. He sat alone in his bright office on the top floor of the tallest of the pen buildings.

Since the growing public concern over the Penal Reform Act—and the Foes' search for martyrs—the state pen had tightened up on visiting, in general only allowing close relatives of the prisoner to attend. Fortunately, Lambert was a member of the sling-gliding club, so I was hoping to squeeze some concession out of him.

For some moments I had to listen while, red-faced, he shouted into the visiphone at some Newspocket reporter who wanted an interview.

At last he relaxed and pushed a button on the desk. "I'm sorry, Joe," he said. "We've been under a lot of pressure here lately—and it gets a man down, you know? All I do here is run this goddamned place the way the Government tells me to—but I'm the one who has to take the rap. Sometimes it seems to me that public opinion is against prisons no matter what they do. People used to object to prisoners being kept in idleness by the State—now under the Penal Reform Act the public object to prisoners being made to work for their keep; they call it slavery."

"I think it's bondage and the Ambulatory Organ Pool that they object to most."

He raised his hands in a gesture of despair. "And what the hell can I do about that? Bondage is merely another facet of the principle of Productive Correction, and the prisoner goes into it of his own free will. And as for the Ambulatory Organ Pool . . . well, that's Bob Gallaugher's department, but I have strong views on the matter. The prisoners in the Pool are the worst kind—rape and murder and robbery with violence and armed assault, all life sentences—and they can't be let out on bondage or work parties; it's not safe. They're little better than animals and to my mind they should be punished to the hilt. They have nothing to offer society except their bodies—and to my mind society is entitled to force them to make what restitution they can."

"But those sort of prisoners aren't quite sane, surely?"

"By our standards they're as mad as hatters. They reject the norms of society in nearly every way."

"Then how can you blame them for their crimes?" I asked. "Obviously a man who rapes little girls must be sick in the head. He isn't responsible. He shouldn't be blamed."

"So what the hell should we do? Spank him and tell him not to do it again? It so happens that I have a young daughter, Joe—and you haven't. So you don't know what you're talking about. We have no hope of reforming criminals; it just can't be done. They found that out years ago. Prisoners are here to be punished, they are here to be locked away safely, they are here to be *used.*"

Bob Gallaugher entered, a rotund precise man in thick-lensed spectacles.

"The Foes are staging another demonstration today, remember, Heathcote," he said.

"How can I forget that?" He laughed ruefully. "Tell me something good, you bastard."

Gallaugher frowned; it seemed Lambert's request was unreasonable right now. "I wanted to speak to you about Rasmussen. He's due out next month."

"Oh, God!" Lambert turned to me. "This is just the sort of thing we were talking about, Joe. Rasmussen is a murderer; he killed his wife. He drew a long sentence and was requisitioned for a donation last year; he gave a leg and a kidney to one of the victims of the Sentry Down disaster— you remember when that antigrav shuttle failed on liftoff? Next month Rasmussen is due for release."

"So he's atoned for his crime. What's wrong with that?"

"For one thing he was a brutal murderer when he came in, and so far as society is concerned he's still a brutal murderer. Ten years in here haven't changed that. But now he gets out and he's free to kill again, and he possibly will— but the Foes of Bondage will make a hero of him. They'll stick him on a platform and roll up his pants leg and they'll say: See the way the state pen mutilates a man. They'll forget the innocent victim of the Sentry Down disaster who can walk again because of the Penal Reform Act, and they'll forget the wife who Rasmussen carved up with a cleaver. The Foes of Bondage will have a martyr, and that's all they're interested in. It's lucky men like Rasmussen aren't released too frequently."

"Are you trying to say he should never be released?" I asked, alarmed at these views from a prison warden.

"That's exactly what I'm saying. And what's more, I feel that he should be painlessly destroyed, once he's donated every useful organ in his body."

Lambert spoke with such transparent feeling that I was forced to conclude he was serious—and that quite possibly he had a point. Gallaugher spoiled the effect, however. "Sometimes I'm at my wit's end to know where the next organ is coming from," he said. "You wouldn't believe the shortage. It only needs an accident like Sentry Down and we're all out of stock, and have to apply for reinforcements of long-term prisoners from other pens."

I stared at him.

"You're speaking to a member of the public, Bob," warned Lambert. "You must be careful how you phrase these things. Joe—remember this. These are criminals, man, criminals. They've forfeited their human rights."

I didn't argue. I felt suddenly sick, and I could feel the sickness all around me. Lambert and Gallaugher were sick too; they were possibly honest men, they possibly believed in what they were doing—but they had become coarsened by the coarseness of the criminals around them, and had likewise lost their moral sense. I spoke to them of generalities for a while, then asked if I could see Joanne. Sensing my mood, Lambert agreed readily and rang for a guard to escort me.

Joanne and I sat on opposite sides of a mesh fence in a long room, at either end of which stood an armed guard. It was sad and awful, just like the movies, and I wondered if perhaps I'd made a mistake coming here.

"Hello, Joe," she said quietly, smiling. "It was good of you to come. How have you been? I haven't seen you for ages. How's Carioca?"

"The same as ever. Are they, uh, treating you well?"

We talked for a while. She wore a short-sleeved dress and I could see where the flesh of her arms merged into the steel of her wrists and hands. The hands glittered in the harsh light and she gestured with them while talking, making no attempt to hide them. As she smiled and chattered it seemed she almost mocked me with those damned hands.

But it was good to see her face again. She looked so pretty, with her snub nose and freckles and blue, blue eyes; and even the rough prison uniform could not conceal the beauty of her full breasts. "I'll be out of here in September, you know that, Joe?" she said brightly.

It was unreal. She should be unhappy and vicious and vindictive but she wasn't. I said, "It's a shame Carioca sent you back here."

"Oh, but it's really the best thing, Joe. This way, Carioca can join the Foes of Bondage and fight against the Penal Reform Act—and once Carioca starts a fight, she never gives up. She's trying to get me an early release as well, you know that? She's really very good to me."

"Joanne," I said impulsively, "when you get out of here I want you to come and live with me, right? We'll get right away from this goddamned Peninsula and all it stands for. We'll get married and sell the farm and buy a boat and go south; would you like that?" I finished breathlessly.

She smiled quietly. "I appreciate that, Joe. We'll just have to see what happens, won't we?"

The white walls and the black guards and the hopelessness

seemed to close in on me until even Joanne looked unreal on the other side of the wire. I wanted to leave, but I couldn't. I wasn't getting anywhere with Joanne, and I never would, and I don't know why the hell I tried. She was smiling, telling me about the food or some goddamned thing. It seemed to go on forever until at last the guard loomed over me, touching my shoulder, and led me away. I looked back, but Joanne wasn't watching me go. She was talking to a female guard.

As I stepped out of the prison gates the sun hit my eyes, and I found a great crowd of women before me, screaming hatred into my face.

7

The Peninsula dressed for spring and April came and went. I settled into a routine again, spending my days at the slithe farm, my evenings and weekends at the club except once a week when I tortured myself by visiting cool sweet Joanne at the state pen. The state of armed neutrality between Carioca Jones and me softened into something akin to our old relationship of cautious friendship allied to business awareness on my side, and effusiveness on the side of Carioca. This mitigation of tension was largely due to Joanne who, in her quiet way from behind the mesh fence, seemed to place personal importance on the relationship between the ex-3-V star and me. Meanwhile Carioca, by all accounts, was spending considerable time and money in her efforts to secure an early release for Joanne on the grounds of a satisfactorily completed bondage.

Often in the spring evenings I would stroll across to the Skipper's Marina and watch the bonded men working on their bosses' boats. I would chat with them as they scraped, painted, and varnished, and try to discover what made them tick. In general they were a cheerful crowd, unlike many bonded men I could mention, and it was rarely that a man would openly admit he was dissatisfied, or that he wished he'd never elected for bondage. At this time it didn't occur to me to question my own growing interest in the penal system.

Perhaps the most interesting of these characters was Charles Wentworth, Doug's man. Even at weekends I would see him there, scraping and painting, preparing the boat for the coming season while the freemen and their loud, made-up wives wandered about the slipway and the wharves, grotesque marine pets flopping at their heels. These weekends had become social events, each man trying to outdo his

fellow in hearty commendation of his own sleek boat, while
the wives vied over such niceties as minipile cookers and
autoflush heads.

Even Carioca Jones appeared on occasion; once she was
wearing the slithe-skin dress I'd made for her, and the skin
turned a faint pink as our eyes met, and we both thought of
Joanne. Her young hands rose to her vulture's throat almost
of their own accord, while her hard black eyes watched me
carefully.

"I must say I'm surprised to see you still come here, Joe,
knowing your views," she greeted me.

"I like to look at the boats."

"Yes, but all these . . . *people,* darling. Aren't they just
terrible?"

"No worse than anyone else, I guess," I said, wishing she
would move on.

One Friday afternoon in May I left the farm in Dave's hands
and again visited the marina. By now the boats were in good
shape, most of the paintwork having been completed; and the
S. P. men were working on the decks and below, polishing
brass, overhauling engines. About twenty hydrofoils stood in
line abreast on their insect legs, looking virile and rakish.

Charles Wentworth was working on the outside of Doug's
boat, lubricating the heavy rollers of the eye. I walked over
and greeted him. He looked up from his work.

"Hi there, Joe," he said. That was one of the things I
liked about him. He was able to treat me as an equal, and
whenever I was talking to him, I forgot he was a state
prisoner and I a freeman.

"When are you going to get her in the water?" I asked.

"About three weeks' time, I reckon." He wiped his hands
on his coveralls and gripped the huge steel loop of the eye in
both hands. He pulled, extending it on well-greased runners
until it projected some eight feet from the hull of the boat—
a giant polished metal D. He grinned at me and tapped it
with a small hammer; it rang like a bell.

Rumor has it that an eye fractured in use down south
somewhere last summer, although it was hushed up. A sling-
glider must have complete confidence in his equipment.
Satisfied, Charles gave the eye a seemingly gentle push. Six
hundred and twenty pounds of glittering steel-titanium alloy
rolled smoothly back into the hull of the boat, the flat upright
of the D—the outermost part of the eye—fitting so snugly

with the contours of the hull that the cracks could hardly be seen.

Charles turned his attention to the whip, which lay on the slipway beside the boat and stretched to a small mooring buoy out in the water—a total length of some eighty yards. This year everyone had bought new Ultrafiber-X whips; they lay rigid across the surface in parallel green lines.

"What do you think about, Charles?" I asked curiously. "When Doug's up in his glider, when the hook hits the eye, what thoughts occur to you?"

He grinned, kneading grease into the attachment where the whip joins the pilot's harness. "There's no time to think. I'm too busy pinning down the whip, rolling out the eye, trying to control the boat at the same time as I'm listening to some idiot observer panicking in the stern. But you want me to say I worry about Doug getting hurt, don't you?"

"It must occur to you."

"It doesn't." Charles stood over six feet, blond and weatherbeaten; he looked the sling-glider type, although hardly the state prisoner type. Not for the first time, I wondered about his sentence for rape, which was apparently the result of some incident on board his boat. Personally, I thought the whole thing sounded very unlikely—and although the Compitrator found Charles guilty, he only got four years. Doug Marshall had known him slightly in the past, and agreed to take him as a bonded man.

I remember thinking: The sling-glider is entirely in his steersman's hands.

I looked at Charles. Surely he must think *something* while Doug was in the air, in that flimsy glider.

He worked on impassively, talking technicalities as he checked and greased Doug Marshall's harness.

It is difficult to define an air of suppressed excitement. It can be observed most easily, perhaps, in the way people will suddenly address strangers, asking their views on whatever is causing the furor. Such an air was in evidence at Skipper's Marina during those last few weeks before the start of the sling-gliding season, as freemen talked competitions and freewomen spoke of the clothes they would wear at the President's Trophy; while at their feet, brought into unaccustomed proximity, land sharks fought barracudas, octopuses devoured micropekes.

The sloping landscape of the long slipway was busy every day and crowded at weekends; on the last Sunday before the season began Carioca Jones came again to the marina, spectacularly dressed, with Wilberforce flopping at her heels. The brute was growing fast; he was now over eight feet long. Doug Marshall was bent double and sweating as he adjusted the shear-pin on one of the props, when the land shark undulated across and lay beside him, watching him coldly and stinking like a fishmarket, oxygenator pulsating unpleasantly. Doug caught sight of the fish suddenly, straightened up, and cracked his head on the keel.

He had never liked Carioca Jones, and now he exploded. "Get that bastard away from me," he yelled, "before I put this drill through its skull." He brandished the whirring power tool like a rapier.

Carioca hurried over and laid her hand on her pet's collar. She was wearing slithe-skin gloves and I noticed they had turned mauve in sympathy with her temper. "Wilberforce is quite harmless." She spoke coolly enough. "There's no call to lose your temper with him, Mr. Marshall. He wasn't doing anything wrong."

"Wrong!" Doug was massaging his scalp. "The swine nearly fractured my skull for me!"

"Come now, Mr. Marshall. A great big brave sling-pilot shouldn't be frightened of a mere fish, should he now?"

Doug recovered, swallowed hard, and spoke carefully. "Miss Jones, that fish is a menace. He's been allowed to grow too big. Look at those teeth. He could have your leg off without batting an eyelid. You ought to have him put down."

"Put *down*?" Carioca's gloves were purple and trembling. Doug met her stare levelly. She looked elsewhere for a scapegoat, and as I was edging out of the scene, Charles descended the ladder from the cockpit and glanced at the protagonists with interest. He was wearing his state pen coveralls. Carioca's gaze lit on the letters *S. P.* and her eyes flashed. "Oh, so you have a *slave* here doing your work for you."

The quick change of subject foxed Doug. "What the hell's that got to do with it?" he asked. "Anyway, Charles is my bonded man."

"Oh, a *bonded* man, is he? I might have guessed. No

wonder you love sling-gliding. Who wouldn't, with a *Spare
Parts* man standing by?"

Doug's eyes widened; he looked at Charles, who seemed
to have been struck speechless. I couldn't think of much to
say myself; arrant rudeness has that effect on me. Fortunately, help was at hand in the unlikely guise of the club
secretary, who happened to be passing. He stepped in
quickly.

"Miss Jones, did I hear you rightly?"

"Who are you, you *strange* little man?"

Bryce Alcester flushed. "I think I heard you use an expression we don't like around here, Miss Jones. Was I right?
Did you use such an expression?"

"Of *course* you don't like the expression, because it's *true*.
How else can men like you summon the *nerve* to go up in
those nasty little gliders, answer me *that*."

"I must ask you to leave the premises, madam. I must
also remind you that you are not a member."

"And I must remind you that the Foes of Bondage will
picket the President's Trophy next week. You haven't heard
the last of this, not by a long way."

Reluctantly, with Alcester's hand on her arm, she began
to move away. Her eye caught mine. *"Frankly*, Joe, I can't
think why you associate with such *cowards*."

After escorting her from the premises Alcester hurried
back to us. There was a tear in the leg of his pants where
the land shark had taken a snap at him. "I'm terribly
sorry, gentlemen," he fussed. He looked at Charles, swallowed, and said awkwardly, "And, uh, I would like to
apologize to you, uh, Charles, on behalf of the club."

Charles smiled blandly. "I've been called names before."

Later that evening, as we drank beer in the cabin, I asked
Charles, "What does it really feel like to be called . . . *that*,
you know?" I must have had several drinks by then. "I mean,
don't you feel pretty degraded? It sort of subtracts from your
individuality."

Charles grinned. "Always trying to pump me, aren't you,
Joe? I often wonder if you're a revolutionary on the quiet,
gathering information."

"Maybe, but I'm not a Foe of Bondage."

"But Carioca Jones is right, you know," he said surprisingly.
"I am a Spare Parts man. I've wagered my body against a
shorter sentence. I went into it with my eyes open and so

far I've been lucky. And I don't mind Doug's sling-gliding, because I've done it myself and I know the thrill of it all. Now *that's* where Carioca Jones is wrong. I know that we would glide whether or not, uh, spare parts were available. Miss Jones doesn't know that. She can't. She's a woman."

I addressed Doug, pushing it a bit further. "Doug, just supposing you smashed yourself up and you needed, say, a leg. Would you use Charles? Or would you spend the rest of your life with a tin leg, watching Charles walk about whole?"

"The beer has brought honesty," said Doug quietly. "And I can say in all honesty that I don't know. And it's one thing about myself that I never want to know."

During those days of preparation there were constant undercurrents at the club, which occasionally surfaced in outbursts of temper or, in the case of the prison governor, a mood of deepening gloom. Heathcote Lambert was becoming increasingly preoccupied, and frequently could only recall himself to Committee business with an obvious effort.

"The Foes causing you problems these days, huh, Heath?" boomed Walter Ramsbottom on one such occasion—and Lambert seemed hardly to hear him. Certainly there had been considerable exposure of the penal system on Newspocket recently; it seemed every time I glanced at my pocket portovee some politician was under fire, some ex-con waving his steel arm at a sympathetic studio audience.

The results of the Penal Reform Act were coming home to roost. The time had come for certain ex-members of the Ambulatory Organ Pool to be released, and the public was becoming suddenly aware that it had created a monster in the guise of social justice—cells-full of monsters, in fact.

I still felt a slow fury whenever I thought of the prison officers' curious moral code and, unfairly perhaps, I tended to identify them as the oppressors of Joanne. They were here and now; whereas the Penal Reform Act was a somewhat nebulous abstraction. You can't punch an idea on the nose, and I wanted to hit at the state pen and those in charge of it.

I didn't at that time think the Foes of Bondage were suitable allies. They were a bunch of female crackpots. Not that I have anything against women—far from it—but there is no denying that the middle-aged unmarried female is more inclined to get herself involved in social and community organizations and action groups than her male counterpart.

Maybe this is indicative of the female's more highly developed social conscience; I would like to think it is. But although on paper such organizations are fine and benevolent bodies, nevertheless the actions they tend to take can be nothing short of destructive. So it was with the Foes of Bondage.

Looking back on those days, it now seems to me that I was becoming obsessed. At times, I would make a deliberate effort to transfer my rancor to the crew of the *Ancia Telji;* this was not difficult, since the recollection of those bastards leaving me to drown was etched vividly into my brain. I made attempts to trace the ship but without success; indeed, I seemed to come up against a wall of silence. I suspected that this was due to a recent fishing dispute with a neighboring Latin country which had caused the authorities to tread very warily in matters concerning foreign vessels. And Warren Rennie was no help at all.

From time to time I would climb onto the promontory south of Black Bay—which juts well out into the Strait—and spend an hour or so watching the passing yachts and occasional merchantman through binoculars, but without success—and I'm not sure what I would have done, had I spotted her. Maybe I was still a shade unbalanced those days; yet at the time my actions seemed perfectly logical.

Then, one windy evening, somebody came into the club and told us that there was an old coaster in trouble, out in the Strait. . . .

8

The strong onshore wind had freshened almost to gale force and this, together with the outcrops of rock in the middle of the rough track, made the journey up to Black Point a difficult one. Finally I killed the engine, and the swaying, bucking hovercar steadied as it sank to solid ground. I looked around at the gloomy twilight, wondering what I had come for. The lights of the state pen gleamed down to my left; in the distance down the right coastline I could see the Skipper's Marina and the clubhouse. Ahead, the gray sea tossed angrily and the area around Wolf Rock was a turmoil of spouting spray. The rain gusted against the windshield and I turned on the wipers. It was a good night for driving quietly home and enjoying a drink in comfortable surroundings.

Then I noticed the activity on the concrete wharf near the foot of the penitentiary walls. A group of men, their oilskins flapping like bats' wings, were busy around a large hoverlaunch. They stripped the covers from around the skirting and climbed in, while other men watched, huddled in their waterproofs. They were too far below for me to recognize any faces.

Spray fountained around the base of the vessel as it slid down the slipway into the turbulent water; seconds later the high whine of turbines reached me. The hoverlaunch was big, probably sixty feet long; but even so it was not the type of craft I would like to ride with an easterly gale blowing straight into the bay. In fact there would be very few vessels abroad in the Strait tonight. From my vantage point I could see the ferry terminal beyond the pen; the big hoverferry was stationary, the service suspended until dawn.

I looked out to sea again, shivering in sympathy with anyone who had to be out on such a wretched night; then something caught my eye. As the windshield wipers cleared my vision I saw a large vessel; then rain flooded down the glass again. I saw it again, long and black. I climbed out of the car; the wind snatched the door from my grasp and slammed it shut behind me. With eyes half closed I peered into the driving rain and now I saw it clearly—a large displacement vessel with the appearance of a coaster, crabbing across the Strait at right angles to the strong current, heading directly for Black Bay beneath me.

I climbed quickly back into the hovercar and looked through the side window, where the rain was not so fierce. The hoverlaunch was well under way, forging through the tossing water toward the wide bay entrance where Wolf Rock stood like a sentinel; I caught sight of the coaster, nearer now, bucking and plunging toward me with the wind behind her.

I think it was the ponderous, heaving inevitability of her approach that convinced me something was indeed wrong. The launch was hove-to now, riding the waves awkwardly in the lee of Wolf Rock, unable to go farther as the steep seas nullified her lift. I wondered what the launch was hoping to achieve, what she was waiting for. One thing was sure; everybody was waiting for something. I could sense it in the stormy air, in the position of the rolling launch, in the attitudes of the huddled men on the wharf—while the coaster came barreling on.

A rocket leaped into the twilight, bursting blood against the dull clouds. I heard the report, watched another trail arch upward, another crimson starburst. Still the coaster came on.

At a guess, the heavy following seas had damaged her steering gear, while her engines were not powerful enough to turn her or even hold her, in those seas. Maybe she only had one screw, maybe that was damaged; I don't know. Whatever the reason for her distress, she plowed on, turned almost beam-on to the waves now, so that she rolled viciously.

She was headed directly for Wolf Rock.

A siren wailed from the tower of the state pen and I saw men running among the buildings as the floodlights came on. I heard the detonation as the coaster launched another distress flare. I watched the tall pen gates swing open, watched the uniformed men pouring through, running down the short road to the wharf.

The beam of a searchlight sprang from the hoverlaunch and eyed the doomed ship like a voyeur. Black hull plates, rusted upperworks glistened in the wetness.

It was all intense and real and here and now, nothing like a 3-V drama as I found myself standing in the driving rain, staring down at the eternal sight of Man losing his battle against the sea. The hoverlaunch was holding at full power, spray gouting unevenly from the sideskirts as the tall waves rolled by. The coaster came on, an ancient ruin, now broadside to the waves and rolling so that the decks were constantly awash. Spray leaped from Wolf Rock just a few yards away.

The coaster struck.

I saw her lurch and after a while I heard the noise, muffled but huge; and I could make out the little men scuttling about the wet deck as though it were an upturned stone. I watched as she pivoted slowly and came free, drifting on across the bay toward where I stood, listing as she took water through the wound where Wolf Rock had ripped the guts out of her. I was aware of other cars arriving, of doors slamming around me, but I paid them scant attention.

The coaster came on, much closer now, and I saw men jumping, God knows with what desperate purpose, into the maelstrom that was Black Bay. I saw the hoverlaunch move in, maneuvering clumsily as the wind swept her around, throwing lines to the struggling figures in the windblown surf, finally pausing at a respectful distance from the coaster, waiting like a scavenger.

Then the guards arrived, a file of uniformed men trotting past me, stationing themselves at intervals along the clifftop. They stood peering downward, leaning against the wind with capes flapping.

A sudden hand tapped me on the shoulder. "I must ask you to leave."

I swung around to find a man in prison uniform with his hands cupped to his mouth, shouting at me against the storm. "What the hell are you talking about?" I shouted back. He wore silver pips on the shoulders of his streaming trench coat and I took him to be some sort of officer; but I am ignorant of ranks and have no intention of learning.

I saw Doug Marshall grappling with another official. "There

are people down there who are going to need our help, for Christ's sake!" he was shouting.

I moved nearer to them; Charles was there too, and a few more besides. It seemed to me that we were strong enough to tell officialdom to go to hell.

I was followed by the officer who had first addressed me; he spoke to us all, rivers of rain streaming down his broad face. "I must ask you people to have some consideration for those poor wretches down there. Their lives depend on the efficiency of my men, and I will not tolerate a bunch of amateurs fouling up the operation. For God's sake, don't you have any pity? Must you gape around like a pack of ghouls?"

Respect and fear for the law is deeply instilled into us these days—one of the consequences of the Penal Reform Act. With a lurching sensation in my stomach I realized that we were trying to buck authority. I began to edge toward my car. "Now get the hell out of here, all of you!" someone shouted.

"Just hold on there," came a new voice, and I paused. It was Charles speaking; he stood lazily above the prison officer, smiling easily. "I really can't see the necessity for this kind of talk," he said. "We're all members of the Peninsula Sling-gliding Club—whereas your men, I understand, are merely prison guards. We've had much more experience of sea rescue than you have. We do it every day. So just shut up and let's get on with important things like lifesaving, shall we? That is, unless you want to find your picture on Newspocket as the man who rejected expert assistance and caused a lot of people to die. We all know there are going to be lives lost here—but I'll make goddamned sure that you're blamed for every one. May I have your name, please?"

The prison officer stared at him for a second, then strode rapidly away toward a stocky figure which I recognized as Gallaugher. They held a short conversation, and the whiteness of Gallaugher's face turned in our direction; after a while the prison officer nodded and began to walk back to us.

So it was Gallaugher who was in charge, Gallaugher who had given the orders for us to be removed. I wondered what the hell he had been thinking of—and why he hadn't addressed us directly. He, too, was a member of the club. I decided to tackle him, took a step forward, but he had gone.

"Take the area of cliff to the right of my men," snapped the prison officer. "You'll find ropes there already."

As we hurried to our positions I wondered how the man would have felt, what his reaction would have been, had he known Charles was a bonded man.

Then there was a cataclysmic grinding, screaming of steel against rock as the coaster struck, immediately below us.

Fortunately the cliff was not sheer at this point; it descended in a steep slope of salt grass and granite outcrops to the jumble of jagged boulders where the waves pounded, where the coaster now struggled. As I watched, the waves caught her and rolled her against the shore, and the tip of her foremast lay for an instant parallel with the slope, so close that I could have almost stepped forward and touched it. Then it swung away and I became aware once more of the struggling people on the decks, large numbers of men and women sliding about, grabbing for handholds, fighting and screaming and being buried against the gunwales by rolling waves and avalanches of tumbling humanity.

We drove the hovercars to the edge of the slope and anchored the ropes to them, then scrambled down the short grass as near to the pitching hull as we dared, and shouted to people to jump. A few did, and we grabbed them as they landed stumbling with flailing arms, and we got their hands onto the ropes and set them climbing to safety. Sometimes they fell, or we didn't grab them in time, and they rolled down the slope to the rocks, where they lay looking up at the hull as it descended on them. They never made much noise; they seemed stunned. They just lay and waited passively to be reduced to so much ground meat—and when the ship rolled away again they were usually gone, and the rocks washed clean. In my horror, this seemed to me a very efficient way to die.

There were people in the water on the far side of the wreck too; the hoverlaunch was picking these up where possible, although I knew that the current would carry numbers of them around the headland toward Roberts Bay and Dollar Bay and the Skipper's Marina. Later, we would have to make a complete search of the shoreline.

Finally there seemed to be nothing more we could do. Hoverbuses had been plying between the promontory and the penitentiary sickroom, and I heard a guard say that a large number of cells had been made ready, and doctors called in from Louise. The ambulopter was busy removing the more serious cases to the Louise General Hospital. We assembled on the clifftop again, coiled up the ropes, and looked at each other while the coaster screamed and groaned below. The guards had spread out and were searching the cliffs farther around the point.

"My God!" said Doug Marshall to nobody in particular. We seemed in no hurry to disperse; the events of the last couple of hours had forged a bond too strong to be broken immediately. We needed to compare people's feelings with our own. We needed to debrief.

"They hardly spoke," muttered Presdee. "They hardly said a goddamned word, hardly screamed even. Like goddamned zombies."

"Shock," said Ramsbottom wisely. "Shock does strange things to a person."

Somebody asked, "Who the hell were they?"

"God knows," replied Marshall. "A crowd of cut-rate tourists, maybe? Difficult to say. They were dressed like tourists, I thought. You know how tourists look."

"Lousy end to a vacation. Not much of a ship, either." Ramsbottom peered down at the floodlit wreck grinding and rolling below us. *"Ancia Telji,"* he read. "Pretty much of an old tub, if you ask me."

After leaving Black Point and, surprisingly, being thanked for our efforts by Gallaugher, we reopened the clubhouse for a much-needed last drink. Later I drove along the coast road home.

It was past three now, and the road deserted. Gusts of rain swept across the low coastal scrub and jolted the hover-car off course; tiredly I fought the wheel, thinking of bed.

Suddenly I jabbed the emergency brake as a figure lurched into my headlights. I saw the flash of bare legs, I saw long hair blowing stringy in the rain. It was a girl; she half-turned and looked back into the headlights, dazzled, lifting her hand to shield her eyes. There was something very familiar about the gesture and I found myself thinking about the sun, and the south; Halmas, the beach, the banana plantation.

I flung the door open and jumped out. "Marigold!"

She saw me coming and collapsed toward me. I caught

her, held her as the wind and rain flayed at our clothes. "Take . . . take the Roberts Bay road," she mumbled, eyes half closed. "You can't miss the place, it's right by the sea—" Her mechanical voice trailed off. She sagged in my arms.

I dragged her into the passenger seat, arranged her comfortably and shut the door, then climbed in on my side and drove away, fast. Eyes glinted in the headlights as a small pack of land sharks watched us go. I had picked up Marigold just in time. I couldn't begin to think what she was doing beside me.

I carried her to the house and was about to call the doctor when she stirred and said something. I laid her on the couch, turned the bath on, and mixed a couple of drinks. When I raised her head and tried to get some scotch into her mouth she kept turning away so I gave up after a while, organized the bath, and took her clothes off. She was as helpless and unresisting as a young baby.

I called several doctors but got no reply; I told myself that this was because they were all busy at the hospital and the pen, and nothing to do with the fact that it was always impossible to get hold of a doctor at night.

Later we sat by a log fire I had lit for the occasion in my old stone fireplace, and looked at each other. Marigold still hadn't spoken properly, but I thought the emptiness was receding from her eyes. Now I was glad I hadn't been able to get a doctor, now that she was dry and warm and comfortable like a sexy kitten. I was still trying to recover from the intensely erotic experience of giving her a bath; and I knew that if a doctor came and found her wrapped up like this, I would feel as guilty as hell. She was like a beautiful doll that I wanted to play with all by myself.

I had placed the drink in her hand but she showed no sign of gripping the glass, so I put it on the table beside her. She watched me gravely as I arranged the thick bath towel around her shoulders, but when it slipped down and fell away from her perfect, plump breasts she made no attempt to adjust it. So I thought, What the hell, and left it there. So we sat in opposite chairs, and I tried to tell myself she recognized me.

"You're on the Peninsula now, Marigold," I said.

"Roberts Bay," she said quietly. "Joe lives there; you can't miss it."

"I'm Joe. Look at me, Marigold. Don't you remember me?"

"Joe will be surprised to see me."

It was the shock, I thought; and the only cure for shock is warmth and rest. I decided to take her up to my room; she could have my bed and I could sleep on the couch. The towel fell to the floor as I stood her up and helped her to the stairs. I half-carried her to the room, sat her on the bed, pulled back the covers, and rolled her in. She lay there, looking up and past me; I think she was asleep with her eyes open. I pulled the bedclothes over her, kissed her lips, and went downstairs, closing the door quietly behind me.

It wasn't until I'd undressed, made up the couch, and had a nightcap that it occurred to me that I was not performing before an audience. There was no need whatever for me to handle this situation in the way a character on 3-V would handle it. Too often we assume that every game has its rules, and I realized how nearly I'd been caught out by trite, meaningless convention.

So I climbed the stairs, entered my room, kissed the sleeping face again, and got into bed beside that warm, wonderful body. I held her close and I went to sleep that way, and why the hell not? It didn't do anybody any harm.

In fact it probably did Marigold a lot of good, because she needed someone to hold her that night, after what she'd been through. Suddenly it was morning; I awoke and found this beautiful girl beside me. I must have been sleeping very deeply after the exhaustion of the previous night; Marigold had awakened already and was regarding me with faint bewilderment. So I kissed her and she smiled, but she didn't speak.

I guessed she'd taken a cheap cruise on the *Ancia Telji* out of Vanhalla; it was all she could afford, and she was determined to see the wonderful Peninsula I'd described to her, and probably to see me too.

By the time I was out of bed and dressed, the responsibilities and the guilt were closing in on me, and I wondered what the hell I'd got myself into with my loose talk down south. I wondered what Joanne would think if she found out about Marigold.

Marigold for her part seemed to accept the situation, if dazedly. After a while I pinned a large white towel around her; we went downstairs and I cooked breakfast. With the coffee and bacon and eggs I returned firmly to my senses.

Marigold sat decoratively opposite me and it was great to have her there, but she didn't belong, and I would have to inform the police before they started cabling her parents at Halmas and triggering off all manner of panic—always provided that the police had a passenger list.

Warren Rennie's tired face stared at me from the screen. "It's you, Joe, is it? Look. I had a hell of a night with this ship business, and if it can wait—"

I explained that I had one of the survivors in my house, and his manner changed. "I'll be right over," he said.

I was surprised and a little alarmed when he arrived with two uniformed men, as though expecting resistance. "Where is she?" he snapped.

"Just finishing her breakfast. She won't be a moment."

"Joe, I'm taking her right now. Let me in, will you?"

"What the hell are you talking about, Warren? Can't the girl finish eating? You can't be that goddamned busy."

He thrust me aside and entered, took one look at Marigold sitting partially dressed at the table—by this time the towel had slipped to her waist—then turned to me furiously. "Just what sort of bastard are you, Sagar? By Christ, Lambert was right about you. That girl's been in shock; she's still not right, by the look of her eyes. What kind of monkey business went on here last night?"

Marigold was standing now, watching us in mild wonder while the uniformed men stared at her breasts. I stepped in quickly and threw my jacket around her shoulders. "Leave her alone," I said as Rennie approached.

He ignored me and took her face in his hands, staring into her eyes. "She doesn't know what the hell is going on," he said at last, disgustedly. "By God, you've got something to answer for, Sagar!"

"Just what are you talking about?" I asked coldly. I was becoming tired of his attitude.

"Do you deny you slept with her last night?"

"As a matter of fact, that's exactly true."

"Christ, man, don't you know what you're saying?"

"Rennie, you didn't listen to what I said on the phone. I know this girl. I've slept with her before, if that's so important to you. Now just what the hell are you trying to say?"

He turned away and walked to the window. For a moment he stood there, looking out at the yard where the slithes trotted about their pens and everything looked normal. "What is she doing here, Sagar?" he asked at last. "Are you trying to tell me you were expecting her?"

"I understand she was on the cruise ship that sank. She couldn't help that, could she?"

He turned back to Marigold. "See she gets some clothes on her and take her to the car," he said briefly. "Now see here, Joe. The *Ancia Telji* was not a cruise ship. We've suspected her before, but this time we've got the proof we need—the only trouble is, we don't know who to proceed against. The *Ancia Telji* was engaged in running illegal immigrants."

"What!"

"It's true. After your complaint a while back, we did a little checking. We got hold of a passenger list—with some difficulty, I might add—and tried to find some witnesses for you. Our agent down south checked up—and get this, Joe. He couldn't find one single passenger on that list. They'd never returned. And then one or two relatives talked. It seemed that it was tacitly understood by the agents that a trip on the *Ancia Telji* was a one-way cruise. Now do you see why they didn't stop to pick you up?"

"It figures."

"They were on their way to make a drop. Now, tell me this again, Joe—were you expecting this girl?"

"No."

There was nothing else I could say, unless I'd offered to sponsor the girl, or whatever the hell it is you do with immigrants. But I couldn't do that, not with Joanne due for release in a few months.

Rennie told me they were holding all the survivors at the pen for the time being, and he assured me that charges would not be brought, that they would be sent home by suitable transport as soon as possible. I felt no better.

As they took Marigold away, she showed her first and only sign of animation since I'd brought her home. I kissed her; her lips were soft but unresponsive, but then I saw a glistening tear creep down her cheek.

"I'll come and see you in Halmas soon, sweetheart," I said in futile misery, but she didn't reply.

She was gone, and I turned away to find Dave Froehlich

staring pensively after the receding hovercar. I waited for some snide comment concerning freemen who abused helpless girls.

"She was . . . uh, very pretty, Mr. Sagar," he said quietly.

9

For a while I tortured myself with guilt feelings over the way I'd persuaded an innocent girl to fall for me—but I had enough sense to realize that the faults were not all mine. It was quite apparent that Marigold was not innocent by any stretch of the imagination, and I was quite sure she knew all about the immigration laws. Then I recalled the poverty I'd seen down south: the barren fields and skeletal cattle, the centuries-old adobe huts, and I felt pity again. I had gone there with my stories of wonderful lands to the north where everyone has enough to eat, where the population growth has been brought under control, where education is for everyone; and I had been so preoccupied with my own ills that I'd never thought of the effect my words might have on a poor and impressionable girl. And she *was* innocent in the true sense of the word; whether or not she'd slept around had nothing to do with it. I wondered why these moral hang-ups still persist in our northern culture.

My conscience was eased somewhat when I met Gallaugher in the club a few days later and he confirmed that no charges had been brought by the police; in fact the immigrants had technically committed no crime, having landed on our shores as a result of shipwreck. The fact of their intentions could not be proved; neither did the authorities wish to. The owners of the *Ancia Telji* had been notified, but it was not expected that they would wish to retrieve the remains of their vessel. The crew and passengers had all been sent home by antigrav clipper at the Government's expense.

By now it was only a few days before the first race of the sling-gliding season and we were all totally infected with racing fever, so I wrote a long letter to Marigold before the urge left me, and promised to visit her later in the summer.

As soon as the letter was mailed I wished I hadn't made that promise.

Then gliding took over my leisure time totally, and I forgot Marigold and the *Ancia Telji*. I spent most afternoons and every evening on the slipway, helping with the feverish last-minute preparations. Sling-gliding has this in common with any other sport where complex equipment is used: no matter how careful the preparations, no matter how long ago such preparations started, there is always a panic at the finish. The Skipper's Marina had placed a truck at the disposal of the club and the vehicle was in constant use, commuting between Louise and the marina with suddenly remembered necessities.

Carioca Jones did not appear, although there were rumors from time to time of the form the picketing was going to take. Some said the Foes of Bondage had hired a boat; they intended to interfere with racing by zigzagging across the course on the pretext that the sea was free to all.

Then, a couple of days before the first race, they were seen with their banners and placards boarding a clipper for Lake William in the far north. It seemed that some idiots were going to walk the glacial coast as far as Wall Bay, a distance of several hundred miles. There were three bonded men and a doctor in the party of ten; it was reported that the doctor was taking a full set of surgical instruments along—together with a supply of the instant tissue and bone regenerator Rediseel—in case of severe frostbite. Not only that, but there were back-up parties hovertrucking supplies to a remote rendezvous where the terrain was too broken and the weather too severe to allow shuttles to get in. The personnel for this hazardous task had been hired from the state pen.

On the Thursday evening before the start of the season I stayed late at the marina; I have a hazy recollection of a party developing in the cramped space of somebody's cabin; anyway, I suddenly awoke with a powerful headache and a desire to be sick, to find that I was lying on the floor in unfamiliar surroundings. I crawled to my feet, got as far as the hatch, and poked my head out into the chill night air.

After a few deep breaths I felt better. I glanced around the cabin and saw a sleeping girl, partly clothed, on one of the berths. Her mouth was hanging open and she was a mess, clothes soiled, hair matted. Crumpled around her throat was a slithe-skin neckerchief, its dull brown hue testifying the extent to which she was drained of emotion. I hoped it wasn't I who had drained her, and thought briefly of Charles and his rape case, and how easy it is to transgress the law these days.

I shut the cabin door quietly behind me and stood in the cockpit of the beached hydrofoil, allowing the night breezes to cool my head. I felt sweaty and stale. Stepping over the cockpit coaming, I found the ladder and climbed down to the slipway.

The next thing I did was to trip over the whip of the unknown boat and fall flat and noisily on my face. Whips are of incredible lightness and rigidity, particularly this season's improved models. The end of this particular whip must have been balanced on a box; anyway, it followed me to the ground with a ringing clatter which set up a sympathetic resonance throughout its entire eighty-yard length, causing it to protest with a wail which must have come close to awakening the very fossils under the sedimentary mud of which the Peninsula is composed.

As I lay there trying not to vomit, there was a scurrying, rustling noise nearby and the hair at the nape of my neck prickled. The brute who had made that noise could have been anything; the appalling Wilberforce was quite innocuous compared with some of the bizarre pets I had seen that spring.

I lay still and waited. The sounds continued; an uneven series which might have been footsteps, an occasional clatter of a can of paint or similar slipway debris being knocked over, and a gasping noise which I tried to tell myself was human. Encouragingly, the sounds were retreating; soon they faded away. I heard the distant whine of a hovercar starting up; then that too receded and all was quiet again.

Obviously there had been a trespasser among the boats. In the morning someone would find their paintwork scored or their rudder pintles loosened. That sort of thing annoys me; I just can't see the sense in it. I wished I'd had the courage to tackle the intruder.

Twenty minutes later I was driving through my farm gates. I got out of the car and listened. Everything seemed to be in order; relieved, I made for the house.

The following morning Dave and I made a tour of inspection. The little reptiles were in good shape; as we threw the fodder over the chicken wire they scurried forward, pink with pleasure, and began to feed voraciously. Dave gave one of his rare grins.

"I've had a call from Sentry Down, by the way," he said. "They're expecting our consignment to arrive on Sunday. Do you want me to take the ferry and collect them?"

"I'll let you know." I always enjoy trips to the mainland myself; they make a change—although Sunday was an awkward day.

Dave noticed me testing the chicken wire with my foot, and his manner assumed its accustomed seriousness. "I heard a garden barracuda went for Doc Lang yesterday," he said. "He was walking the nature trail at the back of the lagoon and the bastard came for him, straight out of the bush, all snapping teeth—you know what they're like. It's getting serious."

I remembered the pack of land sharks I'd seen stalking Marigold; at this moment a car drove up, saving me further anxiety on the subject.

"Hi, Joe *darling*." It was Carioca Jones. "I've just been visiting *dear* Joanne. I thought I'd drop by."

"I thought you were up in the snow somewhere," I said.

"Joe, it was the most idiotic *hoax!* Someone sent me what purported to be a transcript of a Newspocket report up at Lake William and it sounded the most *heartrending* thing. Dozens of poor S. P. men being used as nothing better than *pack animals.* And there were some bonded men with the actual party, going across the glaciers—you know what frostbite is, and they had a surgeon as well. My dear, it was all positively *sinister.*"

"Oh, yes?" I said carefully.

"And when we got there with all our banners and placards, there was nothing happening! We marched down the street singing, and everyone looked at us as though we were *mad*. And it was so cold, you've no idea! So we booked into the nearest hotel—an awful place, full of rough men—and I went to the local Newspocket agency, and do you know, they'd never *heard* of the Great Arctic Trek, as it was supposed to be called."

"You must have been very disappointed."

She shot me a glance of birdlike suspicion but apparently my expression satisfied her. "Quite, and it was dreadfully embarrassing, and we hadn't really allowed for the coldness of it. Some of the girls were frostbitten quite badly. They were quite upset and four of them resigned from the Foes. Evadne Prendergast came in for some criticism, I can tell *you.*"

I nearly asked her. I nearly asked just how badly those four had been hurt and whether, if surgery had been necessary, they had contacted the nearest Ambulatory Organ Pool.

Instead I asked, "Are men allowed to join the Foes?"

"Of course," she said. "Why ever not?"

"I just wondered. They all seem to be women, that's all."

"Oh, but that's the way it works out, my dear. You see, it's *men* who go in for these dangerous sports, it's *men* who get smashed up and need grafts and transplants, so naturally *men* will support the status quo."

"Pardon me, Carioca, but that's garbage. The majority of applications to the Pool are the results of road or air accidents. Only a fraction of the male population can afford to sling-glide, or tramp through the Arctic."

"You men all stick together, that's the trouble. Look at you, Joe. You admit that you're against legalized slavery, yet you have your own bonded man, and you're friendly with lice like Marshall who risk someone else's neck for fun. You wouldn't join the Foes of Bondage if I begged you to—so I won't bother."

Just for the record, at this point I gave Carioca Jones something from the depths of my soul, if I have one. "Dave Froehlich is a good man who I feel I rescued from that stinking prison—and I get no thanks from Dave. I'm friendly with Marshall because I enjoy his personality and to hell with his views—even if his views are unsound, which I doubt. I won't join the Foes because I'd be the only man there and people would look at me as a crank, added to which I don't agree with the Foes' methods. Regardless of whether or not the members are women, my point is that they are exactly the *type* of person you always get in an organization of that *type*. It's a type I don't like. Under the guise of doing good, the members get a vicarious personal satisfaction from the annoyance they cause others. Their methods are wrong, in that they think it right to counter evil with evil."

Carioca's mouth had fallen agape during this. When I finished she hitched it up, thought a bit, then said: "You take the whole thing too seriously, Joe. The Foes are a club, that's all. A woman's club, if you will. This talk of evil is non-sense. When we demonstrate, we just think what fun it is to be doing it together. If it helps you any, Joe, I don't think the members consider the objects of the organization as deeply as you do."

"Then we need a new organization. God damn it, Carioca, they shout obscenities at people."

"Well, isn't it fun to have the chance to shout obscenities at people without fear of any comeback?"

I nearly lost my temper, and a good customer. "I've never felt any desire to shout obscenities at people. That's the mentality of a teen-aged vandal."

She took my arm suddenly. "Oh, come on, Joe. Let's not quarrel. I came to do business with you. You and I are on the same side, basically. It's people like your *friend* Marshall I don't like. It was he who faked the Newspocket transcript, of course."

"Oh, don't give me that, Carioca."

"No, I mean it. It's *typical* of his sense of humor. And I can tell you, it's not so funny up at Lake William for a person of my age, Joe."

It was the first time I'd ever heard her mention her age. I changed the subject hastily. "You said you came to do business?" I smiled to make it sound less mercenary.

"Of course, you must be busy." Her manner had become stiff. "I'd like to buy four dozen slithe-skin wristlets, please."

"Four *dozen?*"

"They're for the Foes of Bondage. We shall wear them at the demonstration tomorrow and they will show the solidarity of our feelings."

I had a mental image of four dozen Foes with fists up-raised but with wristlets unfortunately showing colors of rainbow diversity. "Do you think that's wise?" I asked.

"Look, Joe Sagar. Do you want the business or don't you?"

Resignedly I took her into the showroom. While she was selecting the wristlets she persisted in asking about Charles, his crime, his sentence. She seemed to be trying to work up a feeling of pity for the man.

Although the President's Trophy is the first event of the season and tends to be looked on as a mere hors d'oeuvre to the main course of races later in the summer, it is neverthe-less an event worth winning. The psychological boost to the victor will frequently start a winning vein which in subsequent weeks can be worth a good deal of prize money. And more than any other sport, sling-gliding depends on confidence.

Traditionally, the main body of spectators gathers along the ancient stone seawall which was one of the few human artifacts on the Peninsula to escape total destruction by the tidal waves of the Slide. Here gather the curious, the casual, the enthusiasts—and the Foes of Bondage. Out across the bay, half a mile distant, the gaunt pillar of the fulcrum rises from the calm water.

The Foes had already picketed the entrance to the marina, screaming their epithets at the hovercars as they arrived with pilots, crews, and maintenance men. On stepping from my own vehicle I had been surprised when a woman I hardly knew thrust herself before me and referred to my slithe farm as a "plantation." This was the latest dirty word unearthed by the Foes, and apparently referred to some early phase of Man's relationship with his fellows. When I replied, rather weakly, that I didn't plant anything at the farm—if the growing of crops was what she objected to—she merely uttered a jeering noise and called me a "boss man."

Then Carioca Jones appeared. "My *God*, Joe," she shrilled. "Do you mean to say you're actually taking part in this pantomime?"

Fortunately the press of the crowd took her away from me at this point, so I was spared the embarrassment of conversation.

The President's Trophy is a distance/placement event. The glider flies to a point out in the Strait, drops a marker, and returns, the pilot endeavoring to land at a point as close as possible to the seawall. A buoy, just offshore from the spectators, indicates the optimum. It is this finish close to the crowd which gives the event its popularity.

By the time the boats were cruising about, testing their engines, the Foes of Bondage had positioned themselves at a point near the northern end of the seawall, close to the marina. From time to time their president—the elderly Evadne Prendergast whom Carioca Jones hoped to supplant —whipped them into a frenzy with a few well-turned phrases. She had an imposing, almost Puritanical presence which lent weight to her oracular delivery. From my position I couldn't hear the words, but judging from the cheers of her supporters it was all good stuff.

In the distance a hydrofoil was racing toward the fulcrum. The crowd was still. Behind the boat a tiny glider rose into the sky. It was too far away for us to see the whip as the boat snapped around the fulcrum, but we could judge the fearsome acceleration as the little dart was flung low above the water at a speed around two hundred fifty miles per hour. For an instant we lost it against the trees of the island opposite; then it slipped into view above the Strait. There was a murmur as those with binoculars saw the marker buoy drop away as the glider turned to make its approach. The distance of this buoy from the fulcrum is taken into account in the final placings, encouraging pilots to go for speed and distance instead of merely stalling slowly in for an accurate landing.

Archer was gliding and he was trying to squeeze a little too much distance from his speed. He was coming in fast and low after a wide turn and it was apparent that he would not make the finishing buoy. Skimming the sea so close I'll swear he raised ripples on the smooth surface, he used his last breath of flying speed in a shallow climb, then stalled and dropped into the water about two hundred yards away.

The spectators clapped politely as he struggled clear of his harness and trod water waiting to be picked up. The Foes of Bondage were silent. Their wristlets remained neutral to a woman—neither showing the purple of enraged distaste nor the pink of pleasure. I assumed they had done their homework and established that Archer had no bonded S. P. man.

I caught sight of Carioca Jones at the instant she glanced at me—and suddenly I knew that the Foes' rancor was being reserved for our boat, and for Doug Marshall in particular.

10

Marshall was gliding, Charles was steering, and I was observing, sitting in the stern and watching for trouble. Charles's attention was naturally concentrated ahead, on the fulcrum. I stole a quick glance over my shoulder and saw the black post rising solitary out of the flat sea about half a mile ahead. I looked back and Marshall was waving.

"Right!" I shouted to Charles.

He gunned the engine. The whip took the strain and rose dripping from the water with hardly a sag in its rigid length. A feather of foam appeared at Marshall's skis as he began to move, rising upright with the glider attached to his back like a bright vampire.

The boat rose on its foils and the last of the roiling wake fled astern, to be replaced by twin hissing threads of spray. Marshall began to experience lift and kicked off his skis, raising his hands to grip the controls in the nose of the glider. He drew up his legs, jackknifing and thrusting them back into the slender fuselage. He was flying, the whip attached to his chest harness with a snap-fastening.

He sailed easily behind us at about fifty miles per hour, lying facedown within the tiny glider. I suppressed a shudder; the takeoff always affects me like that, ever since Patterson's mistake last season. Patterson had grasped the controls clumsily, so we assumed afterward; anyway, his glider had plunged down suddenly, watched by some twenty helpless spectators in my boat nearby. It had struck the water at a downward angle and the whip had smashed through the nose, jamming. Then the angle of the whip to the glider had taken it down through the water, deeper, deeper. I think the most terrifying thing was watching the exposed length of whip shortening, shortening despite the deceleration of the boat, as the glider and Patterson dived uncontrollably into the black pressure of the deeps. He must have descended over sixty feet in a very few seconds. . . .

But Marshall was safely aloft and veering out toward our starboard beam, ready to take advantage of the initial effect of the fulcrum post. He had banked and I could see him grinning at us, grinning with exhilaration, a six-foot man in a ten-foot glider.

At moments like this the oddest notions come to the front of a man's racing stream of thoughts. Suddenly I was thinking of Thursday night on the slipway, and the fact that Doug Marshall seemed to be a target, and that the Foes of Bondage had arrived back from Lake William earlier than expected—Wednesday, I'd been told. . . .

Charles hit the water brake for just the instant necessary to swing Doug directly abeam, and, at precisely the right moment, he leaned across to the whip bracket.

And slipped the pin easily into its housing, locking the whip at right angles to the boat. He eased the throttle away and we leaped forward again, the glider riveted to a parallel course sixty yards from our starboard beam and matching our speed of around ninety miles per hour. I exhaled a gasp of relief, which was lost in the scream of the turbines. Just for a moment the thought of sabotage had crossed my mind.

"Coming up!" shouted Charles.

I glanced around quickly and saw the fulcrum post racing nearer, the giant hook jutting out black and solid toward us. In June of last year, I think it was, Bennett had misjudged the clearance and run into the hook.

Charles thumbed a button and the eye slid out from the reinforced portside of the hull. The craft listed as the huge steel loop extended and I made the conventional sign to Marshall—the O of finger and thumb. He dipped in acknowledgment.

"Brace yourself!" shouted the bonded man. He leaned into the padded pillar to the right of the wheel. I huddled in my seat, cushioning my head in my hands.

The hook engaged the eye.

I think I probably screamed a little as the G's hit me; I'm told I usually do. The hook engaged the eye—and snatched the hydrofoil, by now traveling at around one hundred miles per hour, into a thirty-yard-radius turn.

Round about this time I never know what's happening; I just cower there and wait for it to finish. I've seen it from a distance, of course, and it looks quite simple. The pilot has taken his glider to a station off the starboard of the boat, so that when the hook engages the eye, the boat veers sharply away. Despite its rigidity, the whip bends. The glider begins to accelerate as the centrifugal force allied to the incredible strength of the whip takes effect.

I've seen boats circle the fulcrum post on the swiveling hook so fast that the whip spirals like a watchspring, the glider lagging behind at first but accelerating, accelerating until the whip finally snaps straight and flings the glider outward at speeds which can reach almost three hundred miles per hour. A glider ten feet long with a wingspan of perhaps seven feet, made of aluminum and stressed fabric. . . .

There is a certain margin for error. If the observer senses that the glider is not in the correct position, that the pilot is not quite ready, he can tell the steersman to abort at any distance up to forty yards from the gantrylike hook and the boat will veer right, slowing, while the pilot detaches the whip from his harness, closes in, stalls, and drops into the water alongside. This is the textbook procedure, although I've seen teams take a wide, wide turn and approach the hook again without dropping the glider.

As the G's forced my head into the padded rest I again sensed something was wrong. I opened my eyes, saw the dizzy blur of water racing past, the gaunt blackness of the fulcrum partially obscuring my view. Then, climbing rapidly against the sky, the glider. The whip curved back from Marshall, beyond my field of vision. I could see him fumbling one-handed with the release mechanism.

The glider lagged back, dropping out of view as the whip curled. Marshall's snap-fastening had jammed. He could not break clear of the whip. Shortly, all that coiled energy would be spent in smashing him into the sea, or whirling him and his glider into broken pieces overhead.

Once, and once only, I saw a man make a perfect landing on the surface with the whip still attached to his jammed fastening—yet that man died, too. Farrel. . . . We watched from the shore as the eye hit the hook and the boat snapped into its turn at exceptionally high speed; it was the finals of the National Distance Championships. The whip coiled into a venomous high-tensile spring which reminds the over-imaginative of a striking cobra. Farrel had gone into his slow climb and was accelerating as the boat slowed at the fulcrum and the whip began to straighten. Farrel's wife was watching through binoculars and I heard her gasp suddenly, a quick gasp which was almost a scream. I remember the expression on the face of Farrel's bonded man who was standing next to her, as he snatched the glasses from her and clamped them to his eyes. Mrs. Farrel turned to me; her face was twisted and she was only able to utter one word —but it was probably the only word apposite to the situation.

"Why?" she said.

And the boat had slowly descended from its hydrofoils and was wallowing around the fulcrum, while the whip spent its venom in hurling Farrel into a speed of three hundred miles per hour. He had stopped trying to fight the release mechanism now and was concentrating on his attitude, maintaining level flight as the whip straightened and began to slow.

At this point the other spectators realized something was wrong. Sometimes, a foolhardy pilot will delay release until the very last instant of acceleration, taking chances on the control problems which arise with a dying whip. But Farrel had gone past even that point. There was a slow murmur of communal horror.

There were also a few anticipatory chuckles from S. P. men standing near. Except for Farrel's man, of course: he stood like a statue, binoculars jammed against his face.

The whip slowed—although we couldn't tell from where we stood, the whip must have been slowing—but still Farrel retained control, retained his horizontal attitude. He was rapidly losing lift due to the dragging effect of the whip at his chest, but he avoided overcorrecting and plunging into the sea, and he avoided the disastrous stall which would have started an end-over-end spin and a breakup of the glider. He was giving a masterly exhibition.

And it was all pointless, of course. There were murmurs of appreciation from around us and I think some people really thought Farrel was going to get away with it. But they didn't know sling-gliding the way the rest of us did. You *never* escape from a jammed fastening.

Farrel was decelerating visibly now, edging closer to the water, extricating his legs from the slender fuselage and dangling them feet upturned, like a swan coming in to land.

An S. P. man chuckled, watching the whip.

There was a communal sigh as Farrel touched the water and his speed fell to zero. He flipped the nose of the glider up in a last-minute stall. I think, even then, he felt he could avoid the inevitable if he could get the drag of the glider's surface area against the water in addition to his own weight.

He didn't make it. He was probably up to his waist in water when the Whip reacted. The deceleration had coiled it backward, building up a reverse tension which now exploded in snatching Farrel from the water and dragging him backward, end over end in the scattering remnants of his glider, spinning along the surface in a curved, frantic plume of spray.

The whip waved to and fro a few times, gradually losing momentum, until at last it lay quiet and twitching on the surface and the boat was able to cast loose from the hook and pick Farrel up. His neck was broken, his back, his legs were broken; there was hardly a bone in his body which had escaped fracture, hardly an organ which was not ruptured.

It might have been possible to do something about all that . . . but Farrel was dead, too.

It had taken just a few seconds. I remember the look on the face of the bonded man when they brought the body ashore. Absolved of all his obligations, his past crime atoned for, release from his bond by the death of his principal, he was now a free man. A freeman. He turned silently away from the drenched and broken thing they had laid on the seawall, and he walked off, saying nothing.

Then Farrel, now Marshall. . . . Pressed hard against the latex headrest, I watched helplessly as the whip straightened preparatory to coiling in the reverse direction while Marshall stayed high in the sky, transfixed by the tip. I rolled my head against the force which held it and saw Charles fighting his way clear of the G-post. His eyes were wide and dead as they met mine; I knew he was going to try something desperate, but his motives were anybody's guess. He edged clear of the post and centrifugal force snatched him from my view instantly.

All this happened so quickly that I had every excuse for doing nothing; in any case, there was no way I could have got clear of the seat. Then the boat was slowing, the landscape ceased its crazy spin, the fulcrum post became a solid object of iron and rust and rivets. As is the way of boats built for speed, she stopped quickly. I stood, my head reeling.

Marshall was clear, gliding landward, trailing the whip behind him, the broken end dangling a short distance above the surface. I satisfied myself that he was descending quickly enough to avoid a stall—the whip in total length is no aid to a smooth landing—and turned my attention to Charles. He was floundering in the water, twenty feet off the port bow. I grabbed the wheel, revved the engine, and slipped it into reverse; backed clear of the hook, retracted the eye, and motored toward him. I got my hands under his armpits and dragged him up the short ladder and onto the deck. He was a big man, strong and heavy, but he was unable to help himself or me.

"Where's Doug?" he asked faintly.

"Almost down. He'll be OK." I glanced at the rig which fastened the whip to the boat; the steel tubing was bent, the whip itself snapped off short where Charles's flying body had smashed into the swivel joint.

It was one of those occasions when the last thing you want to do is consider the implications. I pillowed Charles's head on a life jacket and spun the wheel, heading for shore. Marshall was traveling parallel to the seawall now, diving to maintain speed and at the same time lose height before the trailing end of the whip began to drag in the water and the abrupt deceleration began. Gauging the point of impact, I drove the boat on at full throttle.

Less than a minute later I was pulling Marshall from the water and extricating him from his harness, aided by men from a milling cluster of small boats. I pulled in against the seawall and we carried Charles to the shore, laying him on the grass while someone ran to call the ambulopter.

Almost instantly, it seemed, the Foes of Bondage were standing over us in force, and I shuddered involuntarily because I'll swear there was something akin to predatory satisfaction in their eyes as they looked at the broken figure of Charles, his soaked life jacket oozing crimson.

Two women were to the fore, the president of the Foes, and Carioca Jones. Carioca was the first to speak; she indicated Marshall, who was bending over Charles and lifting a bottle to his lips.

"That's the man I told you about, Evadne," the ex-3-V star said in a voice sufficiently loud for all of us to hear. "He's the *prankster* who tried to get us all out of the way so that we couldn't spoil his fun. Well, you big brave man," she addressed Doug, "how do you feel now? Your man saved you—and we all know *why*. And now look at him, poor thing."

There was a murmur of agreement from the Foes and I believe someone tried to start up a chant, but some remnants of decency prevailed. A Newspocket reporter closed in with his hand minivid. Not to be outdone by Carioca, the elderly Evadne Prendergast said her piece.

"It is a terrible comment on our society when a man will, quite deliberately, risk his life to save another."

Fortunately there was a diversion at this juncture. A man stepped forward and touched Doug on the shoulder. He was carrying the harness which had been cut away from the glider; he indicated the snap release.

"Look. Like you said, Doug. Someone's been fooling with this. The release pin's been roughed up. You can see file marks."

The crowd had gathered itself without conscious volition into two distinct factions around the bleeding man on the seawall. To the landward side were the Foes of Bondage, an unyielding bloc of womanhood, upright and militant. Along the edge of the embankment, backs to the sea, were the pilots, their crews, and supporters, who up to now had been quietly on the defensive.

The mechanic's words changed this. Doug stood, flushing, and an angry muttering spread through the ranks of the pilots. The Foes backed off guiltily.

"I can assure you all—" began the president, hands fluttering, wristlet yellowing.

Carioca Jones took one glance at her fading leader and knew her opportunity had come. She stepped forward boldly.

"It's quite *obviously* a frame-up. And clever, too. Done by one of your own pilots with the object of discrediting the Foes and, incidentally, getting a competitor out of the way. Your treasurer himself told me he heard someone prowling about the slipway on Thursday night." Her black eyes blazed at the elderly man, forcing a nervous nodding agreement. "So *there* you are. There are no grounds whatsoever for even *considering* the Foes as suspect. Only club members are familiar with the slipway and the gear you use. And only a *slave-owner* would think this way, knowing that a bonded man would risk injury himself rather than allow harm to come to his master."

She bent over Charles. "You poor man," she said. "And you only had a year or so to go." Her voice hardened. "Couldn't you have taken the chance that the bastard would kill himself? You'd have been free, then. A freeman!"

She moved back a little, a theatrical gesture to direct attention to Charles and ensure that we all heard his reply—so confident was Carioca Jones. Faintly, but growing louder, we could hear the hissing whine of the ambulopter. The Foes of Bondage wore righteous expressions as they contemplated their prize specimen, their raison d'être, while he lay bleeding on the seawall.

Charles managed a smile.

"I've been a freeman since Thursday, Miss Jones."

11

Early the following morning I met Doug Marshall and Charles at the Skipper's Marina and we drank coffee in the cockpit of his boat. Doug needed to make a trip to the mainland to pick up a new whip and bracket, and since this coincided with the arrival of my consignment of breeding slithes at Sentry Down, he had suggested that we all go in his hydrofoil. Charles was coming along for the ride; he seemed cheerful enough although his ribs were heavily bandaged and he was unable to move with any degree of comfort.

"A couple of broken ribs, that's all," he explained. "But it seems they take longer to mend than a bone graft. They shot me full of Rediseel; I'll be fine in a couple of days, so they said."

"He was lucky," commented Doug. "We thought at first he'd smashed up at least one kidney. The doctor was talking about a transplant."

"Uh . . . what would you have done about that, Charles?" I asked cautiously.

The big man laughed, then winced at the sudden pain. "There you go again, Joe. It didn't happen, did it? So the question doesn't arise. Anyway, a man can live perfectly well with one kidney."

"It was the principle of Compulsory Donation that I was getting at. After all, now that you're a freeman you're entitled to the use of the Organ Pool."

Marshall poured himself another coffee. "I'll never forget Carioca Jones's face when Charles told her he was a freeman. She knew his sentence but she'd forgotten the remission for bondage."

"In her eagerness for the witch hunt," I added. "Uh, do

you mind if we get moving now, Doug? My shipment's due in around noon."

"Don't panic. We'll leave as soon as Rennie gets here. He's off duty today and I asked him if he'd like to join us."

"Oh. Fine." I hadn't seen much of Rennie since the misunderstanding over Marigold, and I was a little wary of meeting him; but it had to be faced. On the Peninsula, it's difficult to avoid meeting people for long.

In due course the police chief came striding across the wharf and climbed aboard. I cast off, Marshall gunned the turbines, and the boat rose onto its hydrofoils, skimming over the quiet water. Rennie poured himself a coffee and we relaxed in the cockpit in the early sunshine, watching the coastline slide past our portside.

We swept past Black Point and saw the *Ancia Telji* lying more easily now against the foot of the cliff; she was probably half-full of water. Hawsers were strung fore and aft, securing her to the shore and preventing her from rolling onto her side and sliding into deeper water. Watching the peaceful scene on the quiet bay with its bright mirror surface, it was difficult to picture the horror of a few days ago, when that steel hull had pounded men and women to pulp.

"In time she'll become a local landmark," said Rennie. "She'll be almost as well known as the *Princess Louise*. I can't imagine the owners moving her. She's not worth the cost of salvage."

"Have you located the owners yet?" asked Charles.

"Yes. We were able to get a whole lot of information out of the crew, before they were released. It seems the owners were all tied up with a tourist agency down south—at least, they called it a tourist agency, but that was just a front. In fact, it was an unofficial immigration office. Christ knows how many people they've smuggled into this country."

The wreck receded astern as Doug veered east, into the open sea. "Well, it's all over now."

"It's not so simple as that. Somebody had to handle the organization from this end." Rennie stared at each of us in turn, piercingly.

"Well, for Christ's sake, Warren," expostulated Doug good-naturedly. "Don't look at me like that."

"An organization with its own premises and boats would be the ideal front for such an operation. Just for a moment, let's consider the Peninsula Sling-gliding Club."

"All of us?" asked Charles incredulously.

"A small group within us. A Committee member or two, a few members with boats, that's all you need. They have access to the yard and premises at all times—and a certain amount of night work often goes on, under the guise of rush repairs. Just think about it."

"Hell, Warren, you might as well suspect the Foes of Bondage."

"I do. I do indeed. The Foes frequently travel between here and the mainland. Only last week they chartered an antigrav to take them to Lake William. I understand there was a hoax involved, but how do I know? You can't set up passport checks between the island and the mainland; the public would never stand for it."

We thought about this as we raced through the small islands which dot the Strait, and it occurred to me then that if Rennie hadn't been with us, we could have kept some rendezvous, taken a dozen illegal passengers on board, and dropped them off at Sentry Down or some other convenient spot. Lambert had said there were around sixty passengers on the *Ancia Telji;* they wouldn't have been difficult to dispose of.

Soon we neared the mainland; the pleasure craft became more numerous as the low coastline came into view. Sentry Down was built on the site of an old city which had been destroyed at the time of the Western Seaboard Slide; the landing area which is now at sea level was once three hundred feet higher. The black dots of antigrav shuttles swarmed about the sky like silent flies.

I left the others at the boatyard, arranging to meet them there around midafternoon, and caught the monorail for the short run to Sentry Down Spaceport. As the car skirted the perimeter of the field I saw the remains of the latest accident—a shuttle lying like a crushed beetle outside the maintenance depot. The crash had occurred last week; the antigrav units had inexplicably failed shortly after liftoff with loss of some seventy lives and God knows how many serious injuries. I had watched developments on Newspocket and had felt no small fury when the District Medical Officer had spoken of the magnificent response of the Ambulatory Organ Pool, without whose donations many innocent people would have been maimed for life.

My mood was therefore somewhat gloomy as I sat in the

observation lounge drinking and watching the shuttles while
I waited for my consignment. The slithes had come via
Hetherington Crusader and the shuttle from the orbiting
starship was already sitting on the concrete outside; the
delay, as ever, was due to the interminable quarantine department.

To my mind the antigrav shuttles rising and falling gently
outside were soulless black boxes compared with the magnif-
icence of the liquid fuel rockets of my youth. I lived most
of my childhood near the huge spaceport at Pacific Northwest—now abandoned and desolate—where my father
worked as Maintenance Supervisor. In those far-off days I
spent most of my leisure hours watching the thunderous
giants roaring into the sky on a crackling blaze of glory, or
squatting toward me—seemingly descending right on top of
me—with fingers of fire probing my very brain, leaving a
touch of wonder that I have never forgotten.

Then some unromantic scientist fiddled with force-fields,
and came up with antigravity. . . .

In due course I heard myself being paged, made my way
to the quarantine desk, and collected the pair of small brown
reptiles. I caught the monorail and within half an hour was
back on Marshall's boat again, eating smoked salmon and
drinking scotch. The replacement bracket had already been
installed and crutches had been mounted on the bow and
stern to support the sixty-yard length of the new whip.
Although the slender rod overhung the boat by around
twenty-five yards fore and aft, there was hardly a trace of
sag at the ends. This is the proof of a good whip.

We swept away from the quay and headed back toward
the island, and the Peninsula which juts eastward from its
southern end. It was a beautiful afternoon, we'd enjoyed a
pleasant lunch and a good drink, so it was unfortunate that
Doug Marshall had now to introduce his topic—thereby revealing the real reason for his inviting Warren Rennie on
the boat.

"Of course, I've a pretty damned good idea who was responsible for the attempt on my life," he said, steering carefully around a fishing boat and accelerating into the open
sea.

"If it was an attempt," said Rennie carefully.

"You know quite well it was, Warren. You saw the marks
on the catch."

"They could have been caused by your efforts to free yourself."

"Crap. The catch was roughed up so it would stick instead of releasing. It was quite deliberate. Joe—tell him what you told me; you know, about the intruder on the quay that night."

I sipped at my scotch thoughtfully; it seemed that my hazy recollections of that drunken night were forming an intrinsic part of Doug's case, and I wasn't happy about that. "I'm not too clear about it," I admitted, "but it did seem to me, at the time, that there was someone prowling about the yard a couple of nights before the race."

"By which time the Foes of Bondage had returned from Lake William," added Doug.

"Hold it just a minute." Rennie was looking worried. "You're not just stating your opinion that I have a case for investigation. You're pointing the finger. I reckon that's a bit premature, Doug."

Marshall flushed. "Look, Rennie. I don't say that sort of thing lightly. If I tell you that the Foes of Bondage wrecked my gear and tried to kill me, then take it from me I've got good reason. I suggest that you investigate further, and bear in mind what I've told you."

He drank deeply from his glass, scowling. He scanned the ocean, making a course correction, his hands white on the wheel. The experience yesterday had shaken him up more than we'd realized. Charles watched him anxiously from his prone position, then glanced at me with his eyebrows raised.

A couple of weeks passed during which we heard nothing more from Rennie, although rumor in the club had it that investigations were under way and one or two people had been discreetly questioned. I prevailed upon Lambert to allow me to see Joanne again and we had a pleasant though inconclusive talk through the wire. She told me that Carioca Jones had been to see her several times—apparently the ex-3-V star had more pull than I—and that she was getting up a petition demanding her release. Behind the petition was an implied threat that the Foes could make things even hotter for the state pen by stepping up their demonstrations and publicity, if they so desired. It was now mid-June, and although Joanne was due for release in less than three months, September seemed a hell of a way off.

In fact the Foes had been quiet lately, following their public humiliation over the episode of Charles. Carioca explained this to me one morning when she arrived with the monstrous Wilberforce—who was wearing a muzzle, I was relieved to see.

"My dear, we're *torn* by internal dissension," she cried.

It seemed a tactless moment to ask when the Foes were going to pay me for the forty-eight slithe-skin wristlets, but I have never prided myself on diplomacy.

"I really can't say when you'll see your money, Joe," she replied distantly. "The Foes are more than a little fragmented just now, and since that ridiculous trek to Lake William we are really on our *beam ends,* financially speaking. But all that will soon change. Evadne Prendergast has resigned over that *appalling* debacle concerning the man Charles Wentworth—and I should think so too. How any normal person could be guilty of such a *gross* error of judgment I really can't think."

Wilberforce lay pulsating on the grass, eyeing the nearest slithe pen with ill-concealed gluttony. The little reptiles cowered against the far side of their enclosure, yellow with terror; so I stood close to the shark's head, trying to obscure the slithes' view of him. "Who is to be the new president?" I asked.

"Of course that's up to the members, by secret ballot—but I've made it *quite* clear that I am willing to be considered. I am even holding the Lake William Hotel's *exorbitant* bill until the result is known; naturally, I have made it known that I am not averse to throwing my personal wealth behind our great cause. Unfortunately, that *wretched* policeman Rennie is poking about and making the most *bizarre* accusations, and it is becoming so the Foes are *terrified* to be seen in the company of one another. It's only the common cause of dear Joanne that's holding us together."

I made sympathetic noises and Wilberforce slammed his head against my leg, forgetting he wore a muzzle. "What's wrong with this fish?" I asked.

"Joe, that's what I came to see you about. I intend to *confront* Miranda Marjoribanks with him and I need moral support. Will you be a dear and come along?"

In due course we dragged Wilberforce from the hovercar

at Pacific Kennels, Miss Marjoribanks strode up with an in-
quiring look, Carioca whipped the muzzle from the shark's
head and stood well back. "Do you call this a well-adjusted
fish?" she shrilled.

Miranda Marjoribanks eyed Wilberforce cautiously. I noticed that her foot was heavily bandaged—the legacy of
Wilberforce's last visit. "Have you been giving him his pills?"
she inquired.

"Well, *really!* It should be obvious to the *meanest* intelligence that I couldn't get near him, let alone put a pill in
his mouth. Why, it took three hypodarts to get the muzzle
on him—and even then I barely escaped with my *life!*"

"Rosalie! Come over here for a minute, dear!"

"You surely don't intend to let that poor girl near him?"

The bonded girl approached Wilberforce, who stared at
her malevolently. Unafraid, she put her hand out, patted
him on the head, then knelt beside him. She slipped a pill
from the pocket of her coveralls and pushed it into the
shark's mouth, then held his jaws closed while he swallowed.
She stood, smiled at us, and returned to her duties around
the enclosure.

"You *see?*" said Miranda Marjoribanks in triumph. Noting
that the shark's head was drooping she stepped up to him,
rolled him onto his back, and opened his jaws. "You haven't
been filing his teeth," she accused. "Naturally you can't get
near him—I told you he was highly strung."

"I can't get near him to file his teeth. In any case," Carioca
admitted, somewhat abashed, "I've lost the denticure set. But
that's neither here nor there, Miranda, as you perfectly well
know. I've paid you, and paid you well, for a therapy course
which you assured me would cure Wilberforce's tantrums. I
demand satisfaction."

"Leave the fish with me," said Miranda shortly.

Carioca's mood changed so suddenly that I suspected she
was only too glad to have the brute taken off her hands.
"That's *so* good of you, Miranda," she cooed. "I told Joe
you'd see reason. I *do* hope your foot is better."

"I was forced to apply to the Ambulatory Organ Pool
for a graft, no thanks to you. It seems to be taking well."

"The Ambulatory Organ Pool?" Carioca was staring at
Rosalie, who was feeding a shoal of tuna. "But you have a
bonded girl. They don't allow you the use of the Pool when

you have a bonded girl. A bonded girl is supposed to take care of all such requirements."

"It so happens that Rosalie is a good worker and I need her intact—and it also happens that I have a certain amount of influence at the state pen. The officials and I are on very good terms. Naturally, I had to wait a week or two until a suitable donor was matched with me, and I had to pay a considerable amount of money for the treatment. But then," said Miranda Marjoribanks, smiling fondly, "no amount of money is too large when dear Rosalie's appearance is at stake. She's such a pretty girl."

The bonded S. P. girl was leaning against the far side of the enclosure, chatting to a young man whom I recognized as Jonathan Bartholomew, son of Hector Bartholomew the famous artist, and himself a creator of emotion mobiles of no small merit. Young Bartholomew and Rosalie seemed very friendly, and I recalled hearing that Miranda Marjoribanks had acquired a couple of Bartholomew originals recently. There are indeed wheels within wheels, on the Peninsula.

"I question the legality of your operation, Miranda," Carioca was saying sternly. "I also question the morality, but you know that very well. It's bad enough that the Pool should be available gratis to freemen, but to hear that spare limbs can be bought like avocado pears is little short of *terrifying*. You will receive a strong letter of protest from the Foes about this."

"I've no doubt I shall," replied Miss Marjoribanks airily. "If your organization can afford the postage, that is."

It was a difficult morning all around. When finally I got rid of Carioca and arrived back at my farm, I found Warren Rennie waiting for me.

"I'd like a word with you about the alleged sabotage at the Skipper's Marina, Joe," he said. "I've had the lab go over Doug Marshall's harness, and I've made a few inquiries here and there. It seems there might be something in what Doug says. This is off the record, of course."

"Of course."

"Now, I'd like you to tell me again what you remember of that night."

I hesitated. As time went by my recollections seemed to have become more hazy. I saw Dave Froehlich emerge from the factory; he was approaching us. "I've got to make this clear, Warren," I said. "I was stoned out of my mind that night. Here and now, it's difficult to remember just what did happen. Perhaps if we went along to the marina I could reconstruct it. That might be easier."

"Fine. Are you free now?"

"Excuse me, Mr. Sagar," Dave interrupted, holding something out. "Before you go. This letter arrived this morning while you were out."

With an uncertain feeling in my stomach I saw the envelope was postmarked Halmas. I tore it open and read:

> Dear Joe Sagar,
> Sorry we had to open your letter to Marigold because our Marigold is not here since she take ship north. You say in your letter you will visit us later in the summer well this will be very nice. It is sad that Marigold is not here since she take ship, but you say she was with you. Yet we think you are saying she is now back with us well she is not and we don't know where she is. If you know where she is will you please tell us because her mother and all of us are very worried.
> Respectfully yours,
> Aldo Carassa.

Rennie was waiting for me to go, but I needed time to think, to consider the implications before I discussed the letter with him.

"Something's come up," I told him. "Can we leave things for a while?"

He looked at me sharply. "Not too long, Joe. I'd like you at the marina just as soon as you're free, if you don't mind."

12

For a few days I avoided Rennie and the club while I busied myself with very necessary work about the farm, leaving instructions with the S. P. girl nearest the visiphone to tell the policeman I was out, if he called. He did call on two occasions, and later I was forced to creep off into the bush when I saw his hovercar approaching down the track. It was a demeaning experience.

It was Rennie's personality which threw me, and the piercing way he had of looking at me. I couldn't rid myself of the memory of his unpleasantness when he'd decided I'd spent the night raping an unconscious girl. It was apparent he needed only the smallest excuse to mistrust me; and if he found out that Marigold had not arrived home he would quite likely jump to the conclusion that I had her chained naked in some dungeon at the mercy of my lurid perversions.

Yet the overall situation was alarming, even suspicious. Gallaugher had assured me, one night in the club, that Marigold had been sent home with the other immigrants. Was it possible that she'd escaped in some way before the clipper lifted off—or had she in fact completed the journey but was too ashamed to face her parents?

Or maybe Gallaugher had lied to me. He was a small man and too fat for his age, and he wore extremely thick pebble lenses which made it difficult to assess the expression on his face. He drank gin. He was, in fact, an obnoxious character and it was not beyond the bounds of possibility that he had retained Marigold for his own purposes. A rambling prison full of crooks and prostitutes and dope addicts would be the perfect hiding place for a kidnapee.

Round about this stage in my reasoning it occurred to me that I was allowing my dislike of Gallaugher to run away with me. Possibly the man honestly had believed that Marigold had been on the clipper; maybe he had been misinformed. I had got no further than this in my deliberations when Rennie finally ran me to ground, and I agreed to meet him at the Skipper's Marina on the following morning.

On the afternoon before this I visited Joanne in the pen and found her in good spirits. She smiled at me warmly and I felt my heart warm too, and I ached to hold her against me. She seemed to have gained a little weight and her eyes sparkled with mischief as she taunted me, and refused to commit herself as to what she intended to do when she was released. When I watched her face—her bright eyes and pert, snub nose; her freckles and thick hair which fell to her shoulders—when I saw all this loveliness I didn't think about her hands at all. Neither did I think of her hands as I lay in bed that night thinking of her; in my imagination she was perfect, and it seemed to me that she would come to love me, given time.

But the following morning I awoke in a gray mood and the weather matched my gloom as the rain swept the window; and I couldn't bear to think of Joanne because it all seemed so hopeless.

After a while I dressed and went downstairs, ate breakfast, and went out into the yard. I found Dave standing in an empty slithe pen, staring disconsolately at the mud. The rain was blowing in from the sea. He didn't look at me.

"We've lost twenty slithes from this pen, Mr. Sagar. They've disappeared overnight."

"You must have left the gate open."

Now his eyes met mine; there was defiance there. "I closed the gate last night."

"Don't talk crap. No land shark could get over this wire. It's six feet high, man." The slow anger was rising in me. Dave ought to know better than to take me for an idiot, I thought.

Unfortunately the pen in which we stood was near to the factory, and the S. P. girls were crowding the doorway, watching us.

"If I said I shut the gate I mean I shut the gate!" Dave's voice was raised too. "I tell you something climbed over the top!"

It seemed as though the frustration of months was building in Dave, and for some inexplicable reason I had the urge to make things worse, to provoke him until he completely lost his head. "And I tell you I don't believe you," I said harshly. I was sick of his attitude, sick of his shifty looks. "You're making excuses for yourself, Dave."

"You're only saying that because I'm an S. P. man," he muttered.

"What the hell do you mean?"

"I mean you wouldn't call me a liar if I wasn't an S. P. man. Just because I'm bonded to you, you think you can say what you like!"

There was a chorus of agreement from the girls and one of them called out, "Quite right, Dave! You tell the bastard! These freemen seem to think they can treat us like animals! They've made second-class citizens out of us!"

I sighed, feeling unutterably depressed, my rage burned out. It was a new group of S. P. girls but they thought just the same as the old group. I had a wild notion of closing the whole place down, sending everyone back to the pen, then starting again with regular free employees. The profits might be less, but so would be the problems. And it would be great not to be greeted by Dave's surly face every morning.

"Listen to me, Dave," I said tiredly. "Doesn't it occur to you that I'd ball anyone out if I thought he'd left a gate open, whether he was a freeman or an S. P. man?"

"I know what I think," he mumbled, face sullen. The girls scowled at me from the factory door. They were all united in hatred of me—just because I hadn't served time, just because I was honest.

The rage surged up again, quick this time, and maddening. "Well, you know what I think?" I shouted. "I think you're a lot of stupid bastards! You're too goddamned stupid to stay out of the pen! You say I treat you like animals—well, maybe that's because you *are* animals." I tried to recover my composure before I hit someone. "Now get back to work, all of you, and let's hear no more of this crap. The next one who brings up this second-class citizen thing will be reported to the warden."

The fattest and oldest S. P. girl—incidentally the least efficient—stood her ground, arms akimbo, while the others ranged themselves uncertainly behind her. "You're the one who's going to be reported to the warden, Mr. Goddamned

Sagar. You've gone too far this time, speaking to us like that. You'll get no more work out of us."

"Dave!" I snapped. "Ship them back to the pen. Bring me a fresh batch."

"You won't get any more girls here!" shouted the fat one. "Not when Mr. Lambert hears what we've got to say!"

I turned away. "Dave," I said, "you're still my bonded man. I'm directing you to deal with this situation—I have to get along to the marina. Now get these cows out of here. I'll expect to see new faces when I get back, and I'll expect to see them smiling, for Christ's sake. I want no more trouble-making from anybody—and that includes you."

As I drove to the marina to meet Warren Rennie I knew for the first time that the Foes of Bondage were right, all along the line. If it hadn't been for the Foes' composite personality I'd have realized it before; but the sight of a crowd of screaming women is naturally prejudicial to a man's attitudes. But now I knew. The theory of the Penal Reform Act was fine, but in practice it couldn't work—people aren't made that way. Bondage created tensions between principal and servant and was wide open to abuse. Compulsory labor by hired prisoners held connotations of slavery which were never far below the surface, and again clouded the whole relationship between employer and employee. And as for the Ambulatory Organ Pool . . . that was abhorrent, no matter what Heathcote Lambert said.

It was a pity, but it seemed to me the only answer was to go back to the old system of locking prisoners away at public expense. Maybe the real problem was people; and the real answer, the abolition of crime. Whatever the solution, there was nothing I could do about it.

Except, maybe, to disassociate myself from the whole business, release Dave from his bond, hire free workers, join the Foes of Bondage and see if I could bring a leavening of common sense into that benighted organization. Joanne would like me to do that.

Rennie was already waiting at the marina slipway when I arrived; as I walked down the slope I saw him bending over a heap of scrap metal, poking about with a stick. He straightened up, greeted me, and immediately wanted me to identify the position of the boat on which the party had been held.

I looked around. The boats were all gone from the slip-way now, riding at anchor in the bay or tied up to the marina floats. The muddy concrete was bare of reference points from which I could begin my reconstruction; just a few dinghies lay around, and a scattering of smaller objects: odd lengths of rope and cable, broken lengths of whip, timber offcuts, cotton waste, wooden chocks. "Look. I'm not sure," I said. "Everything looks different now."

He produced a large sheet of paper. "I've been able to get hold of something which may help you," he said. "This is the winter slipway plan from the marina office. All the boats are marked. Now, take a close look and tell me where that party was."

I pondered, then pointed at the plan. "I think it was on this boat. Presdee's. That's two boats away from Marshall. You could ask Presdee; he might remember."

"I already have." He smiled thinly. "It seems everyone has the same problem as yourself. There were so many parties on so many nights that they have become confused in people's minds. For the time being, we'll have to assume it was Presdee's boat. Now. Let's stand over there."

He paced out the slipway, found the imprints of Presdee's hydrofoil legs still showing deep in the mud which covered this area, while I tried to remember what had happened after I'd departed from the remains of the party. "There was just a girl left, asleep," I said. "God knows who she was. I climbed out, down the ladder. It would have been about . . . here." I pointed. Rennie placed a small red marker on the ground.

"Which way were you facing, after you climbed down?" he asked.

"That way." I pointed up the slope and to the right. "I started to move away, toward where I thought my car was, and I tripped over a whip . . . that's right. It must have been Presdee's whip. It made one hell of a noise. I lay on the ground for a while—I think I may have been sick—then I heard the noises."

"Where from?"

"Up there." I indicated the approximate area and Rennie consulted his plan.

"That's it," he said. "That's just about the place where Marshall's harness was, on a box, so he said. Now, let's take it from there."

I was finding that the memory was becoming more vivid and I could even recall the direction of the retreating sounds —probably because I'd been so scared at the time. We followed my recollections up the slipway, across to the right where I'd heard the clattering of cans—and sure enough, there the cans were, abandoned and encrusted with solidified paint. Then onto the grass some distance above the slipway, among the scrub; at that time the alleged saboteur must have been searching for his car in the dark. Then across to the left, near the marina office, from which direction I'd heard the slam of the car door and the eventual departure. Rennie and I traced the route, and every so often Rennie placed one of his red markers.

Finally we were finished. We made our way to the clubhouse for coffee. "What's next?" I asked. "You bring the bloodhounds to sniff around?"

He smiled his mirthless smile. "We've progressed beyond that, Joe. We use a little brute from Altair called a land lamprey. It's not very pretty, but it can sniff out anything touched by a human being within the last few weeks. It's a pity about all this rain, but at least we have some idea of where to start looking."

"There may be nothing to find."

"Possibly not. But our man was in a hurry—and it's surprising what traces a man will leave behind when he's stumbling through the dark."

We finished our coffee in silence; then, as he was leaving, I asked him as casually as I could if he'd got any further in his investigations into the brain behind the illegal immigrants.

"No," he said shortly, and I had the impression he'd rather I hadn't asked.

Life went on much as usual for a while, although my latest bunch of S. P. girls refused to work for me after the first week, on the grounds that I abused them physically. Then, on the next day, occurred the spectacular incident which is still talked about on the Peninsula whenever the name of Miranda Marjoribanks comes up.

I happened to be present at Pacific Kennels at the time— as were Carioca Jones, Miss Marjoribanks herself, the girl Rosalie, the artist Hector Bartholomew, and his son Jonathan. The incident served to remind us that in creating pets and playthings for ourselves out of living sea creatures, we do not thereby alter the basic nature of those creatures. The incident is legend now, and the reasons behind it complex, so there is no point in repeating them here.

Briefly, the land sharks in the enclosure at Pacific Kennels went into a feeding frenzy.

Wilberforce started it. For reasons known only to himself and possibly Hector Bartholomew, he sprang from his cage at the enclosure perimeter and attacked Rosalie. There was a large recent shipment of sharks lying around the place, and they smelled the blood and became excited. The next thing we knew, they plunged into the fray, attacking Rosalie, Wilberforce, and one another indiscriminately. Eventually we drove them off Rosalie and got her to safety, but not before a few of our reputations had suffered in the panic. The only good to come out of the whole terrible affair was the death of Wilberforce.

The ambulopter was called and Rosalie was flown to the hospital. Jonathan Bartholomew went with her, and Hector went home. Carioca and I accompanied Miranda Marjoribanks into her mock-Tudor house.

"I trust you realize I propose to sue you for every *penny* you own, Miranda," hissed Carioca, still trembling. "When I think of the way those savage brutes attacked poor Wilberforce and actually *ate* him before my very eyes, I feel sick to my *stomach.*"

A couple of quick gins had restored Miss Marjoribanks' equanimity. "It saves you the expense of having him put down, Carioca dear," she said loftily. "You know perfectly well that he'd got totally out of control. If there's any talk of suing, I suggest you remember what this incident has cost me. I've lost at least six pedigree hammerheads, and I can assure you they don't come cheaply. If your Wilberforce hadn't launched that insane attack on poor Rosalie, the whole thing would never have happened."

Carioca drank rapidly from her glass, her black eyes furious as she sought for a telling rejoinder. In the corner of the room an original Hector Bartholomew sat on its pedestal, mute and motionless. I switched it on in the hope that it would improve the atmosphere, and the arms began to swing pleasantly, the lights flashed, and the soothing music played gently.

"I'll remind you that Wilberforce was under your care at

the time of the incident, Miranda. You call yourself a veterinarian and yet you have no control *whatever* over the animals in your establishment. My *God*. Every time Wilberforce came back from his treatment, he was more savage than ever. You're no better than a *motor mechanic*. Why, by the time your stupid girl provoked him into attacking, he'd become a different fish *altogether*. He'd become crude and brutal—yet he used to be such a *pet*."

Miranda suddenly dropped the pretense. "For Christ's sake, woman, he was only a goddamned fish. They're all only goddamned fish—it's only you and I who pretend they're intelligent and lovable like dogs. They're cold stupid fish and they've no more brain than a walnut. There's a whole goddamned shoal of the bastards out there—take the pick of the litter with my compliments and get the hell out of here!"

"And that's just *exactly* what I propose to do," snapped Carioca, jumping up. "Although no other creature can possible replace dear sweet Wilberforce."

"Uh . . . do you think we might call the hospital and see how Rosalie is?" I ventured.

"Get that woman out of here right now, Joe Sagar!" shouted Miranda, like Carioca jumping to her feet.

Carioca was already flinging open the door preparatory to a sweeping exit. She stopped so suddenly that I almost ran into her. "There aren't any fish there," she said wonderingly.

"What! Of course there are fish there." Miranda Marjoribanks joined us at the door and together we stared at the enclosure. It was indeed empty. The gate stood swinging, the fish—the land sharks, garden barracudas, morays, rays, sawfish, and numerous others—were all gone. "Oh, my God," muttered Miranda. She swayed, and I helped her back into the living room. I don't know whether it was the shock or the gin which had hit her. I laid her on the couch and got her a drink and the visiphone.

"Would you rather I called the police?" I asked.

"But . . . but the police will destroy them all, with guns. All my capital's locked up in those fish. We could never round them up—and a lot of them will make straight for the ocean. What am I going to do, Joe?"

"Are they insured?"

Her face had crumpled; the statuesque, cultural Miranda Marjoribanks was falling to pieces at last—over a matter of

common, sordid cash. "That last big shipment of sharks . . .
I hadn't got around to insuring them yet. This will ruin
me, Joe."

She was stretched out on the couch and I was looking at
her foot; the dressings were off and I could see the thin
white scar around the base of her big toe.

I forgot all about the visiphone and the police.

"Well, I'm sure I feel *terribly* sorry for you, Miranda
darling," crowed Carioca Jones triumphantly. "But Joe and
I must be going now. *So* unfortunate that you're not in a
position to replace dear Wilberforce. I really shall have
to sue you now. Come on, Joe."

I was looking at the toe; the soft, young roundness, the
faint star-shaped scar just above the joint . . . I thought of
the sun and the beach, and the pretty girl with nice breasts
telling me how the spear-gun had gone off by accident; and
now that pretty girl had disappeared . . . disappeared, all
except for one little part of her, perhaps.

I thought of Marigold, and I feared for Marigold, as I
sat in the mock-Tudor house and the sharks and barracudas
and morays and rays and sawfish flopped and crawled into
the rough scrubland of the flat, sedimentary Peninsula. . . .

13

The *Princess Louise* bar was aswill with lunchtime drinkers and it seemed to me that curious eyes were frequently turned in our direction. This was probably because people recognized my companion as the famous Carioca Jones, although I suspected that numbers of them were wondering who that poor fool was, sitting with that spectacular old witch. Carioca had dressed, or undressed, for the occasion; pallid intense face behind Utrasorb hair, dark eyes glowing at me as she leaned across the table with slithe-skin accessories shining lust red. My worst shock had come when I removed the stole from her shoulders; she was naked from the waist up. As I watched her in horror and embarrassment it seemed she consisted entirely of dark hypnotic nipples.

"I can't think why you should have the slightest doubts, Joe darling," she was saying. "I have over two hundred names on the petition and if that isn't enough to make that *poisonous* man Lambert see reason I don't know what is. I shall *demand* that he release dear Joanne *forthwith*."

"But the law is the law," I said helplessly. "It's not up to Lambert. He's just the warden."

Her face became shrewd, not a pleasant sight. "And that's just where you're wrong, Joe. Lambert is in sole charge and if things are made hot enough for him he'll be *forced* to concede. He was badly shaken by our last demonstration and I know for a fact that his superiors on the mainland have told him to play things cool. There's a big public outcry building up and I intend the Foes to be in the *vanguard*."

More drinks arrived. Carioca drank gin and orange; it has been my experience that women who drink gin and orange are always a little peculiar, in one way or another. "I want to know why you're going to all this trouble, Carioca," I said decisively. "Joanne's due out in a couple of months, anyway."

"Would you like to spend even two months in that *ghastly* dungeon, Joe?"

"All right, if it suits your purpose to petition for her release I'll go along with you. But how do you justify giving her preference over all the other prisoners?"

"Well *really,* Joe. You know perfectly well there's no chance of getting everybody released, so why not select dear Joanne as our symbol? And quite honestly she should never have been jailed in the first place; she tells me she was an *unwitting* accomplice in some petty swindle." She smiled like a skull. "Won't it be nice to see dear Joanne outside those dreadful walls again, Joe? Won't it?"

Later, as we walked through the forbidding corridors of the state penitentiary toward Lambert's office, I had to agree that she was right. The pen is a comparatively modern structure in common with all buildings on the Peninsula, yet the architect had managed to retain the traditional atmosphere of gloom and despair which we associate with such establishments. Recently Hector Bartholomew created an emotion mobile so diabolical—the artist has been going through a bad spell—that it struck terror into the guts of all who saw it. It wouldn't have surprised me if the Prison Commission bought it as a feature for the pen's entrance hall.

Lambert watched us guardedly as we entered. Carioca strutted up to his desk and laid down a somewhat scruffy exercise book with an extravagant gesture. "Now just what do you propose to do about *that,* pray?"

The governor of the penitentiary handled Carioca well. He left the book where it was, glancing from it to her inquiringly. "About what?"

"Open it."

Lambert opened the book, flipped over the pages. "It seems to be a list of names, Miss Jones. What am I supposed to do with it? Is it some sort of mailing list? Where are the addresses?"

"It's a *petition,* you fool, as you very well know. All those good people are demanding that you release Joanne Shaw *immediately.* Please be good enough to instruct your jailor to bring the keys, and we will take no more of your time."

Lambert smiled broadly, leaning back in the chair. "I see

no demands for release. All I see is a list of names. Miss Jones, if you want to petition for the release of any prisoner, then I suggest you draw up your document properly and send it to the Prison Commissioners on the mainland. I have no authority in such matters. Right?"

Carioca snatched the book from his desk, flushing. "You know *perfectly* well any such communication would be ignored. Joe—" She appealed to me. "Tell this *wretched* man exactly what he may expect, if he ignores the wishes of the public."

I was on the spot. "Uh, there seems to be a certain amount of discontent."

Lambert interrupted me, frowning. "I'm surprised at you getting yourself involved with these nuts, Joe. Maybe you think you're doing it for Joanne Shaw, but you can take it from me that all your friend Miss Jones is after is power. She wants to build the Foes into a strong political organization—and other branches are doing the same, all over the country. She's not doing this for Joanne Shaw. For Christ's sake, look at her, man. Look at her hands! Those are Joanne Shaw's hands! What sort of twisted thinking are you trying to put across?"

"You wouldn't understand," I muttered. "There's a lot of things happened since—"

"Well, for Christ's sake." He was staring from me to Carioca. "For Christ's sake. Yes, I'm goddamned sure a lot of things have happened. I tell you this, Joe. I've been giving you the benefit of the doubt over the complaints your S. P. girls have been making against you, but now I'm not so all-fired sure."

"Just what the hell are you driving at, Lambert?"

"Any man who can fool around with a woman twice his age must be pretty goddamned strange, that's what I'm driving at!"

"What do you mean, twice his age?" shrilled Carioca.

"What makes you think I'm fooling around, you bastard?" I shouted, losing control.

"For Christ's sake, it's all over the Peninsula!" he yelled back, spittle spraying. "That funny business about the girl from the *Ancia Telji*—and you and this godawful woman here are always together, and you can't keep an S. P. group at your farm for ten minutes without they start complaining you've been feeling them up. I tell you this—you'll rent no more girls from my pen. You're through, Sagar. Get the hell out of here and take a cold bath, that's my advice to you!"

"I propose to complain to your superiors about your *slanderous* insinuations, you foul-mouthed sonofabitch!" screamed Carioca.

Lambert and I were on our feet, glaring at each other over the desk like fighting cocks, while Carioca pranced about nearby. I wanted to take a swing at the man but the desk was in the way. I found a uniformed guard standing beside me, and suddenly the whole sordid business assumed an air of the ridiculous. "For God's sake," I muttered, sitting down again. "Pull yourself together, Heathcote. You know that every time I report one of your girls for laziness, she reports me for rape. It's traditional. It doesn't mean a thing. Maybe you'll apologize to Miss Jones and we'll get out of your hair."

Lambert seated himself, although slowly; and his lips were still trembling with rage. Suddenly he appeared weak and ineffectual and I wondered once again what sort of pressures he was under, and whether he was man enough to handle them. "No apologies," he said curtly, staring at the desk, not meeting my eyes. "A few days ago Miss Jones and the Foes were standing outside those gates calling me every name under the sun. I guess we're quits. Get her out, Joe."

"That sounds reasonable enough," I admitted, standing, turning, and running straight into Carioca, who hadn't budged.

"Are you going to take that, Joe Sagar?" she asked, standing her ground.

"I understand you want to visit Joanne Shaw," remarked Lambert with great meaning.

I took Carioca firmly by the arm and led her from the room.

By the time we reached the bleak visiting room Carioca had composed herself. I felt the usual flutter around the chest and stomach at the sight of Joanne sitting smiling on the other side of the wire. We sat down.

"How have they been treating you, you poor darling?" asked Carioca.

"Fine." Joanne grinned. "Although a scotch would be welcome right now, and that's one thing they don't stock here. Uh, how are the Foes of Bondage?"

Carioca launched into the story of Lambert and the petition's fate, with appropriate gestures, while I studied Joanne. I'd heard that prison life tended to corrupt, that the cells were full of lesbians and sadists and worse, yet Joanne was still as gentle and beautiful as when I'd first met her. I found it easy to believe that Carioca was right, that her conviction and imprisonment had been unjust—a reasonable possibility in these days of manual labor shortages, not to mention organ shortages.

She watched Carioca from her side of the wire with a gentle smile; after that first moment she had scarcely looked at me. And soon I began to feel out of it. She and Carioca were doing all the talking, and there was no contribution I was able to make. Another thing I noticed: Joanne kept her hands out of sight while talking to Carioca, as though she didn't want to remind her ex-boss of anything unpleasant—whereas on every occasion when I'd visited her alone, she'd practically flaunted those steel fingers before my eyes.

Maybe it was the reaction from my duel with Lambert, but I found myself descending into a gray mood as the two women prattled on. God damn it, it was almost as though Joanne held *me* responsible for her disfigurement. . . . And for the first time, I allowed my mind to play with this possibility. And I could see a terrible logic behind this theory. I tried to forget it—and I promised myself that the next time I visited Joanne, I would come alone.

She gave me a special smile when she left, and my heart ached for love of her. It would always be the same, I knew; she could lift me to the heights with a glance, then drive me to suicidal despair with indifference. It wasn't deliberate, this indifference of hers, and maybe I imagined most of it; but when I was with Joanne I always felt that she didn't understand what love was all about, as though we were on different wavelengths.

So it was that when Carioca Jones and I left the long awful room I was in a foul mood of depression, which probably accounts for my attitude when we encountered Lambert in the corridor.

"Heathcote," I said flatly as he tried to hurry past us, "I'd like to take a look at the Ambulatory Organ Pool, if you don't mind."

I had said it. I had put into words the fears that had been with me for days, the fears which I hadn't dared to voice because the state penitentiary is a Government institution and almost as respectable in concept as the National Art Council. A man just doesn't question the workings of the pen.

Lambert thought so too. "What the hell for?" he asked.

"I'm a citizen and I just want to know what goes on, that's all."

He hesitated, puzzled. "Do you know a donor in the Pool?"

"Yes."

"A relative, Joe?" His manner was changing and he watched me almost with sympathy.

"No."

"Then I'm afraid I can't help you." He seemed relieved. "It ought to be obvious why we can't have members of the public snooping around the Pool, Joe; so don't let's start another goddamned argument, huh? It's Bob Gallaugher's department, anyway."

Carioca was watching me with interest, black eyes gleaming as she scented a dispute. As it happened, the rotund figure of Gallaugher appeared at that moment, walking along the corridor toward us.

Ignoring Lambert, I took a step toward him. "I'd like to arrange to visit Marigold Carassa in the Pool, Gallaugher. I'm not a relative but I can have her father here goddamned quickly if I need to."

His eyes flickered. "There's nobody of that name here, Sagar."

"There shouldn't be, but there is." I tried to sound positive.

"Wait a moment." Lambert was watching me curiously. "Bob . . . that was the girl Joe was asking about before, wasn't it? You know, the one from the *Ancia Telji*, who Joe—" His voice trailed off.

"That's right," I said harshly. "She spent the night at my place."

Gallaugher was looking uncomfortable, as though this revelation offended his moral sense. "Uh . . . she left on the antigrav, with all the other immigrants. I told Sagar that."

Lambert sighed with some frustration. "Is that good enough

for you, Joe? I mean, can we drop this discussion and get on with some work?"

"The hell with you all," I mumbled dispiritedly, and left.

I drove Carioca to her house, then headed for home. It was late afternoon by now and I wanted to see Dave Froehlich before he locked up the factory. It seemed we might have to make some concessions to the S. P. girls, to placate Heathcote Lambert.

Near Skipper's Marina I stopped, seeing a number of police standing around. A tiny antigrav hopper was just taking off, and a group of men stood beside a rectangular metal object. I climbed from the car, walked over, and spoke to Warren Rennie. "How's the detective work going?" I asked. "Find any clues yet?"

He frowned at my facetiousness in front of his men. "We had a delay. The lampreys have only just arrived." He indicated the object; I saw now that it was a cage, solid black steel with a mesh at one end. One of the policemen was opening the small door, slowly and with infinite caution. He held a large bag at the widening gap.

The bag suddenly began to twist and billow vigorously as something thrashed inside it. The policeman slammed the cage door—I noticed he wore thick gloves—then plunged his hand into the bag and drew out the lamprey. It was eel-shaped, black, and loathsome with a flat snout. It was about three feet long and four inches thick. It writhed continuously while the man fitted a tight harness over it. Then someone handed him a long pole, to the end of which he attached a trace of the harness. He swung the lamprey out; it wriggled and twisted at the end of its line like a hooked fish—to which it bore a marked similarity. Then he lowered the lamprey to the ground.

"Watch this," said Rennie.

The lamprey lay motionless on the grass for an instant; then it began to move, its snout questing blindly this way and that, while fine tendrils waved like the cilia of a sea anemone. It humped itself and urged forward over the short grass, while the policeman kept the line slack. Meanwhile, another lamprey was being harnessed.

"Their home planet has been declared unfit for colonization because of these brutes," Rennie informed me. "They have the most keenly developed sense of smell of any known creature, and they seem to have an affinity to human flesh in particular. We have to take the most rigid safeguards when we handle them. They wiped out the first survey party on Altair IV to a man."

I backed off as the cilia fingered in my direction sniffingly. Then the brute suddenly stiffened, plunged its snout among a tussock of longer grass, and began to tremble with orgiastic intensity. The policeman swung it away and another man dug into the grass, finally withdrawing an old ball-point pen, the object of the lamprey's interest. It had probably lain half-buried for months, by the look of it. Impressed, I told Rennie that I would be available for any further help he might need, and made my way back to the car.

A scream halted me. I wheeled around. A policeman was beating at his arm, to which was attached a whipping black devil, coiling and twisting, while all the time making the most dreadful low buzzing noise. The man fell, another policeman flung himself down, hacking with a knife at the feeding lamprey. Eighteen inches of severed body came twisting and leaping over the ground toward me and I jumped aside with a yell of horror. The buzzing continued as the police fought to free their stricken comrade, burning with hand lasers at the remains of the lamprey. Smoke rose and stank as I stood watching, blaming myself for not being able to help.

At last the buzzing faltered and ceased. The police drew back, leaving Rennie kneeling beside the unconscious man on the grass. He was working at the wound with a knife, cutting away the sleeve; he threw something over his shoulder. It landed near me and I knelt down, staring at the bloody remains of the lamprey's mouth where dozens of intermeshing triangular teeth still twitched in their bed of cartilage. Surrounding them in a circular lip, the cilia still waved feebly.

After a while I walked back to the car; as I drove away the ambulopter came chattering in from the south. I was badly shaken. It seemed there were creatures around us which were even more diabolical than the so-called pets that Miranda Marjoribanks sold. I wondered about the half-lamprey which had wriggled off into the bush. I hoped it was not capable of reproducing like an earthworm.

The following morning I was awakened from a fitful night's sleep during which strange homunculi stalked through my dreams, to find the Newspocket beside my bed buzzing its warning that an important announcement was about to be made.

There had been a serious monorail accident on the mainland, with heavy casualties.

I tried to feel bad about all those people, but I couldn't help seeing in my mind's eye the inmates of the various regional Ambulatory Organ Pools, called on once more to donate. . . . Coincidentally, the next news item included coverage of a public demonstration against the Pool at the other end of the country. The local chapter of the Foes of Bondage were in evidence, yelling and waving banners; but what caught my eye was the large number of ordinary people, men and women, listening to the speakers and nodding grave agreement.

Treacherously, my brain asked me if those people would have concurred with the Foes' sentiments so readily, had they been involved in the monorail accident and in need of a new limb. . . .

In many ways that was a bad day. I went out into the yard to find Dave gloomily regarding yet another pen from which all the slithes had mysteriously disappeared.

He stared at me belligerently. "And if you say I left the goddamned gate open this time, so help me I'll smash your face in!" he snarled.

It was not the best way for a bonded man to address his boss first thing in the morning, but I tried to overlook it on the grounds that Dave had recently been under much strain. I changed the subject. "How are things in the factory?" I asked.

"Nobody's there," he said shortly.

"What the hell do you mean, nobody's there? Where the hell are the girls?"

"How the hell should I know?"

"Oh, for Christ's sake!" I stormed away to the visiphone, shouting over my shoulder, "Start searching the bush. I want every goddamned slithe back in its pen inside the hour—and this time make sure you shut the goddamned gate!"

A few seconds later the face of Heathcote Lambert peered warily at me from the visiphone screen. I asked him what had happened to my work force. He sighed.

"I thought I'd made it clear yesterday that I'd allow no more girls at your farm," he said.

"Yes, but I was under the impression we'd squared things up. I need those girls, Heath. The factory's at a standstill.".

"I'm sorry, Joe, but I'm responsible for these girls and there have been too many complaints recently. I'm under a lot of pressure, and questions are being asked about employers who exploit prison labor. There's a big political issue building up back East."

"Well, I'm sorry about that, Heath, but what the hell am I supposed to do?"

"You'll just have to find some regular workers," he said shortly, and hung up.

I returned to the yard, but Dave was nowhere in sight. I looked around the deserted factory and shouted his name, but without success.

Then, in the distance, I heard him screaming.

14

—◆———◆◆◆———◆—

The sound of screaming by its very nature arouses conflict in the mind of the hearer. His immediate impulse is to hurry to the scene, to find out what is happening—possibly, even, to see if he can help. This is the curiosity factor, accentuated by the demanding, supplicating aspect of the screaming.

There is, however, a secondary impulse—to ignore the scream, even to remove yourself from the sound. The scream is born of terror, and what terrifies the screamer might well terrify you. This secondary impulse occurred to me as I was running through the low scrub in the direction of a small grove of stunted trees, from which the sounds came. I slowed down and proceeded with caution, glancing around the waist-high vegetation for signs of quasi-terrestrial life. There was a rustling away to my right, but the screams came from ahead.

"In there!" An S. P. man stood nearby, indicating the taller maples. His companion lounged on his shovel; they looked like highway workers.

I paused. "What's in there?"

"Get on in, you bastard," snapped the S. P. man. "Your man Froehlich is in trouble. What the hell are you waiting for?"

"What the hell are *you* waiting for?" I asked.

He smiled stupidly. "Oh, I'm just a poor Spare Parts man and I have to obey orders. My orders are to cut down the brush at the roadside. You wouldn't want me to disobey orders, would you?"

"Follow me, you two," I said harshly, plunging in among the trees.

The sounds had ceased. It was dark here, and gloomy out of the bright morning sunshine. The hairs on the back of my neck prickled as I stared around, while the small copse seemed to be waiting, holding its breath. I jumped as something tapped me on the shoulder.

"Lead the way, boss man," said the S. P. man unpleasantly.

I moved slowly through the dappled greenery, peering under the bushes. I took the shovel from one of the S. P. men and began to hack about more vigorously, hoping that the violence of my movements would cause any strange nearby predators to retreat. Leaves rained about me, twigs and branches cracked. I stopped suddenly, fancying I heard a different sound. All was still. One of the S. P. men made a nervous sucking noise through his teeth.

I slashed at the bushes again, moving forward among the treetrunks, impelled by a kind of energetic terror. The shovel clanged into a trunk and jarred my arm and I dropped it, cursing, while the S. P. men chuckled idiotically. As I bent to pick it up a black shape slithered away. It was probably a snake, or even a land moray, but I jerked back with a grunt of horror, thinking of the appalling police lampreys.

"Scared, boss man?" inquired the voice from behind.

I retrieved the shovel and beat my way on. The brush was thick hereabouts, and several times I heard the unmistakably noisy retreat of a land fish. The grove was beginning to come alive; the enemy was showing itself. After a particularly violent thrashing in the bushes—I even caught a glimpse of silvery scales—I stopped, heart thudding and hands slippery with fear, to recover my breath and courage.

The S. P. men were gone. During my last slashing they must have crept away, leaving me to face the bush alone. I was not sorry. Several times I'd felt that they—following my unprotected back—represented a greater danger than the unknown brutes in the bush. As a result of the recent public agitation, the attitude of state prisoners had undergone a change for the worse.

As I stood there among a scattering of broken branches and torn leaves, something caught my eye; something white under a nearby bush. I picked it up.

It was the skeleton of a slithe, very much damaged but still unmistakable. Particles of skin still adhered to the bones. Although the rib cage was badly crushed and the skull fractured it was impossible to ascertain the cause of death, since this damage could have occurred after death, while the body lay on the forest floor.

There was a tap on my shoulder and I swung around in some relief, glad to have company again.

There was nobody there.

The tap came again, and I swung around in a full circle as terror inserted itself between my thoughts and sanity, and I tightened my grip on the shovel, shuddered, and began to slash wildly. I heard myself groan with fear as the suggestive prod came again, near my armpit—and whipping around again I caught sight of something. I looked up among the branches of the nearest maple.

A thick tentacle hung toward me, feeling through the leaves blindly, as an elephant feels through bars.

I yelled something and swung at the obscene thing as it fingered toward me again. The shovel struck flesh with a meaty thump and the tentacle retracted into the branches above like a stabbed earthworm. Simultaneously I caught a glimpse of clothing through the leaves; the thing had Dave up there. I shouted to the S. P. men but there was no response. Either they had gone, or they chose to ignore me. The grove was quiet again.

I didn't know what the hell to do. I stood there for what seemed like hours, trying to work the thing out. I had no laser, either with me or at the farm; and if I ran to the house and phoned Rennie the thing would have eaten Dave by the time the police arrived with guns. And even if Dave were still alive, the police would quite likely burn him, as well as the creature, in their enthusiasm.

As I stood irresolute I heard the whine of a turbine from the direction of the road. A hovercar was coming. I left the trees and sprinted through the scrub, tripping over brambles, stumbling into gullies, and finally emerging sobbing for breath at the roadside. The hovercar was coming into view around a bend. I waved, too breathless to shout, and it sank to the ground beside me.

"Joe! What on earth . . . ?" It was Carioca Jones.

"Do you have a laser pistol?"

"Well *really*, Joe. Do you take me for a gangster's *moll?*"

"Or any weapon at all? There's no time to get to the house." Since she seemed bent on expressing lengthy amazement, I explained the situation briefly and breathlessly. She opened the glove locker, fumbling helplessly among combs and maps and cigarette packs.

"Honestly, Joe, I can't help you. I thought I might have a little *gas gun;* you know, I sometimes carry one for protection. I mean, a *woman,* traveling *alone*—" She twittered on about imaginary dangers while she rummaged amid the junk, making her short drive sound like an open-legged invitation to every rampant male on the Peninsula.

"What's that?" I asked. It was a small box.

"Oh, that's poor *dear* Wilberforce's denticure set. I must return it to that *awful* Marjoribanks woman for a refund."

I remembered something. "Give it to me." She seemed strangely reluctant, so I simply leaned into the car and dragged it from her grasp. Dave Froehlich might be dying, slowly. I opened it. There was a bottle of pills and a pack of one-shot hypodarts. I took these, threw the box at her, and ran.

As I reentered the grove there was a stirring from above and the tentacle swung low, feeling about. I could see Dave clearly through the leaves, lying unconscious across a branch while his captor, presumably, wondered how to deal with him. He represented a sizable meal, even for a giant squid.

I waited my chance, bunching the hypodarts in a closed fist. Then, as the tentacle groped toward me again I seized it in my left hand and stabbed the six glass needles into the tough flesh. The sinuous limb writhed as I twisted the darts so that the points fractured and the anesthetic, under pressure, hissed from the vials. A certain amount escaped, bubbling over the surface skin, but most of the liquid seemed to have gone home. I stepped behind a tree while the tentacle thrashed about the grove, scattering leaves and breaking branches around me. Other limbs appeared, waving and snatching at whatever they encountered, snatching up bushes and brandishing them in a shower of loose dirt. Quantities of evil-smelling black liquid began to drip from above.

Then the tentacles began to falter, moving tiredly as though in slow motion, and the various uprooted plants and saplings began to drop from their slackening grasp. At last they hung almost motionless, dark-mottled and swinging slightly with the movement of the wind through the trees. I began to climb the trunk.

When seen from close quarters, the squid was frighteningly large. A huge eye watched me dully from amid a mountain of flesh distributed over the thick upper branches of the tree like a spreading cancer, the leathery skin colored so that it was almost indistinguishable from the bark. Ink still dripped, running in rivulets past my fingers, while the horny beak nodded quiescent near Dave's chest. To my relief he appeared unharmed, lying along a thick bough among a mass of bones and empty slithe skins.

"Joe? Where are you?" It was Carioca's voice.

"I saw a rope in the back of your car. Go and get it; there's a good girl."

No doubt overcome at being called a girl she didn't argue, and I heard her pushing her way back through the bushes to the hovercar. Soon she returned with the rope and we lowered Dave to the ground, moving well out of range of the squid, which was showing signs of returning animation. So far as we could tell Dave was not hurt, although his skin was covered with blistering circles where the squid's suckers had gripped. After a while he moaned and stirred, and his eyes opened. Sudden terror showed.

"Take it easy. It's all right," I reassured him while Carioca patted his hands ineffectually.

He struggled into a sitting position. "The bastard took me around the shoulders and lifted me into the tree like I was a kid," he muttered, rubbing his head. An ugly bruise showed at the temple. He looked at me, then looked away. "I guess I have to thank you for rescuing me."

"Well, don't bother," I said irritably.

"There's a whole mess of slithes up there," he said, more strongly now. "That bastard's been at the pens. He wouldn't need to climb in; he'd just reach over the top. Huh?" He met my eyes and this time I looked away.

"I'm sorry, Dave. I should have known you wouldn't be stupid enough to leave the gates open."

After which painful apology we got him back to the house and, presently, the ambulopter arrived and took him away for a checkup. I called the police, spoke to Rennie, and told him to bring men and guns.

"I'm going to sue Miranda Marjoribanks for everything she has," I told Carioca forcibly. "She's no right to let brutes like that escape about the place. Who the hell would want a land squid, anyway? I mean, how could anyone look after a bastard like that?"

"Well," replied Carioca tentatively, "when poor Wilberforce began to get so *snappy*, maybe I did give Miranda just the *tiniest* hint that it would be fun to have a really unusual pet, something nobody else had. But that's no excuse for her letting Medusa escape."

"Medusa? See here, Carioca, is that bastard yours?"

"Oh, no. Nothing was *signed*. And then when there was that awful *frenzy*, and everything escaped, then the sale was void, of course. And I'm afraid it's no use suing Miranda, Joe, because she has no money. She's *penniless*." Recalling that Miranda Marjoribanks was no friend of hers—and Carioca's affections switched so rapidly that it was not always easy for her to remember whom she liked and whom she didn't—she allowed her face to assume an expression of hatred like weathered granite.

I poured drinks and we strolled around the pens. The factory was silent and there was hardly a slithe left on the farm. It would take me months to build up my stock again; and the loss of goodwill through unfulfilled orders would be incalculable. I felt as though I wanted to hit someone, anyone, and to keep hitting them until I was tired. I had been wiped out, and so I wanted to wipe out everyone else.

And so it was not with the best of motives that I became a member of the Foes of Bondage a week or two later—although it was a logical step. I canceled Dave's bondage contract and returned him to the pen; there was nothing for him to do at the farm, which I now closed down completely. In any case, I didn't want him around, reproaching me with his eyes for disbelieving him over the slithes—and no doubt he hated me for saving his life. So I got rid of him, giving him excellent references to ensure that he still received his bondage remission.

There were other reasons for my joining the Foes. On many occasions during my visits to Joanne, she had mentioned the organization.

"Joe, there are a lot of suffering people in here—and I'm not talking about myself. I got off lightly, I reckon. But they won't let us mingle with the prisoners in the Ambulatory Organ Pool, and it's not just because they're long-term prisoners. There's . . . such a shortage of organs now that they're drawing on the short-term prisoners—the labor force, and so on. So they must have some other reason for keeping those people apart—and I think I know what it is."

A thrill of pure horror ran down my spine as I realized the ultimate to which Compulsory Donation could go.

"You may not agree with the Foes," she continued, "but at least their principles are sound. They could do with a man like you, Joe."

This tallied with my own thoughts of recent weeks. It was therefore a combination of factors which caused me to throw in my lot with the woman who had once driven me to a nervous breakdown by her unthinking inhumanity: Carioca Jones. The closing of the farm, the attitude of Lambert, the growing public concern, not to mention my own suspicions, the disappearance of Marigold, the hints from Joanne . . . and, possibly, my dislike of Gallaugher . . . all these factors added up and resulted in my becoming the only male member of an organization consisting of female nuts.

"This is *quite* an honor for the Foes," twittered Carioca, hardly able to believe my decision. "I can't wait to tell the girls."

"God damn it, I'm only a slithe farmer, and a failed one too."

"No, Joe. You don't realize. Your presence will lend an air of respectability to the society." She spoke with unaccustomed gravity. "People do tend to look on the Foes as, well, *cranks,* you know—but with you among us, they'll have to take us seriously. Heaven knows, I'm not devoted to the male sex," she continued surprisingly, "but a few more men like yourself might help to bring some of my girls down to earth. You see, they have this *obsession* that nobody listens to them, merely because they don't see immediate results for our demonstrations. So they get so *frustrated,* and they start shouting all those words you people complain about. And I keep telling them: nobody, but *nobody,* pays serious attention to a woman who screeches obscenities. But they don't listen to me, Joe. They'd listen to you. They'd listen to a *man,* God damn them."

But as it happened the Foes were in fact making nationwide progress. Hardly a day went by without Newspocket carrying the story of another demonstration, another confrontation, another deputation meeting with members of the Government. Other bodies sprang up with similar aims but more moderate methods: the Freedom League, the Blood Brothers, the more prosaically named Western Association for the Reform of the Penal Code.

Now that I was beginning to think in terms of grafts and transplants, I was surprised to observe the differing attitudes of various people toward this aspect of the law. Fresh from a fiery meeting of the Foes, I stepped out of the *Princess Louise* almost into the arms of Rennie, who was prowling the streets in case of trouble, two uniformed men at his heels. I asked after the policeman who had been attacked by the land lamprey.

"Would you believe it, Joe, the poor guy's only just got his new arm? By Christ, I don't know what the Pool's coming to, these days. I had to bring the utmost pressure on that little prick Gallaugher to get any action at all. Sometimes it seems to me the way to stay healthy is to go to jail! Uh . . . they tell me you've joined the Foes, Joe. That doesn't sit very happily on my stomach. It doesn't sit happily at all."

"How are you coming along with the sabotage case?" I asked hastily.

"Building up nicely." He shot me a piercing look, as though hoping to surprise a confession. "I've been able to call off the lampreys; we have all we need. It's just a question of tying up a few loose ends. Yes, I was very sorry to hear about you joining the Foes, Joe."

His suggestive persistence annoyed me.

"Look. Are you trying to tell me Doug Marshall was right? The Foes were responsible for tampering with his gear?"

He wouldn't tell me anything, of course; that wasn't his way. In any event, the audience from the *Princess Louise* was pouring past us and a few curious Foes had gathered within earshot. He merely shrugged and moved away, calling his men to heel. Irritated, I started to ask something sarcastic about the mastermind behind the illegal immigration racket—concerning which all had gone strangely quiet —but he was out of earshot.

As I became involved with the work of the Foes of Bondage I came across more instances similar to that of Miranda Marjoribanks, where a quick and dubious graft had been obtained on payment of a substantial fee. It was becoming increasingly apparent that something was rotten in the state pen.

One day Lambert approached me at the club. His manner of late had become abstracted in the extreme—and toward me, ambivalent. I had changed from drinking acquaintance to political opponent in a few months, and he couldn't quite figure it. He stared at me with eyes red-rimmed, reeking of drink. "Sagar," he said, and people turned their heads. "I've been checking up, and I tell you again that goddamned girl was sent home. Now will you stop asking your goddamned questions?"

"I haven't mentioned the subject for days, Heath."

"Well, for Christ's sake, your goddamned organization has. They've got hold of the story now and they're pestering me, and I can't take much more of it. You've been spreading vicious rumors, Sagar. You're a bastard, you know that?"

"Gentlemen, gentlemen." Bryce Alcester came to the rescue. "We don't want this sort of talk in the club, do we?"

The matter was smoothed over but the question remained; Lambert was unhappy about Marigold. The very fact of his frequent and unnecessary reassurances showed this. He felt there was something going on behind his back, but he couldn't pin it down. It was noticeable that he avoided meeting Gallaugher in the club. The two prison officers came on different evenings, as though observing an unwritten rota.

Then, one August afternoon in that dreadful divided room at the pen, Joanne suddenly said, "Darling," and lunged toward the wire with her hands, as though she must touch me. Instinctively I moved toward her too and my heart was leaping at the love in her eyes which even the zombie guard must have recognized; then her steel hands clattered against the mesh and I was glad she couldn't read the horror in my mind because she might have thought it was for her, not her hands. Nevertheless I touched her fingertips—and felt the sickness of disappointment as she slipped a folded paper into my hand, because her whole performance had been an act and I didn't want some lousy message; I wanted Joanne.

The message was not even from Joanne.

Dear Joe,
    I want you please to help me because nobody here will listen to me when I say I haven't done anything and I shouldn't be here. Things happen here which

shouldn't happen to anybody. Please can you do something, Joe, you're the only man I know.
    Love, Marigold.

I stood outside the pen in the August sunshine, still shocked by Joanne's spurious demonstration of affection, still telling myself it was the only way she could have got the message through, and my confused emotions began to coalesce into slow, insane anger as I knew for certain that sweet, perfect Marigold—who hadn't even committed a crime —had been butchered inside those walls, in the name of the law.

15

The sea was black and the offshore islands bulked dark against the dim pinkness of the late evening sky. From the clubhouse came sounds of revelry; I could hear Ramsbottom's booming laugh contrasted with the shrill cackle of Bryce Alcester. Gallaugher was not in there; I'd made sure of that. In the light from the undraped windows I could see a wisp of steam still rising from the catapult; the boiler pressure was well up, the horse ready to go. I stood for a moment watching the stars come out, the glider heavy on my back and the harness tight, and I wondered briefly how I'd got into this thing.

Then I walked to the horse, lay facedown and fastened the pin, took a deep breath, and kicked the lever. The horse rocketed down the rails with a huge *whoosh!* of expended steam, and I could imagine the surprised silence followed by the buzz of comment and speculation in the clubhouse. Then the horse dropped away from under me and I was streaking low over the Strait; I remember thinking that if I lost my nerve, I could always make a wide turn and land near the club, telling people I'd fancied the idea of a night flight. The lights of the Skipper's Marina receded away to my left and I eased the controls, banking left and following the coast. I saw the lights of a hovercar, bright pools against the darkness inland, moving slowly north.

I wore no wet suit because I didn't want to be restricted in any way, and strapped to my waist was my minivid. I was deadly cold as the wind whipped my clothes untidily about me, and I began to worry about drag. I shifted in the tiny fuselage and felt the bulk of my laser pistol against my leg; the weapon was a concession from Rennie as a result of the giant squid incident and the presence of other fearsome creatures in the proximity of the farm. The lights

of the state pen showed up beyond the dark headland of
Black Point.

I dipped lower, rounding the headland and skimming low
over the water toward the rectangular outline of the pen,
ablaze with lights beyond the water's edge. I was moving too
fast; the masthead light of a moored yacht flashed within feet
of my belly as I fishtailed in, trying to lose speed. I touched
the air brakes gingerly and the glider roared and shuddered; then I quickly released the lever. There were guards
around the base of the pen wall, near the wharf; I'd seen
them before.

The wall loomed ahead, blacking out the sky.

I eased back the controls, gently, and almost stalled as I
slid over the parallel laser beams and instantly into the daz-
zling brightness of the prison yard. Almost immediately I
was out of the lights again and hurtling toward the playing fields. Now I had no choice. I had to set my craft down on
the hard ground—something no glider was designed to do.
I pulled the controls back, the nose lifted, I mumbled a prayer
or a groan or something, and stalled.

I hit with appalling force. I had misjudged my height, and
my forward speed was greater than I would have liked. For
an eternity I bowled along, my head clasped in my hands,
my knees drawn up to my chest, while the glider disin-
tegrated around me and absorbed most of the impact. Eventually all was still and I was lying dizzy among the wreckage,
certain that someone must have heard me. After a while I
was able to move, carefully to extend an arm, a leg; and
I found no breakages, and heard no shouts.

Unbuckling the harness, I climbed shakily to my feet,
checked the minivid and laser, got my bearings, and began
to walk painfully toward the long three-story building which
jutted from the main complex and bordered the far side of
the football pitch on which I'd landed. I heard a quiet whistle
and froze.

The guard sharks were about. I hadn't expected them to
be on patrol until after Lights Out. I moved even more
carefully, slipping behind a row of low shrubs that flanked
the driveway at the edge of the football pitch. I heard a
sound and crouched low, watching and trying not to breathe
as a dark shape undulated along the road, humping its back
with dorsal fin high, flattening out so that the pale belly

slapped the ground. It was a big brute, all of fifteen feet long.

"Slash!" A door opened nearby; a man stood silhouetted. "Slash, where are you, boy?"

The shark's head swung around and its alarm whistle began to shrill, triggered by the accelerated pulse rate. It made for the door at speed, while I made a dash for the wall under cover of the noise. I felt my way along to the fire escape I'd noticed previously, jumped, and obtained a grip on the poised stairway. It swung down to ground level and I began to climb. I had no idea where I was headed, but it seemed to me that the guards would be prepared to deal with breakouts rather than break-ins, and then from ground level. So I climbed to the first platform.

A whistling started, piercing, close by.

There was a shark on the platform; I could see its flat head against the sky as I reached the top of the first flight. It lunged forward, whistle shrilling a frantic alarm as I snatched the pistol from my pocket and burned it down with a bright sizzling. It died but kept twitching, smoking and stinking at my feet. I switched off the gun and listened.

Down below, the other shark still whistled as the guard threw it scraps from the doorway, effectively covering the recent commotion on the fire escape. I pocketed the laser and climbed on, zigzagging my way up the side of the building, passing five more intermediate platforms without incident, then finding myself on the flat roof. Sitting down, I waited to recover my breath and nerve. Below, the whistling ceased as Slash finished his unofficial feed and resumed patrol. I wondered at the mentality of the guard who could, apparently, feel affection for such a creature. A light breeze stirred my tattered clothing as I watched an antigrav shuttle lifting from the spaceport at Sentry Down in the far distance, a tiny dim star rising to lose itself among the other, brighter stars in the night sky.

In due course I recovered and examined my surroundings. The roof was a flat rectangle bounded by the low wall on which I sat, featureless apart from a single dark block rising in the far corner. I crossed to this, found an unlocked door and steps leading down. Soon, I opened another door onto a brightly lit aseptic corridor which ran the length of the building. It was quiet and empty; enigmatic doors opened off at regular intervals. I wondered, not for the first time, what the hell I was doing here and what I hoped to achieve.

I crept along the corridors, trying doors which were either locked, or opened into broom closets or linen stores. The sense of anticlimax grew as I became convinced that I would be caught before I ever found Marigold, or conclusive evidence against Gallaugher, or whatever the hell I was looking for. I heard a noise and darted into a nearby room, pulling the door quietly shut behind me.

Footsteps approached and paused. The door was jerked open. I pressed back against the wall as the light snapped on and revealed the sterile fittings of a washroom, and a uniformed man's back.

"All right, you can come out of there," he rasped, then grunted as I hit him with the laser pistol.

As I have become older I have noticed with depressing frequency the effects of bodily deterioration on my actions. Last summer I fell full-length into a shallow stream which I was trying to cross by leaping from rock to rock—a project which would have caused me no difficulty ten years ago. Last winter, fooling around with kids, I caught a football, rounded an opponent, slipped a perfect lateral to an uprushing tot, all in the space of five seconds. It took me five minutes, lying on the grass with tortured breath screaming in my throat like a tracheotomized racehorse, to recover.

So I should not have been surprised when I missed my swing with the laser pistol and hit the man a glancing blow on the shoulder. He yelled and wheeled around and we traded inexpert blows without actually hitting each other—which was just as well, because he was Dave Froehlich.

"Mr. Sagar," he grunted in surprise, fielding my right fist in his left hand. "What the hell are you doing here?"

I relaxed. "Uh, Dave . . . is there somewhere we can talk?"

His dour expression lighted. "I have a room to myself," he said with pathetic pride. "I'm a trusty, in charge of this floor."

His room was small but private, and it appeared that he was rarely bothered by the authorities after Lights Out. "They treat me fine, Mr. Sagar," he said, sitting easily on a hard chair, trying to prove how much better off he was since I'd sent him back to the pen.

"I'm glad to hear it," I said absently. There was something troubling me. "Why are you in the Organ Pool, though? Shouldn't you be in the main pen building?"

And as his eyes slipped away from mine, I wished I hadn't asked that.

He never did tell me just what form his Compulsory Donation had taken, although he insisted on defending the State's right to take it. "There have been a hell of a lot of accidents recently, one way and another," he said.

"Dave, you only had one year to go. Weren't there any other donors, long-term men? I mean, why *you,* for Christ's sake?"

"You don't understand, do you? There aren't so many prisoners in this place. The crime rate's so low these days, the shortage of organs is chronic. I understand people offer bribes to the warden, and the guards too, so they tell me."

We sat there for some time and he told me all about the internal workings of the state pen—so far as his little niche was concerned—and all the time he spoke as though he enjoyed it; as though he had gained some queer inverted dignity by the revocation of his bondage. As though he had been a slave, but now he was free. Which was nonsense. I found myself wondering if he were a little mad, maybe.

He showed me the charts he kept. He was proud of the charts. There were twenty wards on his floor and four men to a ward, and Dave kept full inventory records of his charges.

But the odd thing was, the inventory was not classified according to men; it was classified according to organs.

There would be six arms in room 5, subdivided into two left and four right, classified according to sizes A, B, C, D, E; with a further classification by color. Room number 5 was lucky; it had seven legs, although it was dangerously low on kidneys. Even more sinister was the implication behind the record that the four occupants of room 5 possessed a total of four hearts, as of today's date.

"There's no connection between my corridor and the women's corridor running parallel," Dave told me, as if it mattered. Fingers, index, left, 63; fingers, index, right, 57.

"If you can go along with this sort of butchery you must be crazy, Dave," I said with sudden harshness, breaking into his maunderings.

"You went along with it yourself until a couple of weeks ago," he snapped back.

"I hadn't seen it, then."

"But you'd heard of it, and you'd had the chance to inquire more closely. It's people like you, people who don't bother, who got all this started in the first place. You could have voted against the Penal Reform Act at any time."

"For Christ's sake, what good could I do? One vote against a majority of millions!"

Dave was grinning at me cunningly. "Come with me," he said. He led me down the corridor a way, then opened a door. There were four beds in the bare room. Six eyes watched me as we entered. "See this man?" Dave pointed. "Now take a good look at that."

I wondered at the foursome's docility, and concluded they must be sedated. The man Dave indicated lay naked; a rubber tube led from his penis to a bottle under the bed. He had no arms, no legs, and his torso was a mass of scar tissue. One eye peered at me malignantly and I thought: This man will soon reach the limit of his usefulness.

Choking back vomit, I ran from the room.

Dave followed me back into his den. "Terrible thing." He was still grinning that horrible fixed grin like a rictus as he spoke. "God, look what humanity has done to that poor wreck of a man."

"For Christ's sake, shut up about it, Dave."

"But listen to this." He held a card up. "This is that man's record. This is what that man did to humanity. John Umpleby. Committed to this penitentiary seven years ago, having been found guilty on eight counts of murder. The victims were all young children, boys and girls under the age of ten, and all had been sexually assaulted before their death." He held the card before me. "Read it. There's more."

I thrust it away. "What the hell are you getting at, Dave?" I think I said.

He stared at me. He wasn't grinning any longer. "I'm telling you that if you're looking for the difference between right and wrong you're wasting your time here, Mr. Sagar. Here, everything's wrong. I've been trying to tell you that for years, but you couldn't see it. Do you see it now? Do you see it, you smug bastard?"

I'd committed no crime. Why did he always try to make me and everybody else feel like a criminal? Did he want me to wallow with him in his comfortable mudbath of despair?

"I've come here because I think Marigold's here, Dave," I said stonily. "If she is, I want to get her out. She's no criminal. She has nothing to do with these . . . people."

I had got through to him at last. "Marigold," he murmured. "You mean that foreign girl; with the—" Whatever inappropriate means of identification he was about to employ, he broke off in time. "Marigold was a lovely girl," he said quietly. "I'd hate to think she was in this place."

"This is the third floor," I said. "What's below?"

"I'm not sure. More corridors, I guess. More rooms."

"Can you show me?"

His bravado was gone; he looked nervous. "If I'm caught, I don't get to be a trusty anymore. That might mean another donation before I'm released. What are you going to do, anyway?"

I showed him the minivid. "I want to get pictures, and I want to have them broadcast on Newspocket, nationwide."

"You don't have to go downstairs for that. There are plenty of donors up here."

"I told you I want to find Marigold. I want to find out why she's here. I want to find out what the hell goes on in this place."

He shrugged. "I'll go partway with you," he said.

I didn't find what I was looking for on the second floor, where Dave left me, or the ground floor, where I found my way through to the women's wing. All I found were more corridors, more doors, most of them with their little cards describing the organs therein, so that suitable donors could be quickly selected in times of emergency. I used the minivid several times. Suddenly I found myself at the main entrance lobby, and quickly ducked back out of sight. Guards paced the mosaic floor; sharks lay nearby. I waited, trying to think.

I'd glanced into many of the rooms I'd passed without finding what I was looking for. The cards outside the doors gave the names of the occupants and I'd seen no Marigold Carassa—not that I'd expected to. Either she'd be under another name or, more likely, she wouldn't be in these rooms at all. In that case, where would she be?

Soon I found the little door. It was set into an alcove and it had a disused, dirty look.

It was locked. Taking the laser, I burned away the hinges and pushed it aside, hoping the guards wouldn't smell the smoke. If they inspected the door, a cursory glance at the intact lock might convince them that all was well. I stepped into a dingy area and lifted the door shut behind me. Laser in hand, I descended a flight of stairs. As I expected, the gloomy basement contained the heating equipment, silent and dead at this time of year. Beginning to think that this was merely the junk area typical of any bureaucratic establishment—there were boxes of old files and papers stacked against the wall—I tried a small door beside a stack of broken chairs, without much hope.

It opened onto a different world.

Another corridor lay before me, similar to those on the upper floors, clean and white in contrast to the dust and debris of the furnace room. I began to move slowly along it, noticing that the doors possessed no adjacent statistics boards. I eased the nearest door open. . . .

I shut it again quickly, gulping.

It was fortunate that there was nobody around, because it took me a moment to recover. I walked along the corridor again, trying doors, closing them again after taking a brief videotape of the occupants. Then a door opened onto a room brighter than most. A powerful smell of anesthetic greeted me. Taking out my laser pistol again I stepped quietly inside and found myself in a fully equipped operating theater. The big central lights blazed down, and although the table was empty, a figure lay under white sheets on a bed near the wall. I stepped across, stared into the sleeping face.

It was Marigold.

I shook her gently but she didn't awaken, and her body possessed the slack feel of the drugged. I rolled her onto her back, kissing her briefly and feeling like crying, when it occurred to me that she rolled too easily.

I drew back the sheets.

She opened her eyes and looked at me without intelligence, without recognition, as I pulled the sheet up again and tucked it around her throat. I felt weak and sick, so I drew up a chair and sat beside her, slipping the minivid and laser on the shelf beside her because suddenly it didn't seem right to videotape Marigold the way she looked now.

I think she may have understood because her eyes moved from me to the little machine and I imagined there was a flicker of recognition there, a flicker of hope.

She was in postoperative shock and although I spoke to her she didn't really know me, and soon her eyes closed again. I sat there, wondering what the hell to do. I suppose I'd visualized myself burning doors open and leading her out by the hand, slipping through darkness past the guards, dealing with peril as it arose like some goddamned knight rescuing his princess, then a final sprint for safety.

But Marigold wouldn't be doing any sprinting.

I felt an enormous pity as I sat looking at her, and if they tell you pity is akin to love, then they lie, because I didn't love Marigold. Yet in that black moment I knew I *had* loved her, just a little, when she was perfect. This is something a woman can never understand: that any man will feel love, albeit a minor love, when he sees a perfect, beautiful girl. This love is not necessarily connected with lust; it is a simple, delighted pleasure, a warm happiness that anything so pretty should exist. Once, I had felt like that about Marigold.

But not anymore. Now Marigold was spoiled, and I didn't love her anymore, because she was imperfect. It wasn't my fault, because I am only a man and that is the way men are made. So I just sat there, feeling as sorry as all hell.

"Now just stand up and turn around slowly, Sagar."

I complied, and found myself looking into guns held by Gallaugher and a guard.

16

"This way," said Gallaugher briefly.

They took me along the corridor to a small room at the end, pausing only to allow me to be violently sick against the wall. My knees were trembling so badly that I could hardly stand upright, let alone walk. I knew they were going to kill me. They had to kill me now; I'd seen too much. And I couldn't do a thing about it; my gun was back in the operating theater with Marigold.

Inside the room they pushed me against the far wall and searched me briefly.

"What the hell were you trying to do, Sagar?" asked Gallaugher.

I didn't tell him about the minivid on the shelf in the operating theater. It was good to know something they didn't know; almost like an ace in my hand—except that I would have no chance to play it. "I knew you had Marigold Carassa here," I said. "I wanted to try to get her out."

"Is that all?" He looked exaggeratedly surprised. "You disappoint me, Sagar. I'd have thought a dedicated Foe of Bondage like yourself would have been snooping around, gathering evidence against whatever it is you people object to."

"I object to you making money out of the Pool, Gallaugher," I said, finding courage from somewhere.

"Do you now?" he murmured, smiling faintly. "Do you now? Well, isn't that just too bad, Sagar. We can't allow him to say things like that, can we, Johnny?" The guard shook his head. "So I'm afraid we're going to have to kill you. I mean to say"—his smile grew broader—"we could *use* you—there's quite a shortage of organs these days, but in your case death would be the simplest thing. Alive, you might prove difficult."

143

"I won't be difficult," I heard myself croak. The wall rasped against my back as my knees began to give out. Abject fear is a most undignified thing.

The interviz rang just as it seemed to me that Gallaugher had run out of conversation and his finger was whitening on the trigger. "Yes?"

I saw the face of a guard on the small screen. "Mr. Gallaugher, we've found the remains of a sling-glider in the grounds."

Gallaugher winked at me as he spoke to the guard. "Post a couple of our men on it and I'll be up with you in a minute. I think we may have found the body of the man who crashed." The screen went blank.

"You can't shoot me," I said hopefully from my sitting position on the floor. "The police will wonder what the burns are."

"They will have been caused by you passing too low over the pen walls and being caught by the beam fence, Sagar. Uh, would you mind standing? I don't like to shoot a sitting duck. Traditionally, as the villain with the upper hand, I ought now to explain the entire setup here—but our organization is quite large and very complex, and it would take too long. So, uh, good-bye, Joe," he said almost apologetically.

There occurred a dizzy moment which I can never quite remember. All I know is that suddenly there was a woman standing in the open doorway. I can remember everything about her, although I don't remember the door opening. She was aged about fifty-five, had gray hair, pale blue eyes, pink sunken cheeks, and an uncertain expression. Her clothes were expensive with a wealth of mink and slithe-skin trimmings, and her arms were pale and skinny. She wore a tiny gold watch and a large number of huge rings. Her legs were thin, gnarled and knotted with varicose veins like snails, and her shoes were green and jeweled.

She spoke. "Mr. Gallaugher, I hope I'm not interrupting anything, but I really am most unhappy about that imperfection you mentioned." Her manner was diffident at first but was rapidly becoming aggressive as she gained confidence. "I mean, you will be the first to agree that the operation is not cheap. But I am a woman of some substance and am accustomed to getting the very best."

Another woman appeared whom I took to be her hired

companion. She said nothing, but her presence tended to lend weight to her employer's words.

"And I will not be put off," she continued as Gallaugher muttered something. "I paid good money for cosmetic surgery and now you tell me the items you have prepared for me are incomplete. Well, I shall not accept them." She was working herself into a fury. "I want you to understand, Mr. Gallaugher, that when I pay in advance for leg treatment I expect a full set of toes!"

Here again my recollection is hazy. I saw the woman looming up; I saw her wrinkled face and pale eyes through a curtain of insanity. Gallaugher's face receded in a spattering red flash and I caught a glimpse of the guard clutching his stomach. Thoughts, images, words pounded repeatedly through my brain like a piston, blotting out reason, blotting out the physical world around me. All consisted of the one thought, the one image, the one phrase: She bought Marigold's legs, *she bought Marigold's legs,* SHE BOUGHT MARIGOLD'S LEGS!

Somewhere in there was satisfaction, was revenge. I don't know what I did to that woman and I don't want to know— and certainly no repercussions came my way, nor even a rumor; yet she must have been a wealthy person. But in some way I can't remember, I satisfied myself on the woman in about ten seconds—and it was not an easy score to settle, because she was responsible for changing my feelings toward Marigold from half-love to whole-pity, and that's a terrible way for a man's feelings to change.

I was running down the corridor. Paint peeled from the wall beside me in a scorching long blister. I swerved and kept running.

As I ran it seemed I saw a parade of women and girls, the ones who had affected my life, and it was not always certain whether I saw that woman with the pale blue eyes —or whether I saw Carioca Jones. Later, I was not sure exactly whom I had revenged myself on, in that murderous moment in the basement of the state pen.

There were guards and sharks in the entrance lobby. I ran up the stairs, through a doorway, up more stairs.

And it wouldn't have deterred the woman with the pale eyes if she'd known what a pretty girl Marigold was, if she'd known what beauty she was spoiling—in fact she would have enjoyed the knowledge, because that sort of woman *resents* pretty girls. They resent every good thing in other women, most especially if that good takes the form of a gift, like Marigold's desirability. Like Joanne's musical accomplishments.

I reached the roof and heard no sound of pursuit.

They are the devils, they are the destroyers, they are the ones who gather evil like knowledge as they claw their way through life.

I clattered down the fire escape and heard the whistling, and paused beside the body of the shark on the last platform. Below I could dimly see the eager shapes licking at the blood as it dripped through the iron steps, about five of them circling and humping and sliding and sucking and feeding, black like widows around their husbands' graves.

A hooter blew. I pulled myself together and the images vanished, although the sharks remained. Doors slammed and a loudspeaker boomed:

"You out there! Come in with your hands up or we release the rest of the sharks!"

I stood there, wondering vaguely how many more sharks they had, how long it would take them to realize I'd taken the top route out. I heard the speaker rasp its command twice more; then there was silence. Then a low whistling in the distance, a chirruping like a multitude of birds.

They came toward me as a dark undulating carpet, with their uncanny sense of smell making straight for the foot of the ladder on which I stood. There must have been twenty of them. The whistling became piercing as they snuffled around in the dirt, dissatisfied with the pickings. There was no way I could get past them; they were all around the base of the fire escape, avidly waiting for something to kill, to eat.

I was thinking more clearly now, and the trembling had stopped. That obscene black mass reminded me of something, of Hector Bartholomew and a fish-girl named Rosalie, and an afternoon of fear at Pacific Kennels. . . .

I knelt, got my hands under the body of the land shark on the platform, and heaved, blood sticky and slippery about my fingers, cold hide rough like sandpaper. The shark shifted saggily, flopped over and showed a pale belly, slid over the edge, and fell among the writhing forms below.

Instantly the whistling became deafening as the sharks attacked their dead comrade, tearing and snapping, munching and snuffling with unearthly horrifying greed. The body was tossed about on a wave of darting snouts and soon came apart, entrails glistening in the dim light, blood spraying.

Above the din, I heard a shout of triumph.

Inevitably, one shark snapped at another as the frenzy increased in a whirling of sinuous forms, a tearing of delicate fins, a brutal lunging and ripping at the flesh of weaker members. More bodies were flung about, twisting and whistling as the carnage ebbed away from the foot of the ladder.

I jumped to the ground and ran for the wall beyond the playing field. With my breath sobbing in my throat I crouched against the brickwork, glanced up. A light mist was drifting in from the sea; the laser beam fence showed along the top of the wall as three lethal bright threads running from one watchtower to the next. Moths danced about the eerie light and vanished in little sparks of quick brilliance.

A searchlight beam sprang from the tower above me and played against the wall of the Organ Pool. A heaving black mass could be seen, and the flash of pallid bellies. I heard a voice.

"That's no way for a man to die, no matter what he did."

Somebody else said, "Well, what the hell did he do, anyway?"

"God knows. The last escape, it was that guy due for his first donation, remember? Just a kidney, they tell me—but the first is always the worst, so they say. He didn't know how lucky he was. The sharks took all of him. Bastards. Vicious bastards."

"Look at that, will you? I reckon they're eating one another now."

"Oh, Christ!"

I edged along the wall to the gate. Here, both guards were watching the illuminated frenzy from a distance of around a hundred yards, chuckling with ghoulish delight as it dawned on them, too, that the sharks had gone cannibal. It seemed that I had sympathizers all around the compound. The dreadful seething continued against the Pool wall and I had the sudden wild notion that the net result would be one single shark of gigantic dimensions, gorged and comatose.

Then a group of men burst from a door and ran toward the struggle, carrying nets, guns, and gas bombs which they tossed among the writhing forms. Above the whistling I heard dull explosions, and vapor drifted pale in the spotlights. The men closed in, nets in one hand, guns in the other. Their faces were alien with respirators.

The guards at the gate took a few paces nearer to watch the fun and I seized my chance, slipping behind them, fumbling quietly but frantically with the catch on the wicket gate in full view of everyone. The catch slid back, the door opened outward, and I fell through, jumping to my feet instantly and running like hell. I bounded over gullies, tore through bushes, running north toward the distant lights of the hoverferry terminal, finally reaching the main highway, and collapsing on the grassy bank, utterly played out.

Eventually the late ferry came in and the hovercars whined past, heading for Louise, and I hitched a ride home.

As I lay in bed that night I tried to think of some good that had come out of the operation, but without success. I made sure all the doors were locked, but it was a long time before I fell asleep.

In the morning Carioca Jones arrived. I explained the failure of my mission as we sat in my living room drinking coffee and watching the early sling-gliders flitting down the Strait in the morning sun. I'd had a bad night, filled with strange visions of creeping homunculi, hunted by posses led by Gallaugher, and I felt exhausted mentally, my body stiff and aching.

"But I think it's *wonderful,* darling," cried Carioca too brightly for my mood. "Before, we only suspected. Now, we *know.*"

"Know what?"

"Why, that those monsters are cutting people to ribbons, stripping them to the *bone* in the name of the law, turning them into immobile *brains* with nothing to do but think their lives away. Are you sure you didn't see any of them suspended in *nutrient fluid?*"

"Carioca, for God's sake."

"But isn't it just too abominable?"

"Yes, but I'm not sure it's against the law. What's illegal is what Gallaugher's doing in his unofficial Pool for paying customers—but we have no concrete evidence that the place even exists."

"Well, we simply *demand* that they throw the place open to inspection!"

I sighed. "And what if they refuse? It's against Government policy to allow public access to the Pools, particularly since the recent outcries. They don't want people to know just what a critical organ shortage means; it would be political suicide. Lambert and Gallaugher have the backing of the entire armed forces, if they want it; the police, the military, even the goddamned coast guard will come down on their side. If we squeal about unofficial Pools and cash customers they'll just assume it's a trick to get inside. They won't even listen."

Carioca said, "They'll have to, if this one particular pen becomes a national issue."

"Huh?"

"Joe, I have the most *wonderful* idea!" She bounced to her feet and started punching at the buttons of my visiphone. The long, sad face of an unmarried woman appeared on the screen. "Yolande!" cried Carioca. "Phone around the girls . . . uh, I mean the Foes of Bondage, at *once*, and tell everyone to assemble at the ferry terminal with banners and as many friends and relatives as they can drag out; and those who live in Louise, tell them to rent people from the beer parlors on my authority, and get the whole *city* out to the terminal, if they can. This is going to be the biggest thing *ever!*"

Faint signs of animation flickered over Yolande's face, although it might have been a faulty connection; I've been having trouble recently. "Will do, Carioca," she said briefly. "The girls need a good demo. Morale has been low recently. Uh, what's our angle?"

"The *abomination* of buying and selling organs like a *cattle market.*"

"Sounds great. Shall I tell them to pack sandwiches? And what about the cost of transport for the hired heads?"

"For *heaven's* sake, Yolande, charge it all to me. Now I must go, I have the publicity to arrange." The screen went blank and Carioca prodded the buttons again.

This time a man appeared, surrounded by charts and stacks of files in a general picture of busy confusion. People passed to and fro behind him. Recognition showed in his tired face. "Carioca Jones," he said with no great show of emotion. "How are you?"

In the course of Carioca's long and persuasive talk it emerged that the man was a reasonably well-known reporter for Newspocket, and that he would not be averse to covering the Foes' demonstration—provided it did not turn out to be a fiasco like the previous time. I concluded that he referred to the incident of Charles Wentworth and the President's Trophy. Carioca assured the man—whose name was Dale Finlay—that there would be no repetition.

Finally she hung up and turned to me. "There," she exclaimed, black eyes bright. "*Now* we shall see some action! You see, Joe? We strike now, before that *poisonous* little man Gallaugher has time to spirit the evidence away. With Newspocket there, and the whole of the country behind us, Heathcote Lambert will have to throw Gallaugher to the wolves and permit a public investigation of the basement at the very least! Particularly since he's maintaining that there's nothing down there!"

I watched her as she paced about my living room in barely controlled excitement, hands clasped tightly so that the graft scars stood out livid around her wrists, and I thought: This is what she's been after. It has nothing to do with the Foes, with the Pool, with Gallaugher. It has to do with Carioca Jones, the once-great but now-forgotten 3-V star who thrived on publicity, then suddenly found her spiritual sustenance snatched away from her by a fickle public. At last she had the chance to get back in the public eye—and soon she would play her big comeback role—as Joan of Arc, maybe.

I remember thinking: For a clever woman she certainly is a stupid bastard.

I was astonished and a little unnerved by Yolande's organizational ability. The crowd at the ferry terminal must have numbered all of five thousand, of which at least a quarter were men—and more than half of those, drunk. Banners waved and epithets echoed around the terminal buildings, causing the motorists waiting for the two o'clock ferry to huddle nervously within their hovercars. The Foes were in trenchant mood with glowing slithe-skin armbands—of varying hues—and I noticed several of the younger members attempting to entice the male motorists from their cars and into the march with all manner of unlikely bribes.

"Are you refusing the young lady?" one drunk bellowed,

pounding on the roof of the hovercar while the driver cowered within, doors locked. We dragged the belligerent quasi-Foe away and Carioca told the girls to cool it. If the public was to take the demonstration seriously, it would have to be conducted in an orderly fashion.

Newspocket arrived in the form of a small bright anti-grav gliding silently in from the east. I talked with Dale Finlay for a while and he seemed a sensible man, if cynical. "If you ask me, they're a bunch of nuts," he said confidentially. "But even nuts can hit the jackpot, newswise. I have a feeling this afternoon will prove interesting."

Then Carioca was screaming into a megaphone and the march lumbered into straggling motion, banners flying.

As a sober male I was a member of an important minority subgroup and, as such, I was made to march near the front. Carioca strode nearby and seemed to feel that it was essential the leaders keep station, although a huge, crudely worded banner kept blowing in my face. The main column walked behind, separated from the leaders by a troupe of delectable youngsters known as the Louise Girls' High School Baton Twirlers. Overhead glided the Newspocket antigrav. All in all, it was a creditable showing at short notice.

About an hour later we arrived outside the gates of the state pen. A truck pulled up nearby; a team of men jumped down and began to erect a temporary platform. The Newspocket antigrav landed and the cameramen set up their gear. Then the entire crowd, for no good reason that I could see, was led by Carioca from the platform in the singing of "Abide with Me," accompanied by a little girl with an orchestrella.

I asked Finlay about this, following the final ragged note. "A nice touch," he said, headphones clamped to his ear. "We sent it out, of course, and I hear there's already been a favorable reaction nationwide." We ducked as a sling-glider swept overhead and discharged an unidentifiable fluid onto the crowd. I recognized Doug Marshall's craft. "It heightens the whole tone of the proceedings, starting with a hymn," he explained. "But don't ask me why. I merely gauge public reactions and act accordingly. For instance, there are things here I'd change right away, if I were in charge. For a serious gathering, there are too many drunks and the Girls' School Twirlers are too sexy. We can correct that with our camerawork, of course."

The flymart, which had been hovering overhead for the last few seconds looking for a vacant space, landed in a flurry of dust. The hatch slid open. The grocery display had been removed; in its stead gleamed a hot dog machine. Music blared. A beer tanker came bumping over the uneven ground from the west, scrub bushes swaying aside from the downdraft. The drunks cheered.

Happy faces were all around me. It was a fine afternoon and people lay relaxed on the grass; some lined up at the flymart and the beer truck was already besieged. The girls wore bright dresses and the hard-core Foes' wristlets glowed pink with content as they gossiped in little clusters. Beyond, the ocean lay blue and serene and a few gliders flitted about the Strait. The little girl was playing a catchy tune on her orchestrella. Carioca trotted toward me across the grass, smiling. "Isn't this *fun*," she cried. "I'd like you and the other officials up on the platform now, Joe. We're going to start." She spotted a camera on her and grinned, laughing gaily.

"Yesterday I found a girl in that prison whose legs had just been cut off," I said. "She was lying under a white sheet, and the sheet bulged quite a lot over her body, because she had nice breasts. But farther down the bed the sheet was flat, flat from her hips to the bottom of the bed, flat like a table, because there was nothing to hold it up, because her legs had been cut off."

She glanced at me abstractedly, waving to someone. "Joe darling, you *must* remember to say that on the platform. The same words, *exactly* like you told me. Now"—she laughed—"let's get started, shall we?"

The whole thing was beginning to seem unreal as I followed her to the platform and gravely took my seat among various other people whom Carioca considered Newspocket material. There was a burst of clapping and cheering as she stepped up to the mike.

"Welcome to you all, friend and Foe alike, on this wonderful afternoon." There was a mild acclamation, then she continued, "Today is no ordinary day, however, and this meeting is no ordinary meeting. Oh, no. We are met here today for a purpose so serious that—"

She continued in this vein and I found myself turning around, my neck prickling. Behind me loomed the gaunt prison wall cutting off the bright warm grass with black shadow some fifty yards away. Two guards stood in the nearest watchtower, looking in our direction, holding rifles. It only needed a word from Gallaugher for them to pick me off. I tried not to think about it, and it was with some relief that I saw several uniformed police among the crowd before me. In the distance I saw Rennie's bright blue hovercar swaying through the scrub toward me, dry dust blowing.

"We are here, good people, to *demand* a thorough and immediate investigation into the *monstrosities* which have been perpetrated in the name of the law behind these stark walls. Indeed—and heaven knows the Ambulatory Organ Pool is evil enough as it stands—I now hear on *unimpeachable* authority that this evil is within itself corrupt! An unofficial Pool has been spawned, born of a mind of *diabolical* cunning, whereby people may *purchase* limbs."

I could feel the rifles leveled at my back.

Of course, Gallaugher would say it was an accident. "A guard's gun malfunctioned. A dreadful occurrence and I can assure you, officer, that the man responsible will be severely disciplined and presented to you. We *had* intended to prosecute Mr. Sagar for trespass, willful damage, assault, and attempted murder—in support of which charges we have influential witnesses—but of course the matter will not now be mentioned. Such a tragic thing. Did he leave any relatives? A girlfriend, perhaps? The state pen would like to make some small token gesture. . . ."

Carioca Jones laughed harshly, arms wide, head back. "*Ambulatory* Organ Pool! Isn't that just too amusing!" She paused, staring fixedly at the cameras as they zoomed in. "Those poor wrecks can't even walk! Their legs have been *ripped* from their bodies! They have no arms, no eyes, hardly a body organ is left to them as they lie immobilized, blind, deaf, unthinking, too sick to care, in *there!*" She pointed; the crowd muttered. "In there! In *there!* In THERE!" she screamed, pointing, stabbing her finger in the epitome of accusation.

Lambert was suddenly beside me, gripping my shoulder. "Why wasn't I told? Why did nobody have the courtesy to warn me of this? We're not prepared in there! By God, Sagar, if this crowd gets out of control— Stop her, why don't you? Oh, my God. Is that Newspocket?"

The crowd was murmuring and swaying. A beer bottle shattered against the prison wall.

"Sacrifice Gallaugher, Lambert," I advised shortly.

"What the hell do you mean, sacrifice Gallaugher?"

He was badly frightened. Carioca Jones screeched on, whipping the crowd into a fever, giving them a masterly performance.

"Don't you know Gallaugher has his own Pool in the basement?"

His eyes were wild. "Not that crap again. Don't give me that crap again, man!"

"I've seen it, Heath. I was there last night!"

"You what? You what?" Suddenly he shriveled up, dropped to his knees beside my chair. "My God, Sagar. Is this the truth?"

I ignored him while he blubbered on, kneading my forearm. Carioca's act was reaching its crescendo, sweat eroded gullies in her makeup, she screamed directly into the cameras, the crowd forgotten.

But the crowd hadn't forgotten her, and they accepted her words, they ate her words, her words nourished their latent hatred of authority and made it grow, and blossom. . . . I noticed the police had concentrated into little groups at strategic points. The guards on the wall held laser rifles at the ready.

Rennie was pushing his way through the crowd, white-faced, sensing the hatred all around him, making for the platform with a dozen men at his heels. I saw several cameras dip and follow him forward.

Carioca stared at the blue sky, clutched at the heavens with slim young hands, lips a livid scar in her wreck of a face. "And we shall *demand* the *heads* of the *bastards* who *degraded*—"

Rennie touched her on the shoulder.

The cameras captured the scene.

Carioca blinked, stared at him. "If you think you can stop *me,* you *fool*—"

I couldn't see their faces. I fumbled out my Newspocket. It was there, in full close-up, in full color. Carioca's mouth was open; it was not a flattering shot.

"I'm sorry, Miss Jones. I must ask you to accompany me to the Louise City Police Station where you will be charged with the attempted murder of Mr. Douglas Marshall, where you will be allowed to summon a lawyer to represent you, following which recording devices will be attached to your person and you will be detained to await trial."

It was the standard caution, just like on 3-V.

The cameras whirred.

17

When somebody is beaten I don't like to see them kicked, no matter how much I dislike them. So I found I was watching Finlay with some disgust as, blasé cynicism cast aside, he capered beside Carioca Jones while she was led away, his goddamned mike stuck in her face, his free hand gesturing the cameras in, demanding that she give her comments to the world at large. Being Carioca Jones she obliged him, of course, and it didn't do her any good at all.

I was still sitting in my chair and I stayed there while the other people on the platform jumped to their feet and obscured my view. I found Lambert still crouched beside me. In the incredulous silence which was gripping the whole crowd, I said:

"Didn't you know Gallaugher was selling organs, Heath?"

He looked like a man who had pissed himself with fear. The immediate danger was over, but there was still an embarrassing problem to contend with. "That's a very serious accusation you're making, Joe," he replied, pulling himself together too fast, too smoothly for my liking. Only a moment ago he'd been practically in tears. If I didn't pin him down now, I never would.

Around us the crowd was beginning to murmur again; the buzz of comment was starting. "I asked you a question, Heath."

Suddenly, shockingly, an idiot technician switched the Newspocket broadcast into the public address system and Carioca's voice screamed out: ". . . incompetent *bastards* for every goddamned *penny* . . ." As abruptly, the man realized his mistake and there was instant silence.

Lambert was standing up. I stood too, not wishing to lose him. "You're way out of line, Joe. The records of the Pool are so watertight that not so much as a toenail could be

156

smuggled out without it showing up. My God, we're dealing with human beings in there. Everything's checked and double-checked."

"I'm saying there's a person in there who never got onto the records. Maybe a number of people."

"I'm sorry. I refuse to pry into Bob Gallaugher's department without evidence. Oh, good. There he is. I have nothing more to say to you, Joe." He began to move toward Gallaugher, who was blowing into the mike.

The crowd was milling about uncertainly, looking for a leader. I saw Evadne Prendergast, the ex-president of the Foes, make her way toward the mike, but Gallaugher shrugged her off. He took a deep breath. "Listen to me!" he shouted. Sweat was running down his plump face and his jowls were tense with determination. The crowd quieted down, people turned toward the platform again, while Rennie's blue hovercar drifted away over the scrub, taking Carioca Jones with it.

"By now you'll all have realized that you've been hoodwinked by an old phony who was trying to make personal capital out of the Foes of Bondage!" Gallaugher shouted. "Now, some of you people are members of that organization—if I can call it an organization—and some are not. What I have to say is for all of you. You have seen what can happen when you allow yourselves to be led by a crooked dictator whom most of you did not even have the chance to elect. This is what happens when democracy is thrown down the drain—the worser elements, the loudest mouths, come bubbling up and taint every honest person with their stink."

Dale Finlay was on the platform again, headphoned, directing the cameras to cover Gallaugher. "He's not bad," he said to me. "It's too early to tell yet; everyone's still in shock. But I think I'm getting some response here . . . yes." He motioned a technician to his side. "Switch the filters now; we're getting a favorable reaction. Pink positive for Gallaugher close-ups and any shots of the guards. Catch them smiling—they're the good guys now. Green for the Foes, and a touch of graininess too, I think. See that old witch up there?" He pointed to Evadne Prendergast, grim-faced and haggard after her failure to stem Gallaugher's oratory. "Switch on the overhead spot for shadows under the eyes

and catch her in close-up. . . . Do a split-screen with her
and Gallaugher for contrast."

I moved away from him as he directed his strange operation which seemed to have no connection with reality as I
saw it—yet which would affect the thinking of millions.
Meanwhile Gallaugher roared on, arms windmilling, calling
damnation on the heads of the Foes, pitying those who
had been misled by the glory-seeking virago who had proved
herself little better than a murderess.

As the crowd began to split into factions, encouraged by
the drink and Gallaugher, isolated fights broke out. Sudden
surges would leave inexplicable empty gaps; by the time the
eye had caught the motion, the flurry would be over. A bottle
sailed over our heads and shattered against the prison wall;
the guards ducked, fingering their weapons. The police were
everywhere, breaking up incipient fights, leading bleeding
men and women away.

"Cover that!" I heard Finlay snap as a group of women
began to manhandle a policeman, their Foes' armbands
blue with hate, knocking off his cap and beating him over
the head with bottles and shoes. "Cut! Edit that out!" he
shouted as the policeman fought back in desperation,
getting in some telling blows.

"For God's sake, stop Gallaugher before someone gets
killed!" I told Lambert.

He avoided my eyes, muttering something about free
speech. Gallaugher raved on, praising democracy, the Establishment, law and order, and the benefits of the Penal
Code—all in such terms that the brawling continued un-
abated and people smashed in one another's faces.

I took time off to glance at Newspocket, secure in the
center of the now-besieged platform. Dale Finlay was put-
ting the issues with consummate clarity now. Gallaugher appeared as a godlike figure silhouetted against the blue sky
and representing all that was good and decent in the human
race, while at his feet, in filthy grays and blacks, fought the
animal mob: the Foes of Bondage, the drunks from the
beer parlors, the rabble, the scum.

It might have lasted all afternoon, had not a diversion occurred in the form of the flymart. Somewhere back in Louise
somebody must have decided from the evidence of Newspocket that his property was in danger, and hastily pressed
the recall button. The little robot helicopter, lauding the

flavor of Island Hot Dogs, rose suddenly into the sky with a half dozen would-be customers still clinging to dubious handholds on its smooth exterior, and headed rapidly south.

The chastened crowd watched them lose their grip, one by one, as the flymart dwindled to a dot on the horizon.

Although the holiday season was at its height and consequently the sling-gliders were out every day, very little was heard of the Foes during the period before the trial of Carioca Jones. I had extended my temporary closure of the farm into an indefinite holiday while I awaited the arrival of new stock by starship—which was likely to take some months. Fortunately I had been able to recover a proportion of my losses from the insurance company, and I had a suit pending against Miranda Marjoribanks for the balance—although it seemed doubtful whether I would collect.

I found it difficult to believe that Carioca could be guilty as charged. True, she had the motive—but such an action was uncharacteristic of her on physical grounds. I just couldn't picture her prowling around the marina at night.

Then I remembered that it was not revenge on Doug Marshall coupled with a coup for the Foes which would have motivated her—it was the prospect of personal glory. And I had to admit that Carioca would probably do anything for personal glory.

Following the debacle at the state pen I had, in rather cowardly fashion, tacitly severed my connections with the Foes while things blew over. I suspected I was not the only renegade, although at an extraordinary meeting which I did not attend, Evadne Prendergast became president once more. For the time being, however, the Foes were in nationwide disrepute thanks to the job done by Newspocket, and it seemed sensible to disown them. They were in no position to help Marigold.

The Foes were not the only victims of Dale Finlay's cameras. It was rumored in the club that Heathcote Lambert's position as governor of the state pen was extremely precarious.

"I mean, Christ, you should have seen him," Doug Marshall was saying in the club one night shortly after the event. "The man was practically weeping on Joe's shoulder. Newspocket caught it all. He went completely to pieces."

"It's a good thing they have a strong man like Bob Gallaugher at the pen," Ramsbottom stated in his forthright manner. "By God, he soon talked some sense into those goddamned freaks."

Charles Wentworth was not so sure. "It seemed to me he stirred them up. There was no fighting before he started to speak. He'll bear watching, our Bob."

The day's gliding was over and we sat at the big window, opposite the bar, drinks before us and comfortably tired—the sort of situation when the problems of the world are solved. The last gliders were coming in, flitting across the darkening sky and splashing into the calm water nearby. From time to time another pilot and his crew would emerge from the dressing rooms and call thirstily for a drink.

"I was extremely glad to see that Jones woman get her deserts," said Bryce Alcester precisely. "After all the trouble she's caused this club. It'll be good to have her out of the way for a few years. I expect you're pleased Rennie nailed her, Doug. After all, you might have been killed."

Doug Marshall looked uncomfortable. "To tell the truth I feel pretty goddamned sick about the whole thing. It's past history now, but the whole affair is going to be raked up again and some of us will have to testify. OK, so it was a stupid trick she played—but I don't think she quite understood the seriousness of it. And another thing. I reckon I'm beginning to think like Joe and Charles here. I'm beginning to agree with some of the Foes' aims. The Organ Pool is pretty goddamned sick, and I wouldn't trust Bob Gallaugher farther than I can throw him. If you want my opinion, Newspocket did a lot of harm with their coverage."

The discussion erupted into two distinct and vociferous factions and would have continued all night, if Gallaugher hadn't arrived shortly afterward. In the following days Gallaugher rode high, and nobody saw any sign of Lambert. It was rumored that he had been transferred to another pen and would be leaving at the end of the month, but we heard nothing official. Since nobody liked to ask Gallaugher direct, our only possible source of information was Warren Rennie—but with the trial of Carioca Jones in the offing, he refused to enter into any discussions concerning Peninsula personalities.

One interesting thing Gallaugher said: "Rennie never moves unless he has a cast-iron case."

Although the big talking point on the Peninsula was the forthcoming trial—there was much speculation as to the form Rennie's evidence was to take—for me the major event was the coming release of Joanne. Carioca's trial had been fixed for August twenty-third after a brief preliminary hearing held in camera due to the public issues involved. With the Foes discredited, the authorities had no intention of giving her the chance for another grandstand performance.

So Carioca might well be imprisoned by the time Joanne was released, and I would have my girl to myself. I went along to the travel agents and booked flights south on the following weekend, choosing a remote resort in the Andes where I determinedly reserved a double room. Maybe I was trying to force Fate to play it my way for once.

At the travel agents I saw a small brochure for Halmas. I picked it out of the rack and was confronted with a bright photograph of the familiar beach; in the middle background lay a girl in sunglasses with outstanding breasts who could easily have been Marigold, and probably was. For just a few moments I felt sick with regret for the wonderful innocent past which she and I would never recapture, and sick with guilt because I hadn't considered her predicament for days. The release of Joanne had occupied my every waking thought, and quite a few of my dreams, too.

On the day before Carioca's trial started I visited Joanne again. They let me through without referring to Lambert or Gallaugher, much to my relief; by now my face must have been pretty goddamned familiar to those guards. It was not strictly a visiting day, but I was worried about Joanne's attitude toward the trial. She would probably be upset—though God knows why—and I thought perhaps I could cheer her up.

She looked happy enough, however. "Hello, Joe," she said, smiling.

I regarded her anxiously. "How are you, darling?"

"You're worrying about Carioca's trial, aren't you, Joe? Well, don't. I'm quite sure everything will work out for the best. And there's nothing you or I can do about it anyway, is there?"

She seemed very calm about it—but then she always was very calm. "I'll have to give evidence," I said. "I'm afraid it might incriminate Carioca."

"It won't. From what you've told me, all you can say is you

heard someone on the slipway that night. It's up to the police to prove who it was."

"That's right," I said, relieved. "Yes, that's right." Although I told myself that my visits were essential to her well-being, just occasionally I wondered who needed whom the most.

"So just don't worry about it, Joe," she said.

I searched for another topic. It was characteristic of Joanne that she never introduced subjects herself, although she would always discuss intelligently whatever interested me. This self-effacing manner was a part of her attraction, in its contrast to the phony loudmouths around the Peninsula.

I produced the tickets from the travel agents and held them up to the wire. "Look what I've got. We're going away for a vacation after you get out."

She looked from the tickets to me and my heart seemed to pause, waiting to find out whether I was to live or die.

She smiled faintly. "That's nice, Joe. I've always wanted to go to the Andes. I really hope we'll be able to make it."

"Of course we'll be able to make it," I said desperately. "I've booked the hotel as well. It's right on the side of the mountain—the view is fantastic. And the food is recommended by Harcourt Cuthbertson. It's just what you need to, uh, put you on your feet again. If you'd rather have single rooms I'll get single rooms, I don't mind. Just so long as you enjoy yourself."

"Thank you, Joe," she said. "You're one of the good guys, you know that?"

That night I sat in my living room, watching the moon on the Strait and trying to place the most favorable construction on each one of the enigmatic things Joanne had said. I knew I was not going to be able to sleep, so I drank instead, and tried not to think about the trial of Carioca Jones in the morning. In the end I gave up; despite the scotch I could not force my mind away from the unhappy juxtaposition of those two names: Joanne and Carioca, Joanne and Carioca. . . .

I switched on the 3-V for distraction. The alcove blurred, wavered, and a familiar figure was sitting in the corner of my room, plump of face with eyes close-set, smiling woodenly as he waited for the announcer to finish. ". . . and most recently, instrumental in quelling a dangerous riot outside the Peninsula State Penitentiary where a rabble of dissidents was on the brink of storming the gates—you will recall the dramatic arrest of Carioca Jones, the attractive 3-V star, which triggered the incident—here he is, the hero of Black Point Pen, Mr. Robert Gallaugher!"

Now Gallaugher was something I could do without, but curiosity got the better of me and I stayed with him.

The announcer concluded: "Of course, we all know Miss Jones goes on trial tomorrow—and the last thing this station wishes to do is to influence the course of justice—but I'm sure we're all interested to know, Mr. Gallaugher, just what prompted you to take the courageous action you did."

Gallaugher smiled thinly and self-deprecatingly. "Well, I could see the thing getting out of hand. The police were doing their best, and heaven knows they're a fine body of men. But there were ugly customers down there—very ugly customers indeed. They were, shall we say, the gangster element behind the innocent facade of Miss Jones and the Foes of Bondage. They were the strong-arm men, the men of dubious political persuasions who are waiting to move in, once a chink is exposed in the armor of democracy. I've said it before and I'll say it again—give the Foes an inch, and you'll find the hoods a step behind!"

"Very true, very true," said the interviewer wisely.

I poured myself another drink while Gallaugher spoke on, and it seemed to me that his voice was just a semitone higher as he pressed home his views concerning the Foes: ". . . You might find it difficult to believe this, but a respected member of our community actually broke into the pen the other day on the pretext of gathering information. This sort of dangerous, unilateral action is exactly what we have come to expect from the Foes of Bondage. Under the cover of their altruistic exterior, they are plotting, infiltrating, and finally seeking to overthrow the forces of law and order— and what are they offering as an alternative to our present system of government, evolved over the centuries? Mob rule, my friends. Mob rule!"

He stared into the camera with piggy little eyes, face bloated. It was quite extraordinary how unprepossessing the man was, seen in close-up. Puny little fists trembled before him as he ranted on. He seemed to be getting hoarse, and

I hoped that he would soon stop. He must have been going on for ten minutes already.

It was a blessed relief when the man paused for breath and the interviewer appeared. He seemed to represent a crutch of sanity, sitting there normal-sized in contrast to the giant sweaty face which had been dominating my room for minutes.

"We have it on good authority that the principle of Compulsory Donation has been—shall we say—carried to the point of inhumanity in some instances," he said surprisingly, in grave tones. He seemed to have switched his viewpoint. "I would like to ask you this, Mr. Gallaugher. How many prisoners have been released from the Pool during this past year, their sentences served? Is it true that some prisoners have donated everything but their brains? Is it true that organs can be bought?"

Gallaugher returned to the screen during the later stages of these quick questions and his expression was unpleasant to see. He snorted, and the lighting pinpointed the slow parabola of a drop of spittle which seemed to be heading straight for me. "It's a load of goddamned anarchist lies!" he shouted. I turned the sound down quickly; his voice was shrill and deafening. "It sounds like you've been got at, just like everybody else!" He was slobbering visibly now; glistening streamers trailed from his slack lips and, in the background, strange dull red flames flickered.

He loomed at me out of the alcove, all bulging eyes and shapeless nose as he screamed hatred into my room, the epitome of evil, while a military brass band pounded away in the background; and just as I felt I could stand it no longer he receded and became the top third of a triangular composite, ranting away near my ceiling, while below and to the left the interviewer watched with pity in his eyes. And to the right was a well-remembered shot from an early movie, showing Carioca Jones as a beautiful and innocent young girl dressed in a white Grecian gown, struggling helplessly with her bonds. She was tied to a rock and the sea lapped at her feet and the monster which approached so relentlessly bore a striking facial resemblance to Gallaugher.

18

"What can you expect from a local 3-V station?" said Dale Finlay. "They completely misjudged the emotional climate of the country as a whole. They thought they had this local hero who was defending us against subversive elements—but all they had in fact was a nasty little fat man!"

"So how did you persuade them to alter their viewpoint?" asked Doug Marshall.

"Newspocket was carrying their broadcast nationwide, and Newspocket is *big*. As soon as he started to speak, we began to get the reaction that viewers didn't like Gallaugher's face. So we got through to the 3-V station, goddamned quick. Gallaugher looked like a baddie, so a baddie he had to be. They handled it quite well, in the end."

We stood on the steps of the courthouse in the downtown area of the city, two blocks from the *Princess Louise*. Police had diverted traffic and a huge crowd was assembling in quiet and orderly fashion. Over the roofs I could see copters and flippers dropping toward the temporary landing field on the outskirts of town. The trial of Carioca Jones had in any event promised to be a big issue, but following Gallaugher's poor showing last night large numbers of craft were arriving from the mainland, and I noticed that the Foes had come out of hiding. There were armbands everywhere, and a large platform was being erected on the far side of the street. Militant banners flew, proclaiming Carioca Jones as a martyr.

I commented on this evidence of pessimism to Finlay.

"The national feeling is that the result of the trial is a foregone conclusion," he said. "In recent criminal cases the police have had a success factor of eighty-six percent and Rennie is known to be a good man."

I murmured some comment and joined a few members of

the sling-gliding club who were sitting on the steps in the morning sun. It seemed that several of us would be called as witnesses, while others had come along to watch the fun. At last the doors opened and we filed in. I heard an unnervingly huge buzz of comment from the gathering crowd in the street.

As courthouses go, the one in Louise is a modern structure, nicely paneled in light wood with a public gallery seating about two hundred—just enough for the media to obtain a good sample reaction. This looks down on the business side of things, the larger area with tables, chairs, equipment, and—in the center of the arena—the Triangle of Justice. A symbolic representation of this is repeated on almost every available flat surface.

"I'd like you at the Triangle, Joe," said Rennie, strolling up. He was casually dressed and in his element; I'd heard he usually conducted his own prosecutions and he looked as though he was enjoying himself. I sat at the big three-sided oak table in the glare of lights and tried not to panic.

Carioca sat on the defense side of the Triangle, dressed in slithe skin, her counsel beside her, his programmer at the defense computer. She smiled at me briefly; her dress was actually glowing a faint pink. The thrill of the spotlights was overcoming the fear of her predicament. Other men sat around the Triangle, their roles unknown to me—although the side of justice was as yet empty. Around the wall of the courthouse arena sat or stood the other people concerned: the later witnesses, court officials, police. A few recorders and newsmen manned machines at scattered tables. The cameras were wheeled into position.

"The Court will rise!" As some minor official yelled this infuriating command I glanced at Carioca's face. Her expression was of anticipation, and I saw the flicker of her tongue moisten her bright lips.

The compitrator entered, an impressive machine in crimson enamel wheeled by its operator, who wore a robe to match. They crossed the floor in stately fashion and halted at the justice side of the Triangle, where the operator plugged the compitrator in. A green light glowed and we all sat down. "The Court is in session," mumbled the operator. "Case L8756B, the State versus Miss Carioca Jones." He nodded to Rennie.

The policeman said, "Fine. I introduce Bryce Alcester."

He turned to the club secretary, who was also sitting at the Triangle. "Tell us about the row between Carioca Jones and Doug Marshall on the slipway of Skipper's Marina shortly before the sabotage incident, will you?"

"On the Sunday afternoon in question I happened to be passing the hydrofoil of Doug Marshall which was at that time drawn up on the slipway," began Alcester in his precise voice, "when I overheard Miss Jones use a certain epithet."

"Warren, could you ask your man to speak up a bit?" called Dale Finlay from the foot of the public gallery, where he held a recording instrument. "We can't hear a goddamned thing over here."

The prosecution programmer was tapping at a machine as Alcester spoke on more loudly, when Rennie suddenly interrupted. "Look, John. Do we need to know exactly what your client said? I mean, this dirty word, or whatever? I'm willing to leave it out unless you think otherwise. It's not part of my case and it certainly won't sound good on the media."

"Thanks a lot, Warren," murmured Carioca's man.

Suddenly Carioca Jones was on her feet, and the first moment of drama occurred. "I wish the whole *world* to know what I said," she stated forcibly. "I will *not* be silenced. On that afternoon I referred to Charles Wentworth as a *Spare Parts* man—which is *exactly* what he was. Like all those poor *wretches* whom Robert Gallaugher is hiding in his *dungeons!*"

"Drop it, Carioca, will you?" murmured her counsel tiredly.

"Leave it out," said Rennie to his programmer. He shouted across to Dale Finlay. "I know damned well you're pre-recording, Finlay. Now if you put that crap out on Newspocket I'll have you thrown out!" He pulled a portovee from his pocket and scanned it. I caught sight of the compitrator being wheeled in; Finlay was broadcasting two or three minutes behind, and Carioca's outburst would go unheard by the nation.

Visibly seething, her dress a bright purple, she sat down reluctantly.

Bryce Alcester continued his evidence while the programmer tapped away. At length he was finished with very little prompting from Rennie. The programmer extracted the metallic card from his machine and slipped it into a slot on the prosecution computer. A green light flashed and the card reemerged. Rennie passed it across the Triangle to the defense, who slipped it into their computer.

"I'd like to put you on after Bryce, Joe," Rennie said.

Two cards had now emerged from the defense computer: the original and another. The defense programmer slipped the second card through a scanner, then spoke quietly to counsel.

"I'm sorry about this, Warren," said the defense counsel, "but our machine thinks it essential that Carioca's exact words are placed on record, Christ knows why. Maybe it's following some sort of previous good character line, showing where her sympathies lie, perhaps. Bearing in mind that we don't have much of a case, that's all I can think of."

"That won't work," objected Rennie. "I have evidence to show that Carioca once received a graft herself. I didn't want to have to bring it in, though. The donor is due for release shortly and she wouldn't want her name all over the country. . . . Finlay!" he called.

"Oh, all right," groaned the Newspocket man from across the arena.

So Carioca's outburst became a matter of court record and was fed onto the evidence card together with a surgeon's testimony of her hand graft of the previous year—but at least Joanne's name was not mentioned. Again the card was put through the defense computer and reemerged with a suggested question.

The prosecution computer answered satisfactorily and for a while the two machines quizzed and tried to outthink each other, with Bryce Alcester occasionally being called upon to amplify. In many instances we didn't even know what the questions were; the cards were merely passed to and fro between the machines without translation. Occasionally defense counsel would check a question. When Alcester's help was needed, the prosecution machine flashed a red light.

At last both machines showed green and the completed cards were handed to the operator, who fed them into the compitrator with a flourish. The wheels of justice began to turn.

About that time there was a low, dull roar audible in the courtroom as the crowd outside reacted to an earlier piece of evidence.

Then I told my story of the night on the slipway while

Carioca watched me intently from the other side of the Triangle.

"You say you heard a gasping," defense counsel said. "Would you say it was a female gasping or a male gasping, or even an animal gasping?"

"At the time I was frightened it was a fish gasping," I admitted. "But I couldn't say for sure."

The remainder of the questioning was conducted between the computers and soon my legal duties were completed. With much relief I left the Triangle and joined the onlookers lounging around the walls. Doug Marshall and Charles were called in turn and described the flight, the accident, and their subsequent findings on examination of the harness, which was produced in court. One or two other club members testified; then we adjourned for lunch.

Due to the crowd outside, which, we heard, had now reached massive proportions, most of us lunched in the courthouse café. As we discussed the evidence over coffee the general opinion was that the case would be over by the end of the afternoon session—when we might expect a huge and lengthy demonstration outside.

"I don't know how many more witnesses Rennie has," said Doug Marshall, "but I can't see our friend Carioca calling anyone." He chuckled suddenly. "Unless she has it in mind to call Joe as a character witness."

I ignored that one. "So far Rennie's proved nothing," I pointed out. "All that's been fed into the compitrator so far is the fact that someone tampered with your harness, and that Carioca Jones had several disagreements with the club."

"Don't forget the preliminary programming by the operator," Bryce Alcester said. "He fed in a large number of undisputed facts about Miss Jones, the club, and its members. I know, because I had a questionnaire to fill out. I have no doubt the Foes of Bondage had a similar form—as did the state pen, the police, and even you, Joe, for all I know. The compitrator takes into consideration every fact which might have any conceivable bearing on the case. Somewhere it will be finding links, spotting discrepancies, and forming theories which would never occur to you or me."

We regarded Alcester with respect. For a fussy little prig, he seemed to know a lot about the law.

"And don't forget the Occupancy Factor," he concluded mysteriously.

Immediately after lunch Rennie produced his star witness. "This is Miranda Marjoribanks, John," he told the defense counsel. "I'd like both our programmers to work on this one because her evidence is pretty damning to your client, so let's get it right first time, huh? Otherwise we'll be here all night. I've been priming her for the last hour, so we'll just let her talk, shall we?"

I edged closer to the Triangle as Miss Marjoribanks began to speak, and I noticed the cameramen doing likewise, jockeying for position. In the background Dale Finlay was directing his men like an orchestra conductor, with pursed lips, waving arms, and a wealth of furious mime.

"I'll start by saying that I can't stand the sight of Carioca Jones, ever since her unspeakable attitude over a most unfortunate feeding frenzy at my establishment, Pacific Kennels, when her disgusting brute of a land shark was killed—and a damned good thing too, if you ask me."

Rennie touched her on the arm. "I realize I asked you to make your sympathies clear in order to save time, Miss Marjoribanks; but I ought to tell you that the computer pays no attention to rhetoric or adjectives. It deals in facts."

"Quite, but just *seeing* that woman makes my blood boil. However—" She collected her thoughts. "Before his death, this woman had been to see me several times with the land shark Wilberforce, who was proving difficult to handle. A course of psychotherapy failed to produce the desired results and no wonder, because the brute was too fat. Fish are not land animals," she explained, "and are not accustomed to supporting their entire weight on their ventral regions. The obesity of the shark Wilberforce was placing a constant strain on his bodily structure and causing him to act with a viciousness quite abnormal in a properly handled fish."

She consulted her notes briefly, then resumed. "So I was forced to recommend other measures. I sold her a denticure set. It's not an item in much demand—in fact that set is the only one I've ever sold. It contained sedative pills, anesthetic hypodarts"—she paused dramatically—"and a medium-sized, case-hardened file, for the shark's teeth. Here is an example." She laid a box on the table, opened it, and displayed the contents. So far as I could tell, it was identical to the set I'd seen in Carioca's car on the morning the squid got Dave.

"Yes, well, you can see what we're getting at," interrupted Rennie, to Miranda Marjoribanks' obvious annoyance. "There's a file in the set, and a file was used for roughing up Doug's harness. We aim to prove Carioca sabotaged the gear with the file from her denticure set." He tossed a file on the table; it had a label attached. "Here's the file found by our lampreys near the scene of the crime. Here"—he tabled a sheet of typed paper—"is a deposition by our lab to the effect that the traces of metal found in the teeth of the file are identical to the metal used in the harness—a comparatively unusual alloy. Here is a deposition by our fingerprints and perspiration analysis department stating that Miss Jones was the last person to use the file."

The cards were passed over and fed into the defense computer. Eventually the cross-examination card emerged and the programmer began to translate it.

While this was going on a policeman had risen quickly from one of the side tables and was speaking to Rennie, who frowned and beckoned Dale Finlay. "Do you want to cause a revolution?" I heard him ask urgently. "There's just been a breakout at the pen, and I can't spare any men to handle it. It's obviously tied in with what's happening outside. Now just play it straight, will you? No angles, no heroes or martyrs, or I'll have your cameras thrown out of court!"

Finlay nodded, for once chastened.

Carioca sat uncaring in her chair, a little back from the table with crossed legs exhibiting an expanse of thigh, her slithe-skin dress still a bland pink. Her eyes met mine and she winked almost imperceptibly. There was no way she could realize just how serious her crime was. I could imagine her on the slipway that night; maybe she'd just been driving by, furious at the abortive trip to Lake William, convinced that Doug was to blame. . . . Then, on a whim, she had stopped the car and taken the only available tool with which to vent her spite.

Eventually the defense counsel received the transcript of Miranda Marjoribanks' evidence and glanced down the list of alternatives. He frowned. "This is a little embarrassing, Warren," he said. "The machine can't come up with any sensible cross-examination, unless you happen to believe in parallel worlds. It looks very much as though we shall have to go straight to the compitrator."

I began to dream of Joanne with her fair hair and freckles.

Dale Finlay was standing over Rennie again, talking quickly. "Look. What sort of goddamned flop is this? I've contracted for two more hours and you're talking about going to the compitrator already?"

"This is a court of law, Dale. I'm afraid your miscalculations have nothing to do with the issue." Rennie was smiling in satisfaction.

"Yes, but what about the public? They're the ones who foot the bill for this goddamned court and all its trappings. What about all those people outside? That's Carioca Jones sitting there, man. The public is entitled to some sort of show!"

"They can have that after the verdict. She'll be asked if she has anything to say before sentence is passed."

Muttering unhappily, Finlay moved away. I was feeling that glow which normally comes only after the third scotch on an empty stomach. I had given my evidence, the whole wretched performance was grinding to a close, and soon I would be able to go home and think about Joanne.

"Are you saying that an accused person is not entitled to any *defense?*"

As Carioca spoke out, there was a flurry among the cameramen and Rennie and the defense counsel looked at her in surprise.

"I was under the impression that we *had* no defense," said her man anxiously, wondering where he had slipped up. "We can only present facts, Miss Jones. And I must admit that the facts are against us."

"Well, *really!*" Carioca was on her feet in an attitude of astonishment, staring at those seated around the Triangle in dramatic bewilderment. "Is this what I've been paying my taxes for? Is this what I hired a legal counsel for? Oh, no, indeed. You're not going to get away as easily as that. Since it's clear to me that you're *totally* incompetent, I am informing you that I'm terminating your services as from this *minute!*" Subtly her stance altered, she struck a heroic pose. "I shall conduct my own defense."

"Well, for God's sake, go ahead," replied her counsel, annoyance conflicting with amusement on his face.

"I call Mr. Joseph Sagar as my witness."

As the thrill of apprehension hit my stomach I saw the cameras swing in my direction like a billion eyes—which, in fact, they represented.

"Oh, for Christ's sake," Rennie was saying disgustedly. "He hasn't been primed, Miss Jones. Are we going through the old question-and-answer routine? It'll take forever."

"Because he hasn't been primed like those other *parrots*, he'll tell the truth as he sees it. The truth from an honest man is worth a *thousand* rehearsed lies from your *minions*."

The operator spoke up for once. "The compitrator isn't interested in truth or lies, Miss Jones. It's interested in the facts."

"And the facts you shall have!" she cried. "Come here, Joe. Now. I want you to cast your mind back to a certain morning a few weeks ago when you came running to me, *desperate* for my help because your man Dave—Froehlich, is it?—was in the terrible clutches of a giant squid. Do you remember that, Joe?"

"I remember."

"I was in my car—and *fortunately* I happened to have poor late Wilberforce's denticure set with me, which now I have unaccountably mislaid, in which there were a number of objects that we thought might be of use. Do you remember *that*, Joe?"

"Yes." Both programmers were tapping away like maniacs. I heard another low growl from the crowd outside.

"In fact we found the hypodarts in the set. You took them and you saved Dave's life with them. Now, think carefully. Visualize the denticure set. In it were the following items: A bottle of pills. A pack of one-shot hypodarts. And a medium-sized tooth file, metallic with a blue handle, bearing the initials *P. K.* Do you remember that, Joe?"

Her black eyes were deep and glittering, her gaze fixed unwinkingly on mine.

I couldn't remember. I honestly couldn't remember. I didn't think the file was there, but it might have been. Rennie's evidence *could* be faked. Miranda Marjoribanks *could* have lied. There were influential political elements behind this trial.

I thought of Joanne, shortly due for release.

Carioca sensed my indecision and her hands rose slightly in supplication. Her smooth young hands. . . .

"You're a goddamned liar, Carioca," I said harshly. "There was no file in that box."

19

Carioca stood still for a moment, allowing her expression of surprise to drift gradually into tragic grief; then she sat down while the programmer finished his tapping and slipped the card into the defense computer. Rennie was grinning at me wolfishly as I wandered away from the table, a little sickened by my own action.

"You don't rate very high, nationwide," Finlay informed me in that remonstrating tone favored by those who haven't made fools of themselves.

"Go to hell," I told him, walking away.

The gallery was still roaring and I felt exposed, down there on the floor. I wondered uneasily how thick the doors were, if the mob outside took it into their heads to come for me. Doug Marshall and Charles Wentworth closed around me in protective fashion. A sudden shower of orange peel descended from the gallery and the court officials began to shout for order.

"Uh . . . that was a pretty good thing you did there, Joe," said Doug. "Don't worry about those bastards. You had to tell the truth in there."

"I'm not sure whether I told the truth or not, you know that, Doug?"

Charles said, "You told the truth. If Miss Jones had wanted to dispute what you said, she'd have had you coupled to a lie detector. But she didn't."

"Charles, I feel as though I've sentenced her."

Rennie joined us. At the Triangle, the operator was feeding the final pieces of evidence into the compitrator. "You've sentenced nobody—the compitrator does that. And even the compitrator doesn't have absolute power. Its sentence is determined by the Occupancy Factor."

The roar from outside came, angry and threatening like

the fringe thunder of an approaching hurricane. "The Occupancy Factor?" I asked, trying not to think about all those people.

"This is where the compitrator really scores over the old system of human judge and jury. The machine is programmed with the trial data as you saw—but its verdict tendency is weighted by the Occupancy Factor. Briefly, you're more likely to get a verdict of not guilty if the state pens are full. Right now the Occupancy Factor is low; this would look bad for Miss Jones but for the fact that she's obviously as guilty as hell, anyway. As it is, the Factor will only affect the length of her sentence."

There was a stir of activity around the Triangle. The compitrator, which had remained thoughtfully silent for the past few minutes, suddenly chattered into life and emitted a tape. The operator tore it off, glanced at it briefly, and spoke, while the cameras zoomed in. "Miss Jones, it is with regret that I must inform you that you have been found guilty of attempted murder. As you know, you are entitled to address the Court before sentence is passed."

"Will that affect the sentence?" I asked Rennie.

"Not one iota. It's traditional, that's all."

". . . avail yourself of this opportunity?" The operator glanced inquiringly at Carioca.

"I most *certainly* shall." She rose to her feet and the gallery, which had been murmuring comment at the expected verdict, was silent. Dale Finlay was gesturing his cameras lower, bringing the lighting back to alleviate the harshness, playing a neutral role until the audience reaction firmed up. Carioca shook her midnight hair away from her face after a thoughtful pause with downcast eyes, then began to speak. "When I first came to the Peninsula, I knew nobody.

"I was a stranger in this country of yours, and I am a retiring sort of person who finds it difficult to make friends. In my loneliness I turned to the first two people I met—a young S. P. girl whom I took into my home and looked after like a daughter, and Mr. Joe Sagar, whom you met earlier.

"It's an old story, and not a pretty one. . . ."

She spoke on in quiet, sad tones, with none of her usual bombast, her usual emphasis. She was utterly convincing as she told the story of my seducing Joanne so that the girl had to be returned to the pen for her own protection; then she began to get more specific about the relationship between herself and me, and Oedipus undertones began to emerge.

"Raise the lights a fraction," I heard Finlay whisper. "We need a slightly older image for this."

Doug Marshall took me by the arm. "Let's get the hell out of here," he said. We made our way from the arena and climbed the steps to the café, Charles following. As we sat down with our coffee, Rennie entered.

"I thought I'd find you here. . . . Joe, I have some news from the pen about the escape. It seems that there's just one man involved—although a guard said something about a girl, a cripple. The man is Dave Froehlich, your ex-bonded man. They say he held up the guards at gunpoint and got away in a hovercar. Uh . . . Would you happen to know where he got the gun from? The guards said it wasn't a police model; it was one of those new wide-beam personal defense weapons. Like the one I gave you a license for." He shot me one of his piercing glances.

"Sorry, Warren. I can't help you."

"I'd like you to put yourself in Dave's position, Joe. You knew him better than anyone. Where do you think he'd head for? Your farm?"

"I doubt it. My guess is, either he'll head up-island or, if it's a calm sea, he'll try for the mainland."

He left, obviously dissatisfied and thinking I had something to do with it. We finished our coffee and looked at one another uncertainly, wondering what to do next. Nobody wanted to return to the courtroom; neither did anyone relish the idea of going outside. We wandered along the corridors while Carioca's speech and the crowd's reaction boomed away dully in the distance. Eventually we came to a window overlooking the street.

Through the glass, the tragic face of Carioca Jones stared at me.

On the far side of the street a battery of projectors had been set up, and the back of the improvised platform extended upward to form a huge 3-V alcove, almost as tall as the four-story building itself.

Within this alcove a giant Carioca postured and wept.

Charles opened the window.

". . . guilty, of course I'm guilty. If fighting for the freedom of slaves is wrong, then I'm guilty. If defending the weak against the might of the unthinking bureaucratic robot

178 _Michael G. Coney_

is a crime, then I'm a criminal. If unmasking the villainy of those who seek to sell our bodies for cash is a sin, then imprisoned I must be. If struggling to save the sight of one little child—"

"Oh, for Christ's sake, will you listen to that crap?" muttered Doug disgustedly as the voice boomed on and the crowd chanted in agreement. "At least she's stopped talking about you, Joe. Shall we go outside now?"

We made our way to the main entrance and left the building unnoticed. All eyes were on the mammoth figure of Carioca Jones which, from this viewpoint, seemed to loom up at us from the very sky. Behind her, faint and ethereal, was the outline of a cross.

Glancing around, I saw Gallaugher standing against the wall, half-concealed by a pillar. He looked frightened, staring up at the mighty image as though it were about to step on him. Rennie walked across and spoke to him and he nodded, biting his lip. Most of the police were around the courthouse door now; people had left the public gallery to watch the spectacular street show which was so much more exciting than the real thing indoors. The courthouse had become little more than a studio.

I joined Gallaugher and Rennie. "Have they caught Dave yet?" I asked. Rennie shook his head. The fear in Gallaugher's eyes was pathetic as he looked from me to the Carioca image and back again, his lips trembling. "There was a minivid," I said to rattle him further. "The illegal donors are all on record, Gallaugher."

"I really don't know what you're talking about," he said primly, almost crying.

"_They_ are the murderers, _they_ are the butchers of human flesh," roared the massive figure from the sky, finger stabbing in accusation. It appeared that the great finger pointed directly at Gallaugher and me. . . . Gallaugher whimpered, and a few people actually turned around and looked at us.

Carioca spoke on, gradually and skillfully progressing from a sad, defeated martyr to a vociferous, rampant evangelist; condemning the Pool, bondage, the state pen, the police, the Government, and a number of individuals besides. As before, my name was mentioned. Then suddenly she stopped, staring beyond us with some surprise. I felt as though I wanted to turn too, to establish the object of her astonishment.

Then she smiled slowly. "Thank you all. Thank you very much for listening," she said quietly, and disappeared.

The compitrator appeared in the alcove, the operator leaning over it, tearing off a strip of tape. The applause for Carioca died away as he waited, eyes on the tape while its significance dawned on the audience. When all was still, he looked up with deep-set eyes. He looked much more impressive on 3-V than in the flesh.

"Miss Carioca Jones, the sentence of this Court is that you be detained in the state penitentiary for a period of ten years excluding remission."

The roar of protest at the severity of the sentence had hardly died down before another figure appeared in the alcove and I recognized the dour face of Dave Froehlich. "Friends!" he shouted. "I've just escaped from the state pen!"

As the audience gaped at this astonishing announcement Gallaugher turned on Rennie, who was whispering to one of his men.

"Arrest him, Rennie! What the hell are all these police here for? Get on with it, man! He's in front of the courtroom cameras!"

Rennie said something more to his man and turned back to Gallaugher, who was bouncing about frantically, sweating. "I'm sorry about this, Bob," he said quietly. "I've just had orders from the mainland to conduct an immediate search of the pen. I'm sure you understand; politicians get a bit edgy when this sort of adverse publicity gets around. They just want to clear the air, that's all." As he said this his eyes met mine, and he showed no expression whatever.

Gallaugher's shoulders sagged and he turned away. "I'll get my coat," he mumbled; and he was gone. Rennie watched him push his way through the crowd but made no effort to follow him.

Meanwhile Dave was talking, jerkily and awkwardly. His expression was morose but his manner seemed sincere, and I wondered what Dale Finlay was thinking. "Mr. Joe Sagar broke into the pen a while back to try to gather evidence with a minivid, which was a pretty goddamned brave thing to do," he was saying, and I began to feel better. "And he spoke about, uh, Marigold Carassa." Here Dave's face reddened dreadfully, and suddenly I began to understand. "I thought about her a lot after he'd gone but I was scared, see? But last night I slipped downstairs and found everything disorganized, you know what I mean? Anyway, I found Marigold Carassa. She had a gun and a minivid hidden in the ward and I thought: Why don't we try to get out of here? So that's what we did. Uh . . . maybe we ought to show the tape, huh?" He spoke to someone off-screen. He was patently anxious to get away from the cameras.

I heard Finlay's voice. "Get him off and get the girl on, do you read me? Forget the tapes. We don't want the police at our throats." He stood nearby, speaking urgently into a transceiver.

Someone gripped my shoulder. It was Rennie. "Sorry, Joe. We all make mistakes. Well," he sighed. "I suppose it's my duty to arrest Froehlich."

"What about Gallaugher, for Christ's sake!"

"I'll think about that when we've searched the pen. Somehow I don't think Gallaugher will be around anymore."

"You mean he's taken off? You've let him go?"

"I mean I've given him the chance to do whatever he thinks fit. Even you must agree that it wouldn't be sound, politically, to allow Gallaugher to stand trial. It would mean a trial of the whole penal system, the Establishment, the Government, even. All because of one man."

"Listen, Rennie," I snarled. "I want that fat little bastard to suffer. I want him to stand trial and be convicted, and to go into the Organ Pool and be *used*, piece by piece, until he can't walk and he can't talk and he can't see, just like those goddamned . . . *things* I saw in the Pool. That's what I want, Rennie, and I'm going to use every means at my disposal to see it happens!"

"You mean Finlay, I imagine? I tell you this, Joe. Finlay has no say in a matter of this importance. He's a provincial reporter, man. It might seem to you that he's shaping national opinion, but that's only because the authorities haven't seen fit to intervene—yet. Right now he's being used, just like everyone else. He's being used because he's useful to those higher up. You overheard the way he chickened out over the minivid tapes? When he goes too far, he'll be stopped."

Then there was a sigh from the crowd: a low, surprised, envious, loving sigh. . . .

Marigold looked down at us from the alcove.

Marigold looked beautiful. It would be possible to describe her appearance at length but it would be pointless. She was dressed in white and the picture was cut off tactfully at the waist, so all the audience saw was a calm, pretty girl with something in her eye which promised everything every man there had ever dreamed of—and yet which caused the women to smile indulgently and fondly because Marigold always looked so goddamned innocent she disarmed feminine jealousy.

"My name is Marigold Carassa and I come from a little town called Halmas, many hundreds of miles away," she said simply, in her charming accent. "I was in love with the man Joe Sagar and I wanted to see him, and I couldn't afford it." I wondered at the pain in my soul, when she described her love in the past tense. "Then I heard of a new travel agency which was offering cut-rate cruises if you didn't mind an old boat and small cabins. Well, I didn't mind that because I wanted so much to see Joe; but what I did mind was that we all began to feel sleepy and funny when we got near this island, and we knew we'd been drugged but it was too late to do anything about it. . . ."

Then she went on to describe the wrecking of the *Ancia Telji* and the subsequent events as she recollected them, which was not very clearly. "For a lot of the time I was drugged, but there were in-between times when I could speak to those around me, and they all said the same thing. They had come on a cruise, and here they were, and some of them had been here much longer than I. And every day—" Marigold's voice faltered at last. "Every day there was not so much of them, and pieces were being taken away. And they would change rooms or disappear altogether. We tried to find somebody in charge but we couldn't. Nobody would listen to us—and there was this awful fat man Gallaugher."

I looked around for Rennie but he wasn't there.

"At first he treated me better than the others, but soon—" She looked down and now she was crying. "I think he became tired of me. Then at last Joe came, I think. Dave told me, after. Joe came and got caught and got away again, and the guards were very frightened, and people . . . began to disappear very fast. The first ones to go were the . . . the smallest . . . the ones who— Oh, Dave, please take me away from this!"

And a huge arm was suddenly around her shoulders, drawing her off-screen; but before she was able to disappear Finlay played his trump, the cameras slid downward, down past her waist. . . .

The bellow of anguish from the crowd was animal in its mindless, sorrowing intensity.

Rennie was beside me again. He said, "I think perhaps Finlay went too far."

20

I was glad Joanne was safely locked away in the pen and was not able to become involved in the rioting of the next few days. Following the appearance of Marigold the crowd had rampaged through the downtown area of Louise, smashing property and beating up every official in sight. The police were powerless to control them; indeed, Rennie had dispatched half his force to the pen to seize the guards responsible for the illicit Organ Pool before there could be any further disappearances.

Having vented some of their despair the mob had paused on the northern outskirts of the city. The pen lay some miles away across fish-infested scrub. I was in Rennie's helicopter at the time, and I could almost see them thinking with one mind as they seethed around the parking lot of the flymart warehouse and wondered what to smash next. They had no leader, and now that their impetus was temporarily spent Rennie felt they might be more tractable. He roared threats and instructions through the loudspeaker; the Foes of Bondage managed to regroup themselves around Evadne Prendergast, who climbed to the roof of a car and gave an impassioned address, pleading sanity.

It had been well into the evening before the mob finally dispersed.

Before that, Rennie took me for a quick trip across the Strait, over the archipelago of small green islands. "I had a report," he murmured. His eyes were searching the flat blue expanse below as the pilot banked the copter. "See that?" He pointed.

A tiny trail sped southward, a land hovercar taking its chances on the open sea.

Rennie sighed. "He'll make out. He'll get to one of those backward countries—maybe even the one where his god-

Michael G. Coney

damned travel agency operated—and he'll change his name and worm his way into some position, and the next thing he'll be running a town and those poor damned people will respect him and think how lucky they are that he came out of nowhere to protect them from the bandits in the hills. But he'll be in cahoots with the bandits, too."

It was a depressing picture. "Or you could take this copter down right now, and shoot him up," I suggested.

Rennie grinned briefly. "Couldn't we now. But that way I'd have to square the pilot, and I'd have you on my back for the rest of my life. Much better to stick to the book, Joe. Besides, I have no official knowledge of who's in that car— and under the circumstances I'd rather not know."

So we watched the silver wake of the hovercar extending southward as straight as a rule; and yet another bastard was getting away with it while the good guys stood by, hamstrung by their own regulations, their own consciences. The weather was set fair and the car could drive to Tierra Del Fuego on a sea like this, and the sun glared hotly through the Plexiglas dome as I eased the laser pistol from Rennie's pocket while he was twisted away from me, staring down.

"Careful with that trigger," Rennie murmured. "I don't think the safety catch is on."

I jammed the gun into the back of the pilot's neck. "Take her down," I snapped.

By the following morning the Foes had got themselves organized and were planning a somewhat prosaic march on the pen; since Carioca had gone out of circulation they seemed to have lost all imagination. I attended the sedate preliminaries in Louise and was gratified to find myself in the position of being a well-loved figure—an unusual situation for me. People shook my hand and complimented me on my part in Dave's break and the consequent exposure of the Pool. I could have had the pick of the maiden ladies of the Foes, had I so desired.

Evadne Prendergast approached me. "I understand you have some influence over Marigold Carassa, Mr. Sagar," she said. "The young lady is proving difficult and I'd be very glad if you'd speak to her."

I found Marigold in a suite at the *Princess Louise*—paid for out of Foes' funds, I deduced.

"They want to wheel me at the head of their march like an exhibit, Joe," she said in distress. "I can't let them do that. And Dave doesn't want me to, either."

"Uh . . . what's Dave got to do with it?" I asked incautiously, because Dave chose that moment to emerge from the bathroom.

He stood beside Marigold's wheelchair, put his arm around her shoulders, and stared at me defiantly. "I'm going to marry her," he said; and I knew he was thinking: *Which is more than you were prepared to do, Sagar.*

"I thought you were back in the pen."

"They . . . didn't seem to catch up with me, yesterday. That Rennie's not a bad guy, for a cop. They've traced me now, though. They'll be here to take me away soon."

I looked at Marigold. "So you're going to wait for him?"

"Of course, Joe."

She smiled at me like a friend, and I smiled back that way. "I'll tell Evadne Prendergast to find someone else for a figurehead," I assured her.

As I left them there I felt as miserable as hell because Marigold was so beautiful; and I thought about the rioting yesterday, which had occurred all over the country and was still continuing today in many places, and which had claimed a few lives and a lot of property, but which was still a good thing because the Government would be forced to act, to suspend the Pool; maybe even to abolish it.

But this reformation would not occur because of Carioca Jones or the Foes of Bondage or any of the other, more sincere reform groups. It would occur because of Dale Finlay's camerawork and Marigold Carassa's beauty.

It seemed a strange reason for political reform, the fact that a girl was pretty. I tried not to wonder what the public reaction would have been if Dave, with his dour face and aggressive manner, had been the amputee.

I told Evadne Prendergast of Marigold's decision.

"That really is too bad," she said. "However, I'm sure we can find a replacement." She gazed with satisfaction at the gathering which was now assuming immense proportions. "I will ask the girls to, uh, ferret around. You will lead the march with me, Mr. Sagar."

I was saved the difficulty of further denying her by the chattering arrival of the police copter which hovered over the crowd while Rennie's voice roared out metallically. "I have an important announcement for you from the Government in cooperation with the local police. An extensive search of the Ambulatory Organ Pool wing of the state penitentiary last night and this morning brought to light certain irregularities, and those responsible have been detained in custody. It is now apparent that a number of inmates are due for immediate release. This is being effected, and foreign inmates are being shipped home, first-class. Further, your Government is very conscious of public sentiments concerning the recent disclosures, and wishes to announce that the Ambulatory Organ Pools in all state penitentiaries will be suspended while further discussions take place, with the ultimate aim of abolishing the Pools within the year."

The roar of applause drowned out even Rennie's stentorian voice and he waited a while before resuming. "Your Government is, however, extremely concerned for the welfare of its citizens under the present circumstances, and in view of last night's incidents must regretfully declare that until further notice all large public gatherings will be considered illegal and dealt with accordingly. I must therefore ask you all to disperse. The purpose of your demonstration no longer exists, anyway."

"Now isn't that really *too* bad of them!" exploded Evadne Prendergast furiously.

It seemed to me that Joanne's release from the pen ought to be a private thing, that I ought to be able to collect her at the gates in my hovercar, take her straight to the antigrav port and away. Nobody else should be interested; it was just her business and mine. But things didn't work out that way.

During the week before her release the Foes of Bondage had been to the fore in nationwide disturbances which followed the release of large numbers of donors from the pens, when for the first time people really saw what Compulsory Donation *meant*. But the riots were not only illegal, they were purposeless; they merely expressed outrage, and when they finally fizzled out a lot of folk were asking themselves what it had all achieved.

Then some smart Foe realized that, in the excitement, the original object of the Foes had been forgotten: the abolition of bondage. Now, the Pool was gone but bondage remained, and bonded men and women could still be called upon to donate to their principals, and the whole thing was just too despicable, too *barbaric*. . . . In a bright mood of resurgence the Foes looked for a figurehead, and found Joanne. A welcoming party was organized for the day of her release, and my hopes of a speedy getaway were dashed.

The large ballroom at the *Princess Louise* was crowded with Foes and a number of members of the general public like Doug Marshall and others who were there at my insistence. Maybe I had some vague hope of bringing the two factions together in mutual celebrations and drinking; I don't know. . . . Anyway, I stood there smiling and talking, with the hotel reservations and flight tickets burning a hole in my pocket as I wondered how I was going to get Joanne away from this mob.

I said to Doug, "I don't see Rennie here."

"He refused to come. He's even more anti-Foe these days, since the riots."

"Did he say anything about Lambert?"

Marshall took a drink of something brown from a passing tray. "Christ knows what's happened to Lambert. I can't think what happened to Gallaugher, either. It's been a funny season, Joe. Maybe when the gliders are all laid up for the winter, things will go quiet again." He eyed a group of Foes around the platform where the band played. "But we can reckon the Foes are going to be outside the marina every weekend until the season ends, shouting their dirty words." He glanced at me apologetically. "I don't include you in that. I imagine you've resigned from the Foes by now."

"Sort of. . . . How many club members have bonded men now, anyway?"

Marshall thought, then grinned. "None, for Christ's sake. I hadn't thought of that. It just so happens that right now we're in the clear, since Presdee's man George finished his time. So the Foes have no reason to demonstrate at the club. Isn't that great?"

"I think you might find they'll demonstrate there from force of habit."

He regarded me thoughtfully. "Uh, Joe . . . are you going to be around?"

"I may go south for a spell. I'll be back some time next year." And as I spoke I was remembering the last time I went south; I caught sight of Marigold sitting in her wheelchair talking to Alcester and for a moment I felt sad.

Then Joanne slipped back into my thoughts like a warm
zephyr and I was myself again. Evadne Prendergast caught
my eye and began to chatter.

"Isn't it exciting, Mr. Sagar? You must be thrilled—I understand you and dear Joanne were very good friends." She
realized she'd put her foot in it. Carioca had denounced
Joanne and me in front of the nation. "Of course, dear
Carioca was just a *mite* prejudiced, I feel. A fine leader, but
impulsive. All things considered, I think the Foes are a much
happier body of women without her influence." The rapidity
with which the Foes' late president had been discredited put
me in mind of an emergent nation. It seemed that Carioca's
brilliant closing performance was already forgotten.

There was a young girl on the stage playing an orchestrella; and as the warm, sweet tones filled the room I remembered that it was only a year ago since I'd first met Joanne.
With all the waiting, it seemed a hell of a lot longer than
that. I'd wanted to meet her at the pen gate but she'd said
no; there were a few things she wanted to do, and the Foes
had supplied a car.

Watching her through the wires, I'd felt a sudden panic.
"You're not going to get mixed up with those women, are
you?" I'd asked nervously.

"No, Joe," she'd replied, watching me gravely. "But
they've been good enough to arrange this party for me.
Don't rush me, Joe. Give me time to get used to things."

And now there was a sudden stir around the ballroom
entrance and conversation died. As I began to push my way
toward the door I caught sight of Joanne's face, smiling as
she greeted people, accepting her first drink in months, being embraced by all and sundry. I managed to reach her and
we hugged, and I tried to tell myself that she hugged me
closer than she hugged Charles Wentworth, or Doc Lang, or
Miranda Marjoribanks, all of whom were clamoring for her
attention. I hadn't realized that she was so well known; then
I remembered that she'd lived with Carioca, who was always giving parties in those days.

She winked at me as our eyes met over Bryce Alcester's
shoulder.

"She looks well, doesn't she?" someone said to me.

The wink was undoubtedly a conspiratorial wink, as
though she knew and I knew that all this business was a

tiresome pretense, but it had to be endured as a kind of payment for the time when we would soon be alone.

"Speech!" some fool was shouting drunkenly.

The Foes were gathering around her like pigeon fanciers and there would have been a sick jealousy within me if I hadn't remembered what she'd said about not getting involved with them. I thought she smiled and beckoned to me as the crowd carried her farther away, but it was Evadne Prendergast she sought. Her hair was thick and fair, and it bounced as she looked from face to face animatedly, chatting in a way I'd never seen her chat before. I'd always thought her a shy girl, retiring.

There was almost a desperation in her brightness.

They had her on the stage and the band was quiet, apart from the drummer who beat an introductory tattoo.

Then Evadne Prendergast said something brief and handed Joanne the mike. The bright metal glittered as her hand shook, metal fingers gripping metal microphone. She seemed to swallow and recover, and her eyes passed me as she scanned her audience nervously. Then she coughed and began to speak.

"I can't tell you how grateful I am for this wonderful party," she said. "It was a simply marvelous surprise to come from that awful place and find that you'd done all this for me, and it makes me feel . . . unworthy. After all, I'm an ex-con and I'd heard people don't treat ex-cons too well. . . ."

For a while she went on like this, expressing fulsome gratitude in a way that wasn't Joanne at all. The crowd loved it, of course, but the unease was growing in me like an embolism and I was scared. I saw a drink on a table and gulped it down; it tasted terrible.

"And, bless you all, I feel terribly guilty too, because I'm going to tell all you nice people something you're not going to like very much—and I hope you won't feel too badly about it. But it's got to be said because it's something I learned in jail and it's *real*, and it means more than demonstrations and marches and riots."

I wanted to sit down. Joanne's voice was almost mechanical now, as though she were overrehearsed, as though she were expelling words like a computer printout.

"You see, in jail we learn to live by the rules. There are rules telling you when to get up and when to eat and when to go to bed and how to speak to the guards, and there are so many rules that in the end they become a part of you, and you don't question the sense of them because they've become solid facts to hang on to, like truth.

"So you can see I was puzzled and not very happy when I heard about all the rioting and unpleasantness over the last few days."

The thought crossed my mind: Had she been indoctrinated? Her audience was beinning to look bewildered, and Evadne Prendergast looked downright annoyed.

"Now I understand that I'm going to be asked to be a figurehead in a campaign to abolish bondage—and I'm afraid I can't agree to that. You see, a great number of prisoners are in favor of bondage. The remission it involves might represent four or five years of their life—and in any case it's voluntary. Are you going to take that away from them?"

"Well, *really*," interrupted Evadne Prendergast, pink with suppressed temper. "I should have thought with *your* experience of bondage—"

"I was unlucky," continued Joanne evenly. "It was a case of an impulsive gesture on the part of a woman who is normally the nicest person—and believe me, nobody has regretted it more than Carioca, in the months since. Most S. P. men and women complete their bondage without hitch, and many go on into outside life as friends, employees, and sometimes partners of the very people they were once bonded to. Huh, Charles?" She indicated Charles Wentworth, who nodded without expression, watching her face.

"My dear Joanne," snapped Evadne Prendergast, moving in on the mike. "I won't ask you to explain the general tenor of your statements, but I will ask you this. Now just name for us *one prisoner* who has applied for bondage recently, since the Foes by their unremitting efforts have focused attention on the iniquities of this diabolical form of slavery! Just one! Because I happen to know there are none! The eyes of the prisoners are opened!"

"Well, not quite," replied Joanne. "Bondage still represents one-third remission, Evadne—and that can be a lot of years. It so happens that years are important to some people. You wanted a name, so I'll give you one.

"Carioca Jones!"

And it was as though with a fanfare of trumpets that the far door burst open and Carioca Jones entered on cue, prancing toward the stage, greeting people with extravagant gestures of delight. Her eyes were startling black jewels in her pale face, all framed by the deeper, sweeping black of her Ultrasorbed hair. Her slithe-skin dress glowed crimson with exhilaration and as her gaze met mine the skin shimmered, her smile became a mocking parody as her eyes said: *I've beaten you, you bastard.*

She climbed onto the stage while people were mesmerized into clapping, and Joanne and she embraced. I glanced quickly around; it seemed that her very presence had filled people's minds; the Foes were smiling, the sling-gliders gaped, even Evadne Prendergast's severe expression had softened —but nobody was *thinking.*

Nobody really considered the significance of her presence; all that mattered was that Carioca Jones was onstage.

Joanne grinned; Joanne was going to introduce her.

My Joanne said, "So here's justification right before you. Here she is, and she doesn't have to live in that awful prison —after all, who would wish that on anyone? May I present my bonded S. P. girl . . . Carioca Jones!"

As Carioca stepped forward Joanne moved back, not quite smiling now as she watched the actress begin to speak.

Presently Joanne reached out with her glittering steel hand, and she took Carioca's soft youthful hand in hers, possessively.

DAW PRESENTS MICHAEL CONEY

Theodore Sturgeon wrote of Coney that "it is heartening to see a good writer become very good."

☐ **THE HERO OF DOWNWAYS.** Though they cloned for courage, it took more than breeding to find the light.
(#UQ1070—95¢)

☐ **MONITOR FOUND IN ORBIT.** An outstanding collection of the best stories of this rising light of science fiction.
(#UQ1132—95¢)

☐ **FRIENDS COME IN BOXES.** The epic story of one death-less day in 2256 A.D. (#UQ1056—95¢)

☐ **MIRROR IMAGE.** They could be either your most beloved object or your living nightmare! (#UQ1031—95¢)

DAW BOOKS are represented by the publishers of Signet and Mentor Books, THE NEW AMERICAN LIBRARY, INC.
